Sleeping with the Fishes

TOBY MOORE

PENGUIN

PENGUIN BOOKS

Published by the Penguin Group
Penguin Books Ltd, 80 Strand, London WC2R ORL, England
Penguin Group (USA) Inc., 375 Hudson Street, New York, New York 10014, USA
Penguin Group (Canada), 10 Alcorn Avenue, Toronto, Ontario, Canada M4V 3B2
(a division of Pearson Penguin Canada Inc.)
Penguin Ireland, 25 St Stephen's Green, Dublin 2, Ireland
(a division of Penguin Books Ltd)
Penguin Group (Australia), 250 Camberwell Road,
Camberwell, Victoria 3124, Australia (a division of Pearson Australia Group Pty Ltd)
Penguin Books India Pvt Ltd, 11 Community Centre,
Panchsheel Park, New Delhi – 110 017, India
Penguin Group (NZ), cnr Airborne and Rosedale Roads, Albany,
Auckland 1310, New Zealand (a division of Pearson New Zealand Ltd)
Penguin Books (South Africa) (Pty) Ltd, 24 Sturdee Avenue,
Rosebank 2196, South Africa

Penguin Books Ltd, Registered Offices: 80 Strand, London WC2R ORL, England

www.penguin.com

First published by Viking 2004
Published in Penguin Books 2005

1

Typeset by Palimpsest Book Production Limited, Polmont, Stirlingshire
Printed in England by Clays Ltd, St Ives plc

... they seem to me to be something Else besides Human Life. William Blake, 'Public Address', *Chaucer's Canterbury Pilgrims*

1

Hughgrant licked his genitals, stretched and padded to the window, raising himself against its dirt-streaked glass to stare at the street three floors below. The Jamaican builders were beginning their mysterious, short working day. 'No woman, no cry, whoa, no woman, no cry,' drifted from a boom box.

That was me, whoa. No woman since Gina had stalked out after our argument. I still thought the idea of dolphin-friendly tuna was ridiculous.

It was nearly a week, but I was trying not to panic. Things had been bad for a while. I picked arguments, it was true. Gina said I was spineless and paranoid, which is not what a spineless paranoid likes to hear. I was smarting. I told her she was insincere and career-besotted, a New York public relations executive, in fact. 'Anyone who thinks it's fine to kill tuna because Flipper lives is just warped,' I yelled at her departing form, elegant and beautiful even in hurt withdrawal. 'Warped.' My last word to her. What an epitaph. ('And before he died, dear friends, Ollie Gibbon thought only of his one true love. Indeed, his last utterance was a memory of her. "Warped," he said. The congregation gasped.'

But the sun was shining, and on this autumn day I managed to leap out of bed. Not everything was bad. There had been another frightening, pulse-racing, bed-soaking dream about Fishlove. They seemed to be happening more often. But there was no hangover and I had a clear run at the bathroom.

The shower spat out the brown liquid it had been disgorging in angry coughs, sputters and retches since the Rastafarians had begun renovating the apartment below eight months ago. Something resembling a thinned gravy dribbled over me. I sang anyway. 'No woman, a free guy, bum, bum, bum, I remember, de government dum de dum down in Trenchtown.' This particular day, this one that started with promise and just the tiniest twitch of loneliness, was a day off work. I hated the getting up, palebelly Brit wobbling in the shower stuff as a rule. But today I was happy. The Mafia series was filed. Done. There were no stories to write, calls to return or newspapers to read. Freedom. It was how Nelson Mandela must have felt on his first day off Robben Island.

I did the breakfast thing, a bowl of nutrimultigrainbranvitaminswithraisins and purged its benefits with a cup of real coffee.

How Gina and I made our latest trip from pleasurable post-coital funk to nuclear winter was still a mystery. We had escalated rapidly from seventies soul, with the obligatory challenge of naming a Bill Withers album without Greatest Hits in its title, which she was surprisingly good at, to canned yellow fin. It had been fermenting since I spotted the fateful tuna purchase from Wholegoodness Grocery, a store filled with expensive worthiness on 24th Street to which I had taken a passionate dislike after spotting scented candles amidst the individually priced organic mushrooms. 'It's like the army describing their machine guns as environmentally friendly because the bullets don't damage the bloody ozone layer,' I said. 'It's public relations bullshit.'

'Oh, and you'd be an expert in the environment,' she fired back pityingly. 'Mr Recycling Is For Retentives. And as for truth, let's not even go there.'

But that was our life, brittle and disillusioned and fractious. We were just another New York couple, only worse, battling blindly, marooned at that point when love has broken down and nobody knows quite why. One minute we were relaxed on neutral territory discussing Azerbaijan, Madonna or an exhibition at the Met; the next her bum was big in that, the other, and everything she ever cared to put on, including that stupid floppy hat, with its torrid display of straw and fake flowers made by her eco-friend, Grace, probably from recycled tins and renewable dolphin skin.

What had tuna ever done for me? Filled a sandwich. And there I was, sacrificing my relationship for a fish. I scowled over the pillow at Hughgrant, our Yorkshire terrier. All New Yorkers seemed to have them, hairy little turds with busy, burnished eyes. Women love them because they fit into handbags, never ask for awkward new positions or switch off the Fashion Channel. Ours was bought so the world would know we were one. Everyone gets a therapist to celebrate being in New York and a dog to celebrate acquiring a relationship, which is that crucial first step to a therapist. The circle of life.

Hughgrant was a proclamation of our love. I was reluctant at first. He was Gina's idea. Then I felt proud, oddly parental. My last creatures were two gerbils during childhood. They died one winter morning, hungry and cold. We bored each other. The little craplet was redemption, a new maturing in my relationship with animals, a chance to see them as something other than accompaniments to vegetables. Gina, confident and beautiful Gina, was my first step forward in serious love. But there I was, turning it into two cold gerbils.

We had a puppy shower for Hughgrant. Friends came with presents, including a studded leather jacket and matching leggings from Hound Dog on Christopher Street, and a set of plastic toys from Gina's banker friend, Travis, who was something in long hours on Wall Street. The toys were designed to improve Hughgrant's mental acuity because this is a competitive city, Travis explained solemnly. 'Dog eat dog, even,' I said chirpily. Everyone looked at me, puzzled.

Gina wanted to call him something robust and hairy-chested, like Troy. But I dug in. Floppy hair? Cringingly diffident? English? I won. But on this particular day on Manhattan's west side, a few blocks from the grey swell of the Hudson River, I was lost, officially on my own, at least until I got around to apologizing or forgetting the apartment keys.

Our last public row premiered at an avant-garde ballet, where the cast walked around a bare auditorium to the sound of a repeating car exhaust. Someone clapped when Gina stormed off. They were relieved to see a performance probably. It was a good display, better than the ballet, which had begun spreading ominously throughout the room, threatening to encourage audience participation. The Tuna Incident was far worse, and I tried to put it out of my mind.

Independence Day Number Five would start with the fitness centre, I decided. Exercise is perfect therapy for the dumped and anyone on a budget, sweatily releasing the same endorphins as sexual intercourse but without the expense of dinner for two. The truth is that I enjoy the liturgy of health-club exercise, the machinery that nobody knows quite how to work, red dots climbing imaginary hills towards improbable, distant goals, all primed by the two most chilling words in the English language, 'mode' and 'settings'. The Trimthunder boasted the physical benefits of a hike in Nepal with those of an intensive cross-country ski in Lapland. It had been endorsed by Sherpa Tupunar, whose lean, brown face smiled beside the words 'Sherpa Tupunar is the registered trademark of Exerfit Inc., Modesto, California'. It worked upper thighs, shoulders and abdominal muscles, whilst letting participants watch cable and check banking details. I could do everything short of run the country and launch a pre-emptive nuclear strike. That was on Level Twelve. More importantly, at the Old Factory Health Club, the Trimthunder often delivered a brunette.

She was a Trimthunder Olympiad, scaling its peaks, skiing the Arctic Circle and paying off her Visa. I rarely got far beyond base camp. I had tried mild flirtation. But she proved immune to my accent, that finely calibrated machine honed to something that I flattered myself resembled the seductive allure of a sophisticated perfume, its notes speaking of Merchant–Ivory, tea at the vicarage and hints of concern about global poverty. Our eyes met once, but not as I had hoped.

During an indecently long ogle as I walked to the idling Trimthunder next to hers, I tripped over a power cable, bringing the machine she was pounding to a sudden, jarring halt somewhere in the Hindu Kush. Lean, sculpted arms flailed in a frantic semaphore for the safety bar and then for an attorney. The trip-up cost me $1,000 for emotional distress and a leg X-ray. She called me a dumb moron.

Friends said I should have been thrilled. She had insulted me and taken my money, which usually counts as a successful relationship in America. I often indulged a virtual date with her still, imagining what sort of body glistened beneath that sheen of lime-green leotard, hoping she was spared mine through its rambling, loose-fitting rugby shirt of uncertain vintage. Perhaps she was taut and defined like the women in the S & M magazine that they used to wrap menus at Romp, the new Tibetan–Swedish fusion restaurant on Sixth Avenue?

The sight of My Lady of the Trimthunder was sometimes too stimulating, releasing a viagra of inappropriate blood. I would hit Level Ten and head for a punishing atoll or a particularly snowy part of Lap. Not that we had ever exchanged another word.

This morning she was nowhere to be seen. I climbed the Eiger at Level One anyway.

Calmed, I headed home, along Hudson Street, ducking down Perry and across to the Meat Packing District, a three-block area where they still carved choice cuts of beef and chicken for distribution to Manhattan restaurants whilst property developers hovered, waiting for a carve-up of their own.

I had arranged to meet Fishlove for lunch. I hurried past the encroachment of new restaurants, places of the infinite minimal that were transforming once bloodied streets into the deepest shade of sanitized cool.

I could hear the telephone ringing as I neared my front door. Maybe Fishlove to cancel? Gina? All I now know for sure is that when the end of the world calls, it always catches you unawares.

2

Life had been straightforward and uncomplicated, with just the usual Manhattan detours through therapy and the colonic of chronic self-absorption. Even rows with Gina were simple, always ending when I accepted my psychological flaws. She said I was closed. I said I was British and didn't want to talk about it any more.

It was a relief to have finished my sizzling – that was the word the *Herald* used on the front page – three-part series on the Mafia. The day off, otherwise known as 'some virus I picked up, should be better tomorrow', was my reward to me.

I had named names, interviewed shadowy capos, met with under-bosses, overbosses, adjacent bosses, postmodernist bosses. My inter-view with Salvatore Rosselli for the final piece was the climax. I warned that this never-photographed mobster was on his way to Britain. I talked to wives and girlfriends in New Jersey, to terrified associates drawn into his 'sickly web' of prostitution and drugs by the lure of 'easy money' and fear of 'swimming with the fishes'. My deep throat, the source of all my 'explosive revelations', worked 'Vice' at the New York City Police Department. He looked like Al Pacino in *Serpico*.

In fact, he was Al Pacino. The whole series was culled from tele-vision and the internet. It was a lot less effort than original research, compensating perfectly for my absence of knowledge about the Mafia and disinclination to acquire it. This would have meant making real contacts and probably travel to New Jersey, with its drab wooden shopfronts and knitting pattern of telephone cables stretching along flat, grey, featureless highways.

My best sources for the series began instead with the letters www. The characters who filled my reports were all Sopranos or bit players from *The Godfather*, *Casino* and *GoodFellas*. Some just came to me, including Jimmy 'The Knees' Garolfo and Freddie 'The Toolbox' Saveria. Albert 'The Vegan' Anacroci was a clever contemporary touch, I thought.

'This is a great read, Ollie,' Tom Harman, the features editor, said during a rare window of sobriety, 11 a.m. in the morning his time, 6-bloody-a.m. in the morning mine, after the first piece had run, splashing across two centre pages.

'Oh, glad you like it, Tom,' I said, voice thick with sleep. 'Even if it is only six in the morning here.'

'Is it? Sorry, mate. Didn't think, thought the clocks had changed,' he said pleasantly. 'You'd think they'd find a way to get us all on the same time, wouldn't you, what with the Euro and everything? Anyway. It was great, fantastic. The editor was well chuffed. Don't know how you got those people to talk.'

'Lucky break. You know how it is. One thing just led to another,' I said cautiously.

'Funny how that bloke Tortellini actually said "you talkin' to me" when you interviewed him and that he was actually eating pasta for breakfast. Who'd have thought it, eh?'

'Life imitating art,' I said smoothly, promising myself a rebuke or five minutes at Level Eleven later for naming characters after menu items at Giovanni's, the trattoria a few blocks away on Horatio Street. 'They love all that stuff, you see. That's the point. It's really just showbiz. They talk like movies. It's uncanny, I agree.'

It seemed to work. 'Look, I just had a quick query on the interview with Salvatore Rosselli,' Harman went on. 'The subs picked it up, actually. Right at the end you talk about a dripping pipe and twisted window frame. It's a small thing, but I was wondering how that happened in a luxury hotel suite in Manhattan, which you mention at the beginning.'

Shit. I had forgotten the casual location shift for my key interview, the climax to the series. It was originally set in the derelict Brooklyn navy yards ('window frames tragic, twisted and torn' and 'the mournful whistle from passing ships'), which I had seen in a documentary. I switched the fabrication to the hotel in midtown after a happy evening with friends getting drunk on expenses. Still, it was definitely a continuity blooper.

'Oh, yes, Tom. Well spotted. I should have picked that up. I was using an old file on the computer, notes from a previous interview that didn't quite work out. I met some guy on the docks, but he turned out to be a bit weak. Must have got left in the system by mistake.' I was counting on Harman's age and inability to understand more than five things about computers.

'Bloody machines,' he said sympathetically. 'I'm always losing stuff. That's fine. I'll just cut it out, then. How's it going with Whitney Houston's people, by the way?' Harman asked suddenly. I braced.

'They're working on it, Tom. She's got a pretty tight schedule, apparently. Big tour coming up. But I spoke to the aide to her assistant's intern and he told me, no almost guaranteed me, that it was going to happen. I've bought some of her CDs. Stunning voice.' Must remember to claim expenses for those, I reminded myself.

'That's fantastic news, Ollie. Fantastic. I know it's hard. Just don't want to see it in the *Sentinel* first.' He then delivered the low blow. 'Not with our new owner.'

'Right, right. Absolutely. I'll be in touch soon. Oh, and Tom, the clocks haven't changed, by the way. We're always five hours behind, six for a week at the end of winter. No prospect of the Euro either, as this is Dollaroland.'

The new owner. The *Herald* was on its third in five years. Nobody knew much about Sir Derek Stanley, the self-made businessman who had bought the loss-making tabloid as an addition to his stable of porn titles.

I missed the call by a few seconds and dumped my gym gear on the floor by the leather sofa, a piece of tanned curvature bought in a moment of weakness from the long-legged saleswoman at some store in midtown. I simply fell for something lurid and tasteless. The sofa was awful too.

There was no excuse. Manhattan just knocks years off you, often the ones when taste is supposed to develop. I had soon graduated to expensive, sexually explicit prints and line drawings. When Gina moved in, she retaliated, subtly, with photographs of nude men. It worked. We compromised on prints of city vistas. She chose a particularly phallic Empire State Building. I responded with a bas-relief highlighting the charms of a naked nymph.

I pressed replay. 'Hello, Ollie. It's Trish from Sir Derek's office. Could you give me a call as soon as you get this. It is rather urgent.' Something cold fluttered near my heart. I listened several times, searching for clues. If I played it backwards, would it sound like a message from the devil? 'Keith Richards. I'm ready for you now. Bring it on, brother.' Some primal instinct warned me not to return the call without preparation. That would have been like tackling a black run without a skiing lesson, or arguing about tuna without much of a fin to flail. Something was wrong, instinct screamed. Why would the owner of the *Herald* want to talk to me?

I needed advice and called Todd. He sold furniture that had been used on film sets. The chairs, tables and screens were intended for the gullible and celebrity-addicted, a market potential covering everyone in the city.

'Whoa, you have reached Hollywood at Home. I'm not here right now or I could be. Store hours are kind of flexible, so if you feel like coming by, hey, just do that thing and . . .'

Involuntarily, my eyes raised themselves in exasperation as the cheery voice drifted from confidence to confusion. When was he going to change that bloody message?

'. . . or leave a few words at the tone. No, it's a bleep thing, OK, but it's kinda long because something's stuck inside, I think. I got this at a state fair in Pennsylvania. Was it Memorial Day? Yeah. I was staying with my cousins. They got this spread near Allentown. Man, it's just great . . .'

I put the receiver down. Todd was there. He only ever remembered to turn on his ancient, eighties answerphone when he was actually in.

*   *   *

By some sort of inexplicable voodoo, Todd had become my best friend during my years in New York. It was cold when I set off, heading down the windowless stairs past Apartment 2B. I looked in. Through the fug of sweet ganja smoke, I could pick them out, just. Headlights would have helped. All three were sitting on upturned boxes in the dismal gloaming.

'How it hangin', Dogman?' came a rich, amused, disembodied voice.

'Eddie?'

'Da same. Come rest dem wearying legs wid us for a while.'

'Sorry, can't. Got to rush. Listen. No pressure. But is there any chance of fixing the water? It's still, well, it's still brown in my apartment and it's been three months now. I hate to keep mentioning it.'

'We done fix it by dis afternoon. We workin' on it right now. Most priority, mon.'

There was a guffaw from the others at this apparent joke. I backed out, eyes streaming, and decided to let it pass. Again.

'Great, great. Really appreciate it.'

I tacked across the fluvial avenues of Manhattan to the East Village, quietly cursing my diffidence, the English disease, and envying the Caribbean cool by which it was always floored. Why couldn't I just have bawled at him? Ordered him to get it sorted out? Threatened legal action? Or worse? If I were American, I would have 'busted his ass' by now with a string of self-righteous, whining invective. But I was English, so I wallowed in resentment instead.

I walked across 13th, down First Avenue and tucked into 8th Street, passed a row of shops selling aromatherapy, grunge fashion lines and other detritus of human life that somehow ends up on student bodies or dormitory walls or both. I passed two women, three blocks apart, each solitary and sobbing gently to herself. I shivered. Maybe I was turning into a version of that child from *The Sixth Sense* and always seeing dumped people. I tried to stop thinking about Gina.

Hollywood at Home was at the end of the street, in a basement down a flight of chipped, stone steps. The door was ajar, still not absolute evidence it was open. I eased my way past a redoubt of battered chairs, tables and a sofa with popping springs. Todd was in the corner, lounging on a fake, green Eames chair, his huge feet propped on the not-quite-matching ottoman. He was reading a copy of *2000 AD* comic.

'Yo, my man, what's up?' he asked, leaping up and beaming widely. 'Hey, have I got something for you.' He disappeared for a moment, returning with a poster of Bobby Charlton circa 1969. 'Way cool, isn't it?' he said. I grunted, non-committal. 'Combovers are just the funniest thing ever, dude. I mean, I got a kick out of the Elephant Man and Prince Charles, but this just blew me away.'

'Well, he was a great footballer, Todd, a sporting legend in my country. We forgave him the hair a long time ago. Much of a market for Bobby Charltons over here?' I asked tartly.

'I'm not too sure. Just kinda hoping there may just be enough of you guys here for someone to go for it. But it's the hair, guy. This could look cool in a retro bar,' he added. 'I mean, you Brits don't bother too much about the looks side of things, do you? No offence.'

I wasn't going to be drawn into that battle, not so soon after the tuna war. It was too early to open up a whole new front on teeth and hair. This was partly because I knew he was right. Our mouths are shocking, abandoned cemeteries to American eyes. Teenagers with braces conjure up our disordered, stained teeth in their nightmares. They wake sweating and pray for Boo Radley or some gentler horror to visit them. 'Maybe you're right,' I said. 'But it was a long time ago – people have a lot more hair these days thanks to New Labour. Listen, I need your help.' I told him about the devil call.

Todd rubbed his square, stubbled chin and thought for a few moments 'Maybe you've been fired,' he said cheerfully, as I sat down on 'Tom Cruise's office chair from *Mission: Impossible 2*', hearing a spring give in some distant recess.

'Thanks a bunch, Todd. Just what I wanted to hear.'

'Hey, you're welcome. I mean, you do send over a lot of prime crap. No offence. I mean Tortellini, the big mob mobster, or was that Tor Tellini the famous Norwegian explorer? Maybe I should write about some big Mexican gangsta Burr Ritto or Enchi Lada, the broad he hung with,' he said mockingly.

'Yeah, yeah, OK.' God, how I wished I'd never let that second bottle of Merlot unlock the dark secret. Everybody had been stunned. Even Todd, who never to my certain knowledge read newspapers. A grisly silence met my admission of serial professional deceit and I missed the mood, driving on, determined to amuse and regale with stories of fake interviews and concocted experiences in the last hurricane season. Looking back, I can see it was the moment Gina started to drift away. Despite a career in public relations there was a limit to how much faking even she could accept. I was furious at the embarrassed reaction.

'Come on,' I said to her on the way home. 'It's not as if anyone believes what they read anyway, as long as it's interesting.'

Gina just stopped in the street. 'God, you really think that? That's so fucked up. You truly have lost the plot, Ollie.'

'Or how about Alloo Gobi, the famous Indian money launderer,' Todd carried on, breaking my reverie and bringing me back to what passed for reality in his world. He was warming to his theme, I could tell. Todd found Benny Hill funny.

'Thanks, Todd. I got the joke first, second and even third time around.'

'Sure, man. Well. I mean maybe they've found out, that's all I'm saying.'

The thought had crossed my mind. 'I don't think so. I mean, I've just talked to the features editor, who told me how wonderful the last series was. Practically asked to have my babies. Everybody loved it. I'm sure he'd have said something. Anyway, Stanley would simply get the editor to sack me. I don't see the owner doing it in person. He must have more important people to sack than a bloody hack in New York.'

Todd drew his hand through brown, tousled hair. He paused, looking wisely and seriously at me. 'Well, that's surely true. But you could say the same thing about shooting a dumb deer. But, you know what, lots of real intelligent people go out and do it, even when you can just pick up the only bits you'll ever need from a deli.' He looked at me as if the very wisdom of Solomon had been laid at my feet, the distillation of sacred, learnt marvels.

'Gosh. Thank you for that, Todd. But I'm not quite sure if that's an accurate comparison,' I said briskly, beginning to regret trudging across lower Manhattan, negotiating the crazies and beggars, for this particular oracle.

'There's only one way to find out. You'll just have to call back,' Todd said. He really did understand the obvious better than any person I knew.

'Duh, clearly,' I said. 'But what do I say, oh Wise Master?'

'How about "It's Ollie Gibbon here and I'm shit scared."' His face cracked open in pleasure.

'Very funny, I don't think.'

'Chill, man. Hey, look, why should they care what you've been up to? You deliver the goods, give them what they want. That's all it's about, isn't it?'

This was a waste of time. 'Thanks, Todd, you've been a great help,' I said, pouring as much irony as I could into the syntax. But he was from the Midwest.

'You're welcome,' he replied breezily. I was turning to leave when he said, 'How's Gina?'

'Gina? Oh, she's fine, absolutely fine,' I lied, missing the trap until it was too late. Todd and Gina used to go out. They still talked. One of the endearing things about organized, motivated Gina is that she keeps everything, shoes from when she was a teenager, sweaters pulled to within an inch of her ankles, posters from the eighties and old boyfriends, especially disorganized and unambitious Todd. They had both been at college together. Todd was the jock type, all sports and babes and big car from adoring parents. He was an easy-going trust-fund kid who glided effortlessly through

13

life on a wave of credit cards, low expectations and fully paid tuition fees. Gina was the spawn of serious East Coast self-improvement entrepreneurs, who had made their first fortune from kitchen appliances, but she had still ended up in public relations. They really were college sweethearts, finishing each other's jokes and sharing dental floss. They had taken the same liberal arts course, Applied Goodness and Frisbee Throwing or something. There was a whole lot more that bound them, a blizzard of good works on their vacations, which probably included months counselling one-legged, single-parent bears in Yosemite National Park.

'It's just that she came around earlier in the week, seemed kinda distracted. You know, a little not there.' He did a quick *Twilight Zone* hand jive. 'Anything you wonna tell me? Free session.'

This was what Todd did and it always worked. He'd invite a confidence when he already knew the secret in question. It was a sort of friendship test. I often flunked.

'No. Nothing at all. What made you think that?' I asked coolly.

'Oh, I don't know. The tears, maybe. When Geeny said she was going to stay with Grace, didn't think you guys were going to make it, said you'd been hurtful. That kind of thing.'

Bloody hell, I thought, furrowing my brow. Americans are quite shamelessly open. She'd probably already posted our split on a web site, auctioned the rights for an off-Broadway production and stuck flyers on lamp-posts for the first night.

'Really? She said all that? Well, we had a row, but nothing, you know, terminal,' I said.

'Some row, man. She said, now what was it, that you wished she had, like, a brain tumour. That sounds pretty terminal to me, man.'

'What?' I said incredulously.

'That's right. A brain tumour.' He looked at me, eyes popped open with disbelief.

'What exactly did she say, Todd? Relax. Take a deep breath. In your own time.'

He spoke slowly, in a concentrated way. 'That you said she was as friendly as a dolphin with a tumour.'

I waited for the full impact to sink in, swim around a bit, back-flip for the paying audience and sink a cocktail before replying.

'Todd,' I sighed quietly, marvelling not for the first time at a man whose brain had apparently been predigested by some small creature before implant, 'we just had an argument about dolphin-friendly tuna. I did not at any point accuse Gina of looking like anything with a tumour or of impersonating a cancerous sea creature of any description, OK?'

He was taken aback, but regrouped surprisingly fast. 'So, what is that? Some kind of love thing between different species in the fish world?' He was determined, if confused. I had to give him that.

'No, Todd, it was an invigorating debate about the way sanctimonious people buy tinned tuna fish and somehow imply that it's absolutely, bloody fine to eat the stuff if the tin says they didn't cause any collateral damage to dolphins when they caught the bloody things. As if the tuna cares. It's all just PR spin. That was my point.'

He pulled his long neck back like a startled giraffe as my onslaught continued. I was on a roll. 'You know: "Sure, catch me, that's fine. Let the other guys live because they've had their own television series and a star on the Hollywood walk of fame."' I finished, flushed and glowering with indignation. 'I may have got carried away. She told me my argument was flawed.' I winced. 'Like me.'

He edged back, but looked blank, as if he'd just heard something glottal, but distinctly threatening, in Serbo-Croatian. 'Whoa, hey, whatever, man. But you guys better sort it out. She was in a bad way. This tumour –'

'Tuna, Todd.'

'– whatever, dude. It totally tore her up. I could tell.'

Oh, yes, I thought, go on, why don't you. Play the concerned, always-there-for-you ex-boyfriend card. I had my suspicions. No two people had a right to rub along that well after a split. I never had, I thought self-pityingly. And what about me?

'I'm sure she'll be back,' I said, managing to resist adding that she always was. A loft in the Meat Packing District with its own entrance, wood floors and a cleaner from Poland was not something a New Yorker surrendered lightly. 'Listen, I've got to go. You're right. I'll call her.'

I walked to the door and noticed a window display baring its teeth. 'And by the way, Todd. I think you may need to have a word with your suppliers. I'm fairly sure that no stuffed otter made it into the final cut of any *Terminator* movie.'

Outside it was starting to darken. The autumn wind had picked up, blowing trash up the street in crazy swoops and dives, paper pieces dancing dizzy paths with invisible partners.

I headed back to the apartment, down Little West 12th Street, past the Gay and Lesbian Center and Alfred's, which sold bright $4,000 sweaters apparently designed to make wearers resemble bumble bees. A dying autumn sun struggling against the high-rise blocks as it sank over the horizon warmed neither the city nor my spirit.

Gina. Stunning in a raven-haired, determined New York sort of way. Our paths first crossed professionally. I had talked myself into a ticket to some sort of opening. It was another British film sent over the Atlantic as a 'triumph', probably something set in the north of England about a young boy coming of age with a desire to apply lipstick competitively on the international circuit. She was doing the publicity.

It was a few years ago when flares were back, and so was having a Brit on your arm, that is, if you really wanted to make the Manhattan scene. Todd was there as well. Handsome, genial, untroubled, decently tall Todd. I hated him instantly. Jealous. I went into self-deprecating charm overdrive to win her. The whole bit. They had been going out for eight years and the itch was nagging her, I could tell.

Incredibly, Todd took the loss in his stride, as, I was to discover, he did just about everything. But he still remained loyal to Gina, like one of those street dogs in Mexico that adopt you for the duration of your tortilla con queso, then linger hopefully despite any visible remaining evidence of either tortilla or queso.

I envied his ease, height, thick hair, even the ludicrous stab at a business venture of stunning inconsequence. His extraordinary clothes. He invariably wore a baggy, shapeless tweed jacket over a succession of faded t-shirts and ripped jeans. It gave him, infuriatingly, an air of academic superiority wildly at odds with any reality I could ever detect.

'Have you got everything you want?' she had asked, as the night drew to a close.

'Yes, absolutely.'

'Great. So you won't be wanting sex tonight with the actress who plays the supermodel. That's fine. I'll take you off the list.'

My jaw must have hit the floor. Then Gina just laughed and laughed. 'I'm sorry. I don't know why I said that. But that woman is a total bitch. Please don't write that.'

I promised not to mention it. What else did I see in her when we met? Well, everything, as it happened. It was a low-cut, priapic summer night, and she was wearing a diaphanous dress. She was poised, confident and knowing.

What did she see in me? It took me a while to work out. At first, I think it was because she was twenty-five and Todd was her provincial past. I offered an intriguing, foreign future. We found the same things absurd. Or so we thought.

But in moments of honesty, it still remained a mystery. I was another mildly argumentative, cynical Englishman with a doubling chin and the sort of face they reconstruct after commuter train disasters in the hope that somebody will identify Mr Pleasant Looking But Slightly Indistinguishable.

Then I started to make her cry. Her own broad, sunny, ambitious American optimism hit my diminishing self-esteem. She hadn't signed up to struggle with my demons. With Fishlove.

3

'Hi, Trish, it's Ollie Gibbon.' There was a pause. 'The New York correspondent,' I prompted. 'You left a message.'

'Oh, yes, of course. Silly me. Thanks for calling back, Ollie. Sir Derek wants to see you as soon as possible.'

I paused again, this time for the retch of terror that came in those final moments before the suicidal advance towards enemy lines. 'Fine. When?'

'Monday.'

'What? Next Monday? I mean, it's Friday now.'

There was a muffled giggle. 'It don't take two days to come from New York to London, now does it? Even I know that and I flew Virgin.'

'No, of course not,' I blustered defensively. 'It's just, it's just, well, a bit sudden. What does he want to see me about?'

'Can't say I know, sorry. But it sounds very important, so you'd better shake your booty, or whatever it is you Yanks say. Shall we say four o'clock?'

'Sure, I'll see you then. By the way, I'm not a Yank, Trish. I'm a Brit, which should explain this faintly familiar accent.'

'You are a laugh, Oliver Gibbon.'

The rest of Friday passed in a blur. I blew Fishlove out. I couldn't face his skilled, forensic probing masquerading as concern. This was a man whose only known hobby was the solitary pursuit of jigsaws, the more complicated the better. Rumour had it that he managed a 3,000-piece puzzle based on the work of a Spanish abstract artist, an entirely yellow canvas, in one afternoon. He worked for the *Daily Sentinel* and was my main rival. He was talented, thorough, conscientious and had accurate shorthand. Beneath a calm exterior lurked a creature of quite awful skill and commitment. Fishlove took carnal pleasure from the incomprehensible, delighting in complex stories, gnawing away at them patiently for days. Not for him the easy rewrite of American newspapers. He never made anything up, didn't need to. I rather hated him.

I took Hughgrant for a long walk along the Hudson towards Battery Park, generally something I looked forward to doing.

There is just something about the river, wide and busy and strong and unlike the lost and lovelorn Thames. Ferries cut through purposefully, up and down and across to New Jersey, bringing workers from their neat, white homes to their ambitions in the financial district. The Statue of Liberty, sulphurized copper-green, guarded it all, dwarfed by the powerful flow. Kermit with a torch and only marginally more serious features.

The daytime light is good in New York, a place free of those low, doleful clouds that fill the skies just above the pavement in London. But I was barely noticing. It was not giving any clarity to my situation. I knew something was going to happen, something so unusual that it could not be spoken about over the telephone or, evidently, communicated by e-mail.

Gina had called by the time I got back. I played the message. 'Hi, it's me. I'm still with Grace. Don't call. We need to spend some time apart. Think things over. I'm not sure I can handle all this arguing.' There was a momentary pause for what sounded like a sorrowful sniff and I pursed my lips. Then her tone changed to the familiar and practical. 'I just wanted to tell you not to forget Hughgrant's therapy on Monday and he must, absolutely must, be given his seaweed pellets.'

Hughgrant was seeing Dr Kleinman, an expensive dog psychologist on the Upper West Side. There were issues. An abused puppyhood, we were told. I wondered what went on when Hughgrant climbed on the couch. Kleinman was shocked when I asked, insisting gravely that the sessions were covered by doctor–canine confidentiality. What did that wretched, pampered animal say in there? Kleinman promised to tell us only how we should modify our behaviour to help the little Urine-a-tron regain his self-esteem. I asked if this would be the same day the little delight stopped cocking his leg against kitchen units, chewing the curtains and dumping turds on the Persian rug.

Gina was much more understanding, which was easy for the daughter of Depak Firman, the famous and photogenic New Age guru. His breakthrough book, *We are Cubes*, was now on course reading lists. I read it once, some reviews, anyway, as part of our courtship. We are all small cubes on the outer reaches of the universe, surrounded by larger ones that affect our lives, multi-facets and so on. The usual stuff. Firman was, shrewdly, business friendly, describing corporations as secular religions, servile enough to sustain invitations to lucrative executive empowerment seminars.

The first book was mentioned on *Oprah*, sold a gazillion copies and the rest was history. Or, in Firman's case, a huge estate in California where many people were employed to mow lawns, cook, drive and do other menial tasks for the great man, freeing him to concentrate on the cubeness of it all. He also kept a place on the Upper East Side, which, as I once joked to a stony-faced Firman on a rare meeting, is actually a very square neighbourhood.

After listening to Gina's message I called Mrs Romstein, who lived in a tiny basement apartment in my building, and asked her if she would dog-sit whilst I was away. Oddly, she adored Hughgrant. They must have bonded over poor bladder control. 'He's perfect,' she once purred, adding coquettishly, 'Just like his owner.' I'd smiled and tried not to flirt back. She was 5,000 years old, after all. It's that British thing: open your mouth and Mr Darcy from every Masterpiece Theater ever broadcast pops out. The problem was her age. Being trapped at one of Joan Collins's weddings was a recurring nightmare of mine.

But I flattered myself. Mrs Romstein, delicate and hunched, really had her eye on the even older Mr Kapachutski, who lived down the hall. I knew this because she once confided to me that he was a 'real gentleman'. Nobody does something for nothing in this town, including offer praise, without sight of a bottom line. The object of her desire was single, severe and erect. He walked without the aid of a frame but with comprehensive health insurance. This made him rarer than diamonds on the sidewalks in Greenwich Village. I knew little except that Mr Kapachutski had fled some brutal Eastern European regime many years and several dictators ago. Fortunately, I'd always managed to get away before learning much of his story. There was probably a great cabbage famine.

I had hurried home after the walk, passed the shops hawking lurid displays of forced, primary-coloured flowers, navigating between office workers heading to the subway for clapboard homes in Hoboken, Queens and Brooklyn. A few heritage gays cruised the streets in leather, cadaverous men with defiant moustaches and sunken cheeks mixing it with the heterosexual financiers and computerists who were taking over the neighbourhood, softening its edgcs.

There were transsexuals, echoes of a less sanitized past. They hung about on my street corner. 'Hey, you want some action? I'm talking to you,' one in a group of three screeched at me as I headed back. 'No, but thanks anyway,' I replied warmly. 'Just eaten.' God, I even sounded apologetic. 'Probably got a small dick anyway,' I heard, followed by raucous cackles and the slap of high fives.

I knocked on Mrs Romstein's door. Of course, she would love to have Hughgrant for as long as I wanted. Yes, she could manage the seaweed. No, I couldn't stay for a little bite to eat. Yes, she could do the walks, twice a day and always before 10 p.m. Shc could put the sleeping mask on him and would try to remember the ear plugs as well, but her hands were a little shaky.

'Because he's so well behaved,' said the observant Mrs Romstein, 'he can sleep in the bedroom with me. I could even spank him if he's naughty,' she added, winking one rheumy eye at me.

I ignored the bait. 'Gina doesn't approve of hitting dogs, I'm

F/2044611

COUNTY LIBRARY

afraid,' I said coolly. 'Just a few angry words will do. He's in therapy.'
She looked disappointed.

I didn't bother calling Gina back. She would have been furious.
She hated Mrs Romstein, and I was forbidden to leave Hughgrant
with her. Maybe it was jealousy.

4

The *Herald* rose out of a London mist to resemble some becalmed wreck, a piece of the City inexplicably aground on the ugly reaches of a listless South Bank still awaiting reclamation by developers, optimists, lifestylists and latte sellers. The top three floors hung in cloud and were barely visible.

I had arranged to meet a colleague, Guy Armitage, the paper's gossip columnist, at the nearby Old Printers' Nark pub before the appointment with Stanley. I was early. The Nark was lined with famous *Herald* front covers from a distant heyday. The smell of disinfectant and years of drunken brawls and soaring egos hung in the air. I bought a pint of Old Curleycue and waited, glancing out at the Thames, unused but for the odd barge pressing past. I had a *Herald* to read. Weird headlines leapt out, baffling testament to my years abroad. It might as well have been Sanskrit: VAN BERGER JOINS HAMMERS; STREET'S RONA: 'I QUIT' SENSATION'; SACKED CIVIL SERVANT CLAIM: 'IT WAS BROCCOLI'.

Armitage finally strode in, purposeful and pink, an animated meringue of a man, chin high. Sumptuous. He had a huge, improbable beard and legendary appetites, some of them legal. He might have been Alexander Solzhenitsyn's brother, the debauched roué everyone in the family kept quiet about.

There had clearly been a brandy or ten already that morning, if his red face and weed-withering breath were an accurate guide. He unknotted his stained fuchsia tie and sighed heavily. It never rained, but it poured. Usually doubles.

'So lovely to see you again, Ollie,' he said, shaking my hand limply. 'What can I tell you?' he went on before I even asked. 'Things have changed, you know. Everyone who isn't an estate agent has their own reality television show,' he added dolefully before brightening. 'But what an honour indeed to have a visit to the Evil Empire from its exiled son. I say, Roy, bring me over a sensible brandy, will you, and another whatever it is for Luke Hackwalker here.'

'On its way, Guv. Scratchings?'

'No, no, no. Perish the thought. Far too early.' Armitage scrunched his face in distaste, turned and leant forward, ready for the dead drop of choice gossip. There was a dramatic pause. 'The library's going, you know,' he announced triumphantly.

'You're kidding,' I said, sounding appropriately shocked. 'Where to exactly? On sabbatical?'

'Going as in curtains. Kaput. Finito.' Armitage looked pleased by my incredulous expression.

'You can't be serious?'

'You have been away too long, dear boy. It's the usual, of course. Cost-cutting. Some teenage whizzkid's been in and persuaded Stanley to get us all on to some global online cuttings service. Apparently, it cuts the newspapers in Fiji and Mauritius. It's based in the Cayman Islands. As, indeed, we are these days, of course.'

'Fat lot of good that is when your readers all live in Bolton,' I said.

'Quite. But that's not the point, is it? Readers never seem to notice. You're well out if it, Ollie, believe me,' he said, sipping on his 'sensible' drink, at least a triple Rémy Martin. 'We're going to hell and there's no union to speak of either.'

'You don't belong to the union, Guy,' I noted mildly.

'Of course I don't belong to it,' came the tetchy reply. 'But I do expect it to put up a little resistance when one's workplace is being dismantled, torn apart from under one by some Visigoth. Tell me, is that unreasonable?' He stared at me. I muttered of course not. There was an awkward silence.

Armitage took another, longer draw. 'You know that United Nations report last week saying that the earth was now so polluted Alaskan Inuits were going to be cultivating bananas soon and that East Anglia would be colder than Siberia?'

24

I nodded.

'Well, Stanley said it was all too depressing and ordered up a pull-out on the lighter side of global warming. I mean, I ask you.'

'Has anyone found it?'

'We're all on it. Showbiz, Sport. Books. Even me. The editor said I should write a nostalgic piece about how I could remember when 45 was a record size, not a sun protection factor.'

'How's it going?'

'Quite well, actually. I'm rather pleased. It had better get a good show or I'll be livid.'

Outside, the mist had risen clear of the river. The bar was filling with tubby young office workers, lads nudging and joshing, ordering and draining, talking about the games of life, the new temp in accounts, the match last night. Armitage glanced at a bearded, overweight man standing alone by the bar. 'Oh, dear. Look what he's wearing.'

'Shirt, jacket, tie,' I ventured. 'Or am I missing something?'

'There are two things that are always very suspect on men over forty-five, Ollie, tie dyes and Thai brides.' Armitage sounded appalled. 'Just look at that thing around his neck. Ghastly.' He waited for me to inspect the sartorial failing.

'Anyway, to happier topics. So, is Greenwich Village still a gay heaven? It's been so very long since I visited.'

'Still.'

'How wonderful. Gentrification has been the curse of the cruising classes over here. I've been dreadfully worried by the spread of those single-occupancy loos. You know they actually disappear into the ground. Most antisocial. I do miss America, really I do. But in America, not London, that's my point. Yanks are a bit like rats over here these days. You're never more than ten feet from one.' He sipped delicately. 'They've ruined Spitalfields.'

'Rats?'

'No. Americans. Those ghastly wooden-floored flats are their fault. It's all come over the Atlantic.' Armitage paused, lost in some quiet recollection of architectural outrages or fumbles past. 'What's someone like you doing in the Village anyway?'

I humphed. 'Making a stand for straight rights in a cruel, gay world, Guy. Soon we'll be properly recognized: they'll have fundraising concerts where pretty women with shaved armpits play soft rock and flirt with us.' The Curleycue was going down very well. 'Actually, I got a good deal on a loft in the Meat Packing District. Couldn't pass it up. It's hell trying to find anything in Manhattan these days. Much else going on here?'

Guy thought for a second. 'Not really. Things don't change much, you know. Everything that had angles now has curves and appliances come in any colour, as long as it's grey.'

I drained my warm beer, savouring the celebrated foulness that regularly won Old Curleycue real-ale awards. 'Listen, Guy, have you got any idea why he's called me over?'

'Not one, and I did ask around. You know me. But I doubt it's the old heave-ho. He'd have got his creepy sidekick Bleaker to do that.'

I had, of course, heard of Bleaker. He was the new staff director and Stanley's right-hand man, so it was said. I had made it my business not to get to know him in much the same way gazelles learn not to know lions.

'What's he like, this Bleaker character?'

'Pukemakingly awful,' said Armitage vehemently, raising his eyes towards the stained ceiling. 'Hush Puppies. Lives in Purley, needless to say.'

Armitage had survived on the *Herald* for years and to accuse someone of living outside four chosen postcodes of London was his most vicious insult. I looked at him over my pint glass. There was a private income somewhere. It was rumoured he owned an Aston Martin and drove at weekends down the King's Road. Come the next Ice Age, only cockroaches and Armitage, the *Herald*'s 'Beady Eye', would survive to recolonize, or, in his case, to occupy, the first reclaimed snug bar.

It was said that he always made a point of digging up dirt on the revolving door of owners who took on the declining *Herald*. But it was hard to dig up dirt on a man who lived in it. Armitage, long past middle age and belted by incremental pay increases, felt the fear of passing time. Why rock the boat? That was the job of the union, he had decided.

'Little boy's room,' Armitage said abruptly.

I watched him glide head high, navigating knots of drinkers to skirt the door marked TRADERETTE and head for TRADER. I thought about his sad diatribe. The *Herald* used to be *On the Waterfront*, a contender. Not any more. There were once reporters in all major countries. I was now the last one left outside central London. Maybe that was why I felt so insecure?

'Yes, it's all very strange these days,' Armitage said on his return, picking at a bowl of olives that had appeared unbidden, part of the Nark's grudging softening of its own edges for the twenty-first century.

'Hardly any expenses. Himself signs off on everything, you know. Sits up there late at night, just a candle flickering, going through our claims.' He shivered. 'I don't even try slipping my Veuve Clicquot through these days. I have to disguise it as taxis. Takes hours, a complete waste of my time when I could be out having dinner with contacts. Can you imagine? I should tell him, but what's the point?' There was outrage in his voice.

I grunted in sympathy. It was nearly 3.30. I felt better after three pints of Old Curly, nerves calmed, palms dry. Yes, they had definitely helped.

Armitage pulled a pack of blank Old Printers' Nark receipts from his blazer pocket and handed me one, asking me to fill in a figure. 'How much has this been? Fifteen quid? Put £46.50.' I scribbled the number.

'Any advice?' I asked, as we rose to leave.

'Yes,' Armitage replied, leaning over to whisper softly. 'Suck on a few mints before you go in. He's teetotal, you know.'

I didn't.

5

'It's a bloody good work-out,' the chairman of World Media barked from behind the drum kit, hands moving at bewildering speed, sweat soaking through his blue shirt, a dark stain penetrating its white wing collars. 'Now, I think Buddy Rich is the best drummer there ever was, although I've got a lot of time for Charlie Watts too. Met him once, you know. Great laugh. Tea? Coffee? Kiwi fruit?'

'Er, tea would be fine, thank you. No fruit, if it's all the same,' I said, my ears ringing from the lengthy tattoo.

'This is Mick Fleetwood on 'Tusk'. You probably recognize it. Oi, Decca,' Sir Derek Stanley shouted. A tall man with a crew cut walked in through a side door. 'Get our guest a large coffee and a kiwi, will you?' he barked over the din of beaten skins. 'Fucking good for you, kiwi. Packed with vitamins. Dozens of 'em. How many do you eat a day?'

'Well . . .'

'Guess how many I do.'

'Actually, tea would be better –'

'Go on, go on, howmanydyerthink?'

'Four,' I blurted. 'Five, maybe,' just in case.

'Four! Five! Don't be a plonker. Two a day is what you need, eleven and four o'clock on the dot. The great thing is that nobody actually handles them inside. That's what counts. People don't wash their hands. You see it wherever you go. Disgusting. That's why this country is so filthy. Apples and pears are bleeding death traps. But with the kiwi it don't matter, see.'

'No, I suppose not.'

Suddenly, the display was over. Stanley sprang from behind the drums with the agility of a primate honed by the ministrations of personal trainers, his upper body stiff with muscles, a sweat-glistened tan suggesting hours spent under the sun lamp or at some holiday home in Nice or Essex. He moved nimbly, swinging past a dark leather armchair and a glass coffee table to reach his desk, a vast empty tract devoid of papers that dwarfed him as he plopped into place. A computer linked to stock prices flickered on one side. There was a pause whilst he adjusted his shirt cuffs, buttoning a pair of diamond-encrusted cufflinks. He lit a cigar.

'Loved your Mafia series. Terrific,' he said suddenly, puffing gently, obscuring himself in a thick, scented fug. 'That's what news-papers are all about,' he added ruminatively.

'Thanks. It was fun to do, Sir Derek.' I was alert, tingling and aware.

'Amazing that they actually eat pasta for breakfast. Unfuckingbelievable.' He suddenly leant forward and steadied his eyes on me. 'I didn't believe it.'

I felt that sensation the condemned man has as his final moments approach, the last Momma's crispy fry in battered marshmallow from the concluding meal consumed, the electric chair in sight.

'Not a word.'

I sat, stilled, waiting to meet my maker, or at least my unem-ployment. There was nothing to say. I began to open my mouth. Hell, I might as well confess. Who cared? He was obviously going to sack me and wanted to do it in person. Perhaps it was a poisoned kiwi these days to avoid the redundancy cheque. Still, it had been a good run. Sooner or later someone would watch the same tele-vision programmes, surf the identical internet sites.

I opened my mouth to speak. Dead Reporter Talking. But Stanley had leant closer.

'Was it pesto or pomadoro? Only the wife wondered whether they freeze-dried the pasta and added sugar to make it like a cereal. I told her, "Don't be daft, whoever heard of pastabrix?" I ask you. Women, eh?'

It really is surprising how much air the human body can exhale. 'Tomatoes usually. Usually,' I stumbled, but recovered my compo-sure. 'Sometimes they might add basil, but not often. Depends

29

really on which family you're talking about.' My confidence swelled as he watched. 'It's all wrapped in tradition. Sicily, Omertà, codes of honour, blood debts, that kind of stuff.'

He looked pleased. 'That's what journalism is all about,' he said, slamming the desk.

There was a pause.

'Pasta?' I ventured cautiously.

'Don't be fucking daft. No, all that stuff you see on telly. People want celebrities, pop stars, big weddings, football. They don't want to read about those bleedin' war trials with what's his name, Solobo, Sloba, Milos, Veriditch. You know, that bloke from Yugoslavia. Now do they? I mean, it just makes you fucking miserable. If you want terrorism and vegetarians, go somewhere else, I say. Not in my paper. But a wedding. People love a big wedding.' I was about to agree when a new voice arrived.

'Sir Derek spent some time in America, you know,' it said silkily from over my shoulder. I turned, momentarily startled. A short, suited figure stood close by. He had entered silently.

'Yeah, well, I don't think we need to go into all that,' said Stanley, shifting awkwardly in a way that invited no further questions on the subject. 'Oh, you two 'aven't met. This is Trevor Bleaker, been with me ferrever. Used to drive the Roller, didn't you? Then I thought, what's the point? I can drive, but what I need is someone to watch the journalists for me, keep control of everything. It give 'im something to do as well, 'cos he's a bit of a brush.'

So this was Bleaker, I thought. He shook my hand and stared straight into my eyes. It was like clutching the skin of a snake.

'He's got four degrees now, you know. Keeps getting them,' Stanley said, giving me a welcome excuse to turn my gaze back to him. 'All genuine, although I did offer,' he added with something approaching familial pride.

'Really?' I said with polite interest.

'Yes,' said Bleaker, sitting carefully on the white sofa next to me and stroking his Zapata moustache. 'Two in social sciences, but only one was applied, naturally, and a couple in religious studies.'

'Must be useful in the newsroom,' I suggested.

'Yes, they are. Most valuable for spotting the shirkers, the time-wasters, the fiddlers,' he said calmly, stilled eyes fixed on mine. 'Religion is all about the quest for some controlling force, after all, meaning and value, enlightenment through our shared existential experience.'

'That's it, innit,' Stanley added with sudden, frightening energy. 'Force and value. Right. Bleedin' reporters. They got one hand in my pocket the whole time, scrabbling for the change. And they bugger up the bottom line something rotten.' He spooned the four o'clock kiwi fruit into his mouth with a small silver spoon, its bowl tastefully fashioned with the marquetry of a football.

'I mean, what are they for? Does anyone actually read them? I don't. You know what I always say?' There was an uncomfortable silence as he squinted in concentration and clicked his fingers. 'Come on, come on, Trevor. What is it I always say?'

'A picture paints a thousand words,' Bleaker prompted patiently.

'Yeah, yeah, that's it, a picture paints a thousand words and, more importantly, it saves paying for a thousand words.'

There was another pause. I thought of my conversation with Armitage. Maybe he was right after all. The Visigoths had returned, better dressed and even musical, drumsticks instead of two-bladed axes. But Visigoths all the same.

'Look, the reason I told you to drop by was that I need you to do me a favour in New York.'

There was a pause as Stanley removed kiwi pulp from its skin with the practised precision of a hunter extracting a baby seal from its pelt.

I had a moment to digest the 'drop by' from across the Atlantic, the cramped flight on a *Herald* accounts-department-approved airline, the national carrier from a faraway land of consonants, the meal that resembled small lumps of illness.

'I've got many business interests,' he began, sitting back expansively. 'They're spread over a wide area of publishing and related media, as you know. But what I can do without is a rival coming

31

over here and setting up. Not at this delicate juncture. Have you read *Shaved Crack* by the way?' he asked conversationally. '*Wet Lapper*?'

'Not, not for some time.' I coughed uncomfortably.

'I'll get some copies for you to take back, something to show people.'

He pressed a buzzer. Decca returned and was instructed, even before I had a chance to say that I was quite happy to buy my own.

'I want you to bundle up some magazines for Mr Gibbon here. Give him a few copies of *Crack*, *Landlords' Wives*, *Barbados Bombshells* and *Gents*. Oh, you might as well chuck in last month's *Collar*.'

He leant over the desk. 'Don't read *Collar* myself. It's for all those pervs who want sex with Great Danes. Disgusting. What they need is a good spanking and not the kind they pay for, if you get my drift. Oh, yeah, Decca, you might as well chuck in *Hog Tied*. Sells very well in the Vatican,' he added matter-of-factly.

'Now, don't get me wrong. I'm very inclusive myself. I don't object to no one. In fact, there's a lesbian in marketing.'

'A lifeguard,' Bleaker amended softly.

'What?' Stanley barked.

'A qualified lifeguard, Sir Derek.'

'Yeah, yeah. Anyway, you get my point, don't you?'

I nodded keenly.

Stanley spun his chair and stared out of the window.

'I expect people to give their all to this company,' he said finally. 'And business these days is a ruthless game, ruthless. Now I've got an old-fashioned view about competition.' He pulled on his cigar until the tip glowed with the fury of a stoked furnace. 'I want it out the way. Out.'

There was a pause as he sucked further on the Cohiba, something of quite impressive proportions that a clever engineer might have converted into a small nuclear submarine. Where was this all going? I wondered, moving uncomfortably on the sofa. The soft leather had sunk luxuriously beneath me, forcing my knees to within inches of my chest. I noticed this had not happened on Bleaker's side. How was that possible? He sat erect, sensible, adult, rapt. I was six years old again, struggling with posture.

'I'm going to talk freely. Don't worry, I had this place swept for bugs by my director of security this morning. Now what I want you to do, with your good contacts in the underworld, is find someone prepared to, now what's the words I'm looking for here, Trev?'

'Kill someone,' said Bleaker.

I felt my eyes widen.

'Yeah, that's it. Now this would be for cash. I realized reading your piece about that bloke Rosselli that I'd got to move now.' He slammed the desk hard. 'They're massing, obviously planning to come over. I mean, if he's thinking about it, they all are. One bloke in particular. Sol Goldblam. He's brutal. *Handcuffed by Naked Jam Eating Angels* is already coming in by mail-order, as you probably know.'

I stared at him, unable to hide my obvious and utter confusion. I heard the words, but they didn't make any sense. Was this some kind of joke? A test?

He tutted at my startled face. 'Come on, come on. Don't look so fish-walloped. I just want Goldblam removed, wiped out, done away with. Simple.'

Simple? He might have been asking me to nip out and buy a bar of chocolate. I opened my mouth to speak, but only a jumble of syllables came out. 'Look, I don't know that I –'

'Listen. Your pieces showed the way,' he continued, leaning forward, a weird, messianic glint in his eyes. 'It was like a bulb going on in me head. I thought, if that's how they get things done over there, we should do it over here as well. Modernize.' He puffed thoughtfully. 'Look, I don't want you to do anything more than find a meathead, give him a name and then walk away. Simple. We'll pay $50,000. You can pay 20 per cent up front as a deposit. I don't want any wire transfers into bank accounts so we'll pay it into your New York bank account. If anyone asks, it's a bonus for your good work. In fact,' he said, 'it's a bonus for your Mafia series. How about that?'

'Wonderful idea, Sir Derek,' interjected Bleaker.

Stanley wasn't even looking at me by this point, but continuing with the confidence of someone who knew my willingness to help was not in any doubt, even as I raced mentally to catch up, wondering from a growing crowd of wonders how I was going to explain all or any of this to Gina. She had enough problems with how I went about my job: with the fantasy and plagiarism that had come to define my work, with the increasingly desperate attempts to bulwark myself against cutbacks and the superior talent of Fishlove. 'I think you've got confidence issues, sweetheart,' she would say, the weight of my world on her shoulders.

'Bill-paying issues, Gina. They're different. More English,' I'd reply sharply. 'We Brits have got confidence coming out of our rear-end. Trust me.'

'So, think you can help,' he said. It was a statement, not a question.

I tasted Momma's crispy fries again.

'I'm not sure quite how to –'

'Gawd love me. Those guys you talked to,' he said, impatience creeping in to darken his features. 'Any of them must be able to point you towards someone big enough to have a little chat with. I'm sure you can manage. Listen, show them some of the product, so they know we're legit. You know, not police. They can check with Bleaker any time. There's a mobile number. Now, I don't want anything traced back to this office. I am assuming here that these people are careful. I mean, I don't want some geezer ringing up talking about hits or stuff like that, not on the phone. I've got a reputation to think of.'

'The code word could be badabing,' added Bleaker, a grim smile spread across his face.

'Badabing,' I repeated weakly. 'Why not.' By some astonishing effort of will I kept my own features in a rictus of calm and mature interest. But just below the surface, I was roaring the awful scream of the damned, my eyes were on stalks, fire licked around my ankles. Was this some godly revenge for my years of indifference to journalistic ethics?

Bleaker looked at me, a hunter with an eye on cornered prey. 'Sir Derek's got great faith in you, Oliver. I must admit, I did have my doubts about that Mafia series. It was so, how can I put it, cinematic.' There was a pause as he looked straight at me. 'It seemed so clever of you to get such a detailed insight into their lives, so many confessions that had eluded the police and the FBI,' he said, staring intently at me. 'But I was evidently wrong. You obviously do have the contacts to help.'

He saw something in my eyes. 'Sir Derek believes that it is very important for all members of staff to look to the good of the company as a whole. And the good of the company is not to have Goldblam or his Goldpump Publications setting up in business over here. Nothing must be traced back to the office, obviously. You do understand, Oliver? It goes without saying that this conversation never took place. It will be your word against that of Sir Derek and myself.' He smiled and put an arm on my shoulder, adding kindly: 'Nobody would believe you if you suggested the owner of a national newspaper wanted a killing arranged, so don't even think about it. If it gets out, Oliver, you're finished, sacked, and we'll sue you for libel. We'll take you for every penny you've got.'

Stanley had by now leant very far back in his chair. I was staring at a pair of yellow-stockinged feet resting on his desk. They were ringed by a halo of smoke.

'You're more than just the *Herald*'s New York correspondent, Oliver,' the ventriloquist's feet said. 'You are the representative of something bigger. Of me.' He rose suddenly with outstretched hand. The meeting was over.

'You should stick around for the afternoon news conference,' he said blithely. We might have been discussing the weather.

'That would be great,' I muttered. 'Great.'

'See you later, then.' He winked. I rose, disembodied from whatever reality had once existed in my life.

'By the way,' he said, as I rose. 'Saw you'd claimed for two Whitney Houston CDs. I've knocked them off your expenses form. Cheeky monkey.'

6

Bleaker guided me from the office, through the outer security door and the ante-room with its small peephole and triple locks where I had been frisked on arrival.

'Sir Derek would hate to have to bring you back from New York,' he said, as we reached the lifts. 'The only vacancy here is for a local government correspondent. We're looking for someone to fill it. We've heard Fishlove might be poachable for New York, should you need to be recalled.'

The message was simple. Deliver or be delivered. The prospect of falling back into the arms of the newsroom with its grinding, tedious specialisms was too grim to contemplate. The thought of Fishlove taking over from me was beyond intolerable, unbearable. Decca bustled over just as the lift arrived and handed me a bundle of magazines wrapped in brown paper and a small, sealed bag. I looked at him quizzically.

'Your kiwi fruit, sir,' said Decca.

I might even have said thank you.

'Oh, Oliver. We need badabing by the end of September. You've got ten days.'

I went for a walk along the Thames to digest the enormity of what I was being asked to do. I sat down on a bench and watched the river. It reminded me of the Hudson and home. Had Stanley really asked me to set up a hit? Another thought struck me wildly: perhaps it was all part of some reality television show and my craven acquiescence was going to be broadcast for millions to ridicule?

I could have been outraged, of course, laughed and stormed out, defying him to do his worst. A better man would have done that. But then a better man would not have been me. 'Think of yourself as a soldier,' he had said. 'They kill strangers all the bleedin' time.'

If I'd refused, Stanley would have sacked me, colleagues assuming that I had buckled under the pressure of covering New York. I could see them in the Nark, revelling in the stress finally getting to me; how I couldn't deal with the competition from bloody Fishlove. My description of what he had asked me to do was so preposterous, so fraught with legal problems, that even if anybody believed me, no newspaper would go near it. I could hardly blame them. It sounded insane.

A survival instinct kicked in as I sat, absorbed by misery. In a world where unspeakable things were being done in improbable places by people accessorized with bombs, where was the particular enormity in my crime? I then asked myself a standard question, the one asked by all reporters in times of crisis when others might look to morals for guidance: was there anything in it for me?

A gamine jogger glided past, reminding me of My Lady of the Trimthunder, of Gina. It was a lot to give up and it wasn't as if I was actually being asked to kill someone personally, I reasoned, building the defence for my acquiescence. I was just the middleman. My finger was never going to be anywhere near a trigger. And it wasn't just the job. If I had to come back, I would certainly lose Gina at this precarious stage in our relationship.

I headed gloomily for the afternoon news conference. The editor, Ken Dawson, sat at the head of a long table in the second floor conference room. Dawson, who maintained a low profile both in and out of the office, looked pale and apprehensive, with Bleaker impassive at his side.

Stanley was jogging gently on a running machine. It was placed on a slightly raised dais at the far end of the room. I noticed a small hand bell and a buzzer attached to its front stabilizing bar.

'We've got an exclusive from the government on how the government is winning the war on drugs,' said Marty Johnson, political editor and the first to speak.

That must have been hard to prise out, I thought unkindly.

'The figures are really interesting,' Johnson went on.

'Could make the splash,' said Dawson, glancing anxiously towards Stanley. 'Is there a crackdown or anything for the headline?'

'Not as such,' replied Johnson carefully. 'But I can make some calls to Number Ten and get one.'

Ring, ring. Suddenly, shouting rang over the room. 'Nah, nah, nah,' said the voice, puffing gently. 'What a pile of crap. I'm not having that on the front. Too fucking depressing. Haven't you got a property story? I mean, where's your imagination? Prices must be going up or down, right? And another thing, I want more asylum stories. It's a scandal. They're everywhere, taking over. I've got four of them doing my bleedin' garden for a start.'

Everyone looked at each other. Who would be brave enough? A florid, freckled man with a perpetual frown stirred. It was Jim Hornet, the home news editor. He glanced at Dawson, who nodded gratefully. 'Both very good issues, Sir Derek. Thanks.' He paused briefly. 'But while we're working those up, we've got the mad cow disease kills topless model story, an interview with the girl's parents. Great pics of her –'

Ring, ring. 'I don't want no bleedin' death-bed pictures in my paper, for crying out loud.'

'Great pics of her during her underwear modelling days,' Hornet persevered. There was an audible sigh from around the table.

'That's more like it,' said Stanley pressing the buzzer, his voice rising above the thump, thump, thump of trainers on rubber. 'Next!'

'We've also got the new Euro campaign being launched by the government. Great pics of Jordan at the launch in Westminster.'

Buzz. 'Yes. Next.' And it went on. Dawson sat mute throughout, I noticed, to the game-show sounds as the news department laid out its menu for inclusion or rejection.

'Prince Charles is talking tonight at the Guildhall about the need for people to search into their souls for fewer material values. His people say it's a major speech.'

There was an ominous silence. 'Is he mentioning Jordan, do you know?' asked Dawson quickly.

'No, don't think so,' came the perplexed reply. The editor smiled slyly. 'I think we have our splash. PRINCE SNUBS JORDAN IN MORALS WARNING should fit nicely across page one.'

Buzz. 'Nice one, Ken. Glad to see you earning the obscene amounts of money you're getting from me.'

The mood lightened. 'There are some new figures on breast cancer screening and how it's failing to detect people with the disease despite government claims. Again, I thought we could use a picture of Jordan.'

'Good idea,' said Dawson, adding spiritedly after glancing nervously at the dais. 'Those figures do sound a bit depressing to me. They need cheering up a bit.'

The news editor continued. 'Then we've got the Rebel Yell concert at the Albert Hall. Sir Sting is playing. I think it's in aid of his Rainforest for Wiltshire campaign. The Queen will be there. There's talk she may join in a version of "We are the Champions". Still trying to confirm that with the Palace.'

Buzz. 'I don't want any green loonies ranting about tofu,' said Stanley. 'Let's just stick to the music and the girls. Any big weddings?'

The news editor nodded no. There was a sadness in his eyes.

'Sport?' said Dawson.

'Yeah,' said a smokey voice. 'Man United tonight. Interview with Ferguson. Fulham are after the Dutch striker Van Whanke.'

Buzz. 'Lovely,' said Stanley.

'We've got an interview with his brother, says it's a done deal and it'll be sewn up by the weekend. We've also got a piece on Beckham's hairdresser. He's been done before, of course. But this is the first time he's spoken about the different lotions.'

The buzzer was hit an enthusiastic three times. Dawson looked relieved.

'Showbiz?'

'There's Michael Jackson's new nose,' said showbusiness editor Steve Clockx.

'Didn't we have that last week?' asked Dawson.

'No, that was the last one.'

'Oh, I see. Anything else?'

'Well, there's the Madonna tour kicking off at Wembley. I think we should know what kind of bottled water she plans to have in her dressing room in time for the first edition. We've also got an interview with Steve Surge from Cringe. He's denying the gay rumours, says his family always designed their own clothes.'

Buzz. 'He bloody well is gay,' said Stanley ferociously. 'I heard him going on about helping refugees the other night before he sang that soppy song. Christ. Look, I don't want gay stars, I want girl stars. How many times I got to tell you?'

Clockx carried on, tacking against the storm into recovery territory. 'Pamela Anderson's had a new tattoo under her bikini line. Apparently it glows under a back light. Everyone's getting them. Thought we could go out and do some sort of survey.'

Buzz, buzz. 'Now, that's more like it. We'll put her on page one and have the mad cow model on page three. I don't want dead women on the front, I don't care how pretty they was. Scatter Jordan about a bit, chuck in a couple of asylum stories.'

'Foreign?' asked Dawson.

'Nothing,' said a smartly dressed young man confidently.

And so it went on. If only they knew the story they were really sitting on, I thought. Deranged Owner Orders Reporter to Set Up Hit. Does Not Ask Jordan.

'Oh, Ollie, can I have a word,' said a voice as the meeting broke up. I wheeled around. It was Jim Hornet. 'Just heard there might be a chance of getting Whitney. She'd make a great page three for us, we could cross-ref to your big interview. I hear on the grapevine that Fishlove is after her, by the way. He's sharp, isn't he? I thought his stuff on New York prostitutes and the way they hide their earnings off-shore was brilliant. How about a drink after work?'

No, thanks, I said to myself privately. 'Yes, love to, Jim.' Bloody Fishlove.

'Smashing. What are you over for, by the way?'

We had reached the newsdesk, a bank of tables littered with telephones, newspapers and coffee cups filled with cigarette ends.

'Oh, Stanley suddenly wanted to see me. Something to do with putting a face to the guy who, as he put it, "costs me all that fucking money in America". We just chatted about this and that.'

Telephones started ringing. 'Grab one of those, will you? Thanks, mate.'

I lifted the receiver. 'Newsdesk,' I said. There was a long silence. 'Hello?' What sounded like heavy breathing came down the line. I was about to hang up.

'It's Gilbert here in the Manchester office,' a voice said, slowly, menacing, deliberate.

'Oh, hi, Gilbert. It's Ollie Gibbon. Just answering the phones for Jim. Anything for the list?'

'Welcome back to the asylum. Anyway, got a great story for you. It's about a vicar running off with a teenage girl and setting up a love nest in a caravan near Blackpool. Girl's parents are devastated. Interested?' He spoke carefully, savouring each word. Gilbert Trench was a legendary figure, famous for turning up the most improbably lurid stories from Harrogate, Scarborough and other dens of decency in northern England. 'I'm sure we are, Gilbert. Any chance of an interview with the girl's father?'

There was a pause. 'You're talking to him.'

7

'Can you explain these, sir?' He was tall with crew-cut blond hair. His pale blue eyes stared with the venom of a born-again Christian discovering voodoo dolls in his Christmas stocking.

Outside the white, windowless room I could hear aircraft roaring for take-off into the night skies above Kennedy Airport. Inside, a bright overhead light bathed the room and my luggage, its contents spread over the long aluminium table like some beached, foul detritus. 'Look, they're just, just samples of what my company produces,' I said exasperated, the put-upon victim of some awful misunderstanding: the small-appliance salesman forced to peddle a line of saucy underwear after an unexpected corporate amalgamation. What could you do? I hoped my eyes asked.

'But your visa says you're a journalist, Mr Gibbon,' Blondie persisted. He nodded his head in disgust a few more times. On his wrist he wore a golden bracelet made from the interwoven initials WWJD. A lover?

'I gotta be straight with you. What this luggage says to me, sir, is that you are entering the United States to distribute pornographic material, not to write about our country. That is serious misrepresentation. Fraudulent entry. Visa fraud.'

I felt prickles of sweat on my back. Nobody messed with the Immigration and Naturalization Service. Not any more. They could slap you in jail with Bubba for months before a judge even heard your name.

'Honestly, I know it looks weird,' I went on sounding weary, feeling panicked. 'But the company I work for also produces, well, adult magazines as well as a quite ordinary, decent newspaper that is the bit that I work for. I can't help it. I just went back and the owner lumbered me with this lot to help him make some business contacts here. Give them a call in London. They'll confirm it. I can give you a name. Anyway, is it illegal? I mean there's porn everywhere in Manhattan? What about free speech, the First Amendment? You know, the right to bear arms and show bare.'

'This isn't about the Constitution. I'm talking visa violations, sir,' he said, stone-faced. 'You appear to be entering America under false pree-tenses. That's what we're talking about here.'

I sighed, hoping there was just the right amount of resignation, defiance and blazing sincerity at work in the exhalation. But I could see Blondie wasn't buying it. I wondered idly if he had met his wife at the church group? Was she chosen for him? Was it a mass wedding ceremony at the Church of the Latterday Applied Gospel and Vinyl Record? I noticed to my dismay a tattoo on his right arm. SAVED BY JESUS, it read. Just my luck.

'I'll have to get my supervisor, sir. This looks like distribution to me and, I gotta tell you, someone comes in with this stuff,' he said, staring at me, 'he's a distributor. Plain and simple. I'd advise you to have a list of those contacts ready, sir, so we can check out your story.' He walked out.

One hour, two hours, three hours passed. I lost track of time. Eventually, a burly man walked through the door and sat cop-like astride a chair, resting his head on the back support as he faced me. It worked for Christine Keeler. She had the sort of body made to sit suggestively on a chair. Lt James D. Resin did not. He had a Passion-for-Budweiser body. I tried to look blank. He swept a hand over his balding head.

'See, here's the problem, Mr Gibbon. Your visa says you're a journalist and the company you work for is a newspaper. Sure, it checks out. We ran you through the computer. But here you are coming in with all this, this pornographic material.' There was a pause. 'But you check out,' he said again, sounding disappointed. 'I guess you're free to leave. But let this be a lesson to you. I'm signing this off as for personal use. We have your name on file. If we even get a hint you're importing this stuff to sell, we'll haul you in. Got it? We'll be watching you, my friend.'

'Got it,' I replied, relieved. 'Great. Look, truthfully, I'm not peddling porn, really I'm not. But thanks for all this. I appreciate it, the chance to explain and all that.'

He raised a hand to stop me. 'Hey, look. I don't need to hear anything, OK? I just don't expect to see you again with this, this garbage.'

As I walked out, Blondie caught up with me. 'See this,' he said, dangling his bracelet in front of my face.

'Yes, I was wondering about that,' I said, which was true. 'I had Wilhelmina for the first name and Doris at the end. Got stumped by the middle two.'

He looked confused. 'They ain't no names. They're a question and one you'd do well to ask yourself each and every day.'

'Really, and what might that be?'

A look of smug satisfaction spread over his face. 'What Would Jesus Do?'

'I'm sorry, I don't quite follow.'

'That's the question you gotta ask yourself every day. Just think of the letters.'

I thanked him coolly and fled to the taxi rank, privately offering my own alternative translation: Wholesome Witless Just Dopey.

It was a 45-minute ride back to Manhattan under the hellish tutelage of a Mr Singh. The sweat cooled on my back as the air conditioning churned out its memories of Siberia. I tried to replay it all as we shot along the Long Island Expressway, ricocheting through the Midtown Tunnel. The humiliating and painfully public initial exit through customs, skin mags spread over the table as if they were the remains of some decadent, debauched feast, made me wince. Customs officers, all women as cruel luck would have it, flicking pages, glancing up at me, fingering my boxer shorts with the amusing motif of an electric eel, poking their fingers through the fly, for goodness sake. Occasionally, I'd glimpse some flesh impressively tangled around a four-poster bed, or wince at an animal, as pages were revealed. Behind me a family group stared. Mum, dad and their two little dinkums. I shrugged my shoulders.

'Research,' I muttered apologetically. The adult lips pursed back in acknowledgement, telling the children to 'go play over there'. 'It's for a book.'

I glanced up at the windows and the lit urban canopy of lower Manhattan. God, I needed a friendly shoulder and a huge whiskey. In either order. My heart leapt as we lurched over cobbles to my street and Mr Singh screeched to a halt, hitting the kerb hard. Another New York taxi journey survived. The light was on. Gina was back! I bounded through the front door and the puddle on the landing, oblivious to the water dripping from the ceiling above me. Up the stairs in a minute. Breathless, I turned my key. Stop. I smelt her scent and closed my eyes to savour the moment.

'Hi, there, it's me,' I shouted, awash with pleasure, yearning for that protective cocoon lovers give each other.

She came around the corner, cool and poised. We hugged. 'I've missed you,' I said and meant it.

'If that's an apology, it's overdue,' came the measured reply. But a smile was playing over her lips. 'You know, you really can be a stubborn asshole.'

'I know. But everyone should have one. An arsehole, I mean.'

'You're funny, Ollie. I've always liked that about you,' she said. Her deep blue eyes looked at me. 'But can you explain this?'

On cue, a small green ball of fur rounded the corner into the hall.

'That's amazing,' I said. 'How are you controlling it?'

'Look again.'

'Good grief. Hughgrant?'

'Apparently,' came the curt reply. 'You took him to Mrs Romstein's again, didn't you?'

I cleared my throat nervously. 'Well, yeah. I mean. I can explain. I didn't have any choice. Look, I got called back to London, there wasn't time to book him into Doggy Rest and you weren't here.' I took a closer look. 'Christ, what the heck has she done? I only asked her to take him to Kleinman's and give him the seaweed pellets, Gina, that's all. It can't be the seaweed, can it?'

She sighed. 'Don't be ridiculous. It's dye. God, Ollie. How many times have I told you? That woman is crazy, insane. Nobody gives their dogs to her any more since the washing-machine business. I don't know why you leave him there. You'd better sort it out. And when I got back she was downstairs with Hughgrant and those supposed workmen. Jeez, Ollie.'

'Listen, I'll go and find out what happened.' I headed out, chastened in that way only Gina could manage. At least she had not commented on why I was home fully four hours later than I had said in the message left, optimistically, with Grace. One lie less to deliver.

I knocked on the basement door.

'Who is it?' came a quavering voice.

'It's me, Mrs Romstein. Ollie. From upstairs.'

'Just a minute, please.'

I sighed.

There was a peal of keys jangling, a pulling of bolts. 'Love is just a glance a way . . .' drifted out. Minutes seemed to pass by, whole life cycles completed. Species may have come and gone in the time it took Mrs Romstein to unlock her heavy front door. I leant against the wall, closed my eyes. 'Strangers in the night . . .' Eventually, it creaked open. The air hung heavy with Eau de Nondescript Flowers. She had applied rouge halfway up one cheek and three quarters of the way up the other. Her artificial eyelashes were curled rakes. Something seemed to move in her huge head of jet-black hair, a rigid edifice that rose from her skull in architecturally spirited twists and twirls. A stray Boeing 747? That missing platoon?

'Oh, how perfectly lovely of you to drop by. Lonely?'

'No, not at all, Mrs Romstein. But thanks for asking. I, well we, Gina and I, were just wondering. That is, we were just a little surprised about Hughgrant's colour.'

She looked at me blankly, her eyebrows knitted in puzzlement, head cocked to one side. 'His colour?'

I plunged on. 'Yes, his colour. When I left he was a sort of mottled-brown Yorkshire terrier au naturel, as it were. Now he's a green one.'

She looked pleased. 'Oh, that. It was nothing. Nothing at all. Just bring him back when it wears off and I'll do it again. It was the seaweed pills that gave me the idea. Such a lovely shade, don't you think? That nice man Mr Eddie had some spare paint powder. I had a cigarette with him the other day. It was quite delicious. He said it was a "special import" from his country. Such a gentleman. Well, we got talking and somehow Hughgrant came up. He offered me red, but I said no, which I think was the right decision, don't you?'

'Yes, I suppose so,' I said, disturbed by the direction this was going. 'But I wish you'd said no to green as well, that's my point. Will it come off, Mrs Romstein?'

'Oh, I have no idea. I'm so sorry. The choice was a little limited, you see. I know, I should have waited. The paint was only' – she counted off her fingers – 'eight dollars. I could come by and pick it up this evening.'

'No. Better not. Gina's a bit tired. Look, I think I've got it here.' I fumbled through my pockets for notes and found a $10 bill. I handed it over.

'I haven't got any change,' she said.

'Don't bother,' I replied. Anything to avoid her meeting Gina.

'Well, you must drop by again, when you're feeling lonely.'

I left quickly, pursued by hope.

'I used to tango, you know.'

'Really? Thanks, thanks,' I shouted back down the dark corridor.

'Should I have chosen the yellow? Oh, dear.'

8

I thought we'd go out. Somewhere special. Make up. Forget about Hughgrant. Not that he seemed to mind. Then I remembered that dogs were colour blind. We headed down to SoHo and a dark side street off Prince. My brain was still failing to process the enormity of what I had been asked to do and craved diversions.

'Where's the wretched door?' I asked.

'I don't know. You booked the place,' Gina said with a sigh.

Eventually, after trying a few buzzers at random, I found it, the entrance to Fade Out, the latest, hippest, absolutely must-be-seen-in place of the moment. The restaurant was behind a hidden door, some contemporary take on the old speakeasies of Prohibition. I doubted it was Happy Siam Party Supplies. Perhaps it was Maggio Beef Importers? I settled for the small intercom with no writing anywhere near it and pressed. 'Fade Out,' said a voice.

I could barely hide my relief. 'Hi, I have a reservation. Name of Gibbon. No, G.I.B.B.O.N. Like the historian. All right, then, like the monkey. That's it. You don't? But I called a few hours ago? What other number? Well, someone took my reservation. No, I wasn't sent a key. What? Nobody mentioned a security code.' I played my ace. Nobody was going to get between me and my reconciliation. 'Actually, I'm writing a newspaper review, if that makes a difference.' It did.

Inside, a disturbingly beautiful blonde in *Barbarella* white leather took our coats. 'This way, please. I'm sorry about the confusion. I did find your name. You just hadn't been keyitized.'

She led us down a corridor painted with groovy green and red spirals, and I tried to stare at the walls, but felt dizzy. Our white plastic table was beside the white plastic bust of Andy Warhol.

Gina seemed to approve, which was the important thing. I toyed with the white cutlery, turning the fork a few times. It was clever the way goldfish swam in the chairs. Gina said nothing, of course. It was up to me to build the bridges.

'Look, I'm sorry about Hughgrant. I am. You're right, the old lady's bonkers. I should have thought of something else and I'll have a word with Eddie tomorrow. Apart from anything else, that water in the lobby can't be doing us any good, West Nile Virus and everything, and the shower still hasn't been fixed.'

'And?' she asked.

'OK, I'm incredibly sorry about our row the other night. It was bloody stupid of me.'

'I was hurt, Ollie. I mean, you can be very cruel. Daddy says you have issues. You should see someone. It isn't about dolphins. All I want is for you to have a successful newspaper career, to feel good about yourself. That's all he wants as well. You can do better than making things up. I know you're worried about your job and about Fishlove scooping you all the time.'

'Really?' I felt a tuna moment well up. What did she know about working for a British tabloid? 'Well, I don't worry about Fishlove scooping me all the time, for your information,' I said, bristling indignantly, delivering my first lie since returning. 'Also, I'm not sure your father is an authority on my life, given that we've barely actually met.' She didn't pick it up. I let it pass. This was no night for living dangerously, for telling her that it wasn't just Fishlove, that people would kill for my job or, for that matter, that I was about to kill indirectly to keep it. Why ruin the making-up moment?

'Your old man's probably right. Listen, let's have the seared tuna and to hell with the dolphins,' I threw in with mock braggadocio. 'God, I need a drink. Excuse me, excuse me.' I flapped a hand in the air. Prada-clad waiters sashayed past.

'Oh, God, Ollie,' said Gina, raising her eyes. 'Hi,' she said in a firm assured tone, instantly drawing attention from one of them. 'Two Cosmopolitans.'

We sat in companionable silence. Order was restoring itself to our universe. The stars, temporarily in disarray, were realigned. I was being diffident, Gina was being commanding, which I'd always loved about her, although she often said she wished it was the other way around.

A tall, muscled man with shaved head and enough earrings to hang a shower curtain or receive Radio Albania hovered over the table. 'Our specials tonight are cumin-glazed sea bass served on a frisson of lettuce in a lemon blueberry jelly-bean reduction with a wastage of oregano,' he said, peering into the middle distance, glazed himself. 'I also have chopped pork and spices rolled into a smooth cylinder, grilled and served with potatoes that are boiled, drained, then crushed with a twist of butter.'

'Would that be sausage and mash?'

'Excuse me, sir?'

'That last one. The cylinder. It sounds familiar. Oh, never mind. I'll have it anyway, the chopped pork cylinder thing with crushed potatoes.'

'And I'll have the chicken,' said Gina. 'Crushed potatoes and mineralized spinach on the side, please. Does the chicken come with folic acid and vitamin C?'

'No, ma'am,' said the waiter. 'But I can have them added.'

'That would be good, thank you,' she said. The waiter stood up well to some further close-quarter questioning about the chicken. Was it organic? Had it been soya-fed? Was it stroked regularly? How were the feathers removed?

Finally, we were alone. Gina wanted to know about my trip, now that I had apologized for forcing her to go on one of her own. I wondered what to tell her, settling for most of it. Most. I told her about the kiwis, which she thought was funny, and the praise for my Mafia series, which produced a derisive snort.

I made no mention of the airport. Gina took a dim view of pornography. I could assume that her opprobrium would stretch to facilitating a murder. Our relationship was too fragile to tell her what Stanley had asked me to organize. I knew she would accuse me of being craven, if she believed me at all. I said instead that he wanted a new series written about the Mafia, an interview with an actual hitman.

'He called you over for that?' she asked, suspicious and surprised.

'I think he has some, well, some business to conduct with them after I make contact. For the interview,' I said guardedly. 'Nothing dodgy, of course. He just didn't want to discuss it over the phone. He wants me to make connections. All legit.' I tried to sound breezy and casual, as if it were the most ordinary request in the world.

She gave me one of her long and pained expulsions of breath. 'I really don't get you at all these days, Ollie. Why can't he make his own connections? I mean, you're a reporter. He obviously doesn't want another series, he wants you to do his dirty work. Don't you see, honey? Why didn't you stand up to him? Tell him it was absurd, completely outrageous that he should ask you to find dubious business connections for him. And, really, who wants to make legitimate deals with the mob, for heaven's sake? You're so passive. God, it's annoying. It sounds like he walked all over you.'

I felt anger worming its way inside, but kept it under control, which is what a good passive–aggressive does, bottles it all up for a tuna war. 'That's easy for you to say,' I said tightly. 'You don't work for him. He just thinks I know people and it's good for me that he does, surely? And God knows I've certainly given that impression with that last series of articles.

'The thing is, it's all just one business to him,' I forged on. 'I can't go on about how it isn't my job to do whatever. Stanley pays the bills. I don't really have much choice. He can ask what the hell he likes at the end of the day. Don't you see? He's the reason we can afford to live where we live.'

I looked up. She nodded slowly, lips pursed. The prospect of losing the apartment proved to be the season clincher. She beat a dignified retreat. 'I still think it's disgraceful, and you're being totally lame. What are you going to do, then?'

'I don't know, yet. Sleep on it. Hope it'll go away. Make some calls tomorrow.' I had no clue. 'Look, when it's over, I'll change. I promise.'

Gina looked at me with a particularly sad intensity. 'I just want you back, Ollie. I want the self-assured guy I met in my life again.'

'You'll get him,' I promised.

We walked back to the apartment, content in an imperfect way. I opened a bottle of wine, and Gina put the fire video on. It crackled romantically. We thought about snuggling up and reading by the warm glow from Hughgrant. But then Gina had a better idea as the Detroit Spinners sang that life ain't so easy when you're a ghetto child. 'Come here,' she said, pulling me by the trouser belt and turning up the fire volume. We kissed deeply and collapsed onto the sofa, making love just like in the movies, except for the Day-Glo dog at our ears. I haven't seen that in the movies yet.

9

I went to see Todd the next day, a moth to a bright place, a sinner to his priest, a diversion at least. We went over the road to Brew Bar. A strong wind was blowing through the canyons of lower Manhattan. I ordered a small cappuccino; Todd asked fluently for a magnifico grande double espresso, double skinny latte with flat top. His command of coffee orders was impressive. I told him the problem, or at least the part of it I was prepared to share: that I needed to meet a genuine hitman for a feature article. We worked through blueberry muffins the size of small Polynesian islands. I looked for some sign of recognition, of sympathy for my predicament. Instead, he smiled that big Idaho smile.

'What's so funny? It's a bloody disaster. I don't know anybody involved with knocking people off. I mean, I can hardly call the Chamber of Trade and say, "Give me a list of your finest hitmen." How on earth am I going to find anyone?'

He listened attentively until I finished, spent of frustration. His eyebrows furrowed, and he looked at me with an intensity disturbing in someone who spent a disproportionate amount of time watching the Cartoon Network. For a moment I thought he was going to do his Tor Tellini routine again.

'I just might be able to help you, my man.'

I paused and looked incredulous. 'Oh, sure?' I mocked through the still dulling jet lag. He looked straight at me. 'Don't tell me,' I said. 'Just dial 1 800 HITZDONE and ask for killers in the 212 area code.'

There was something unsettling about his stare. He actually seemed knowing. I faltered.

'You are joking, aren't you?' I said slowly, narrowing my eyes to try to see him in sharper focus, to catch a glimpse of what was beyond that vast veldt of openness. He smiled, and I surrendered to the incredible, letting a sun appear on my personal horizon for the first time in days. It was strong enough to obliterate the rain lashing against the Brew Bar window. 'You're not, are you? You actually know someone, don't you? You bloody do.' I felt ecstatic. 'I can't believe it. How? Who?'

He basked for a moment and then leant over, looking around to make sure that neither of the no other people in the place could hear us and whispered, 'OK. Let's just say I know a guy. He works out of a restaurant on Mulberry Street near old St Patrick's. He's connected. Could be just the dude you're looking for. I'll give him a call, suggest you guys meet up. He'd be a fine interview.'

I had no idea Todd knew mob people. Todd! It seemed incredible. Maybe everyone in New York did and I was the odd one out, the poor sap from out of town who didn't know any Wise Guys, someone for whom the city was merely an architectural drama abandoned by its director, residents the bit players providing noise and spectacle. Look at him walk down the street. Don't laugh, children. Don't throw stones. He can't help it. He's British. My spirits lifted. Obviously, the plain fact was that everyone knew somebody a bit shady. This was New York, a toddlin' town of dive bars and tenements, of tribal loyalties, of Yankees and Mets, heroes and villains, intricacies and insecurities, Broadway stars and Bowery bums. This was the brash house that Babe built. I felt dizzy with it all. Maybe he even knew Whitney?

'That would be fantastically kind. I mean, if it's no trouble,' I said, gratitude and blueberry muffin crumbs tumbling out.

'Sure, man. No problem. Tell you what, I'll call him later today.'

Maybe I'd been wrong about Todd after all. There are about 280 million Americans. Only 40 million of them had passports and Todd was not amongst them. It had always coloured my opinion of him, encouraged a tingle of superiority. He had better hair, sure, but I had been to Malaysia, the country, not the nightclub. Todd had never even been over the border to Mexico to get drunk on mesquite. The world outside America was to him what it was to

most of his countrymen: a weird place of imperfect teeth, unreliable air-conditioning and small portions all best seen filtered
through television screens.

'Todd, I'm really, really grateful. Have I ever said you're not only
talented but also a great pal? Listen, just anybody I can hook up
with to keep the beastmasters in London happy. Anybody.'

I felt wonderful sauntering back home, excited, exhilarated,
thrilled. I just might pull this off. I thought of pay rises, promo-
tions, congratulatory e-mails. I might be given a column to write,
one with a beautifying photograph like the ones other columnists
use, the sort taken ten years ago.

Later that night, Gina and I were watching *Seinfeld* when Todd
called. It was set up. For tomorrow. I was to be at the restaurant
by 8 p.m. I thanked him again. Outside it had started to snow, a
freak early shower. Let it snow, let it snow, let it snow, I hummed.

'You seem in a good mood,' said Gina.

'I am. Todd may have solved my little problem. Says he knows
someone who might be able to help.'

'Really?' She sounded suspicious.

'Yes, really. What's so strange about that?' I said airily.

'Nothing, I suppose. I'm just surprised Todd knows those sorts
of people. I didn't know he knew any hitmen. He's certainly never
mentioned it.'

She had a point, but I wasn't going to concede it.

'It isn't exactly the sort of thing you boast about, is it?'

Our relationship was still navigating treacherous waters, places
where malevolent tuna lurked. Todd had helped me and that was
all that mattered, I said to her, adding with quiet relish, 'Maybe
you don't know him as well as you think you do.' She let out a
knowing laugh.

It was a man thing, I told myself. This was what mates did: lay
down their contacts for their friends, selflessly. I felt goose bumps.
I was lucky to have such a good pal in this city.

'It's probably through his mad shop,' I said, gnawing at it a bit
longer. Gina was right, of course, it was spectacularly out of

character. 'Someone coming in to buy all those "original sofas from *Godfather II*" or something,' I speculated.

It was getting late and I decided to take Hughgrant for a walk and put any uncertainties about Todd out of my mind. Hughgrant glowed at the end of his leash, zigzagging across the dark sidewalk, a demented, widdling beacon. People stopped and stared. Dogs are little people here. They get the vote next year.

'Hey, what species?' said a voice from the dark.

'Oh, he's a miniature Überstrurmbanführer,' I answered cheerily.

'Really? Wow. Great coat, man.'

'Thanks. Yes, they're German hunting dogs. Their prey think it's a small mop or large caterpillar and don't bother to run away.'

'You don't say?'

'Absolutely. It's all down to evolution.'

'Oh, yeah? I know it, that store on Broadway and 12th, right?'

'No, not the clothes shop, the theory of species development.'

He looked at me doubtfully. 'Well, whatever. Way to go.' He waved and disappeared into the flurries.

I got home and knocked back a congratulatory nightcap of Maker's Mark bourbon, an expensive treat to round off a perfect day. Gina was already in bed, which was on the mezzanine floor and looked straight out over the Hudson. A huge moon hung over Hoboken and cast its shine on the stilled, grey water. I wanted to tell her how much I loved her, what a low life I'd been over the tuna business, how she made it all worth while in this lacquered and lonely place of yearning strangers united by restless, often frustrated ambitions and health club memberships. Why I could not imagine being without her. How I would change, do some real reporting once all this was sorted out.

Todd, the great Todd, was connected to Gina by that mysterious cord that binds all Americans, stretching from pre-school through to fraternity house, secret ties sealed by intimately placed tattoos. Todd and Gina. My frat house. Maybe we should get our own tattoos?

Then I heard gentle, deep breathing. I smiled. It could wait until tomorrow. I would tell her then. Hughgrant glowed contentedly in the corner. The only sound was the steady, urgent complaint of traffic on the West Side Highway. I once heard that men fantasize about having sex with as many different women as they can. But they hope to be in love just once. I was in love, I thought. Meanwhile, I'd have another drink, just to make sure that I slept the sleep of the deserving innocent, of the connected. I kissed Gina gently on the lips and later dreamt of My Lady of the Trimthunder. She was riding a huge yellow-fin tuna across the Pacific towards me. There was no sign of Fishlove.

10

'Puth from the hip, you puthy, this ain't no relaxation exercise.' Dimos strode around the leg extender. 'Puth, one mo' time. You can do it.'

No, I couldn't, I thought miserably, clenching my teeth. Both legs remained stubbornly locked around my elbows in some hellish Kama Sutra illustration or an especially unhappy birthing contortion. Constipated grunts failed to move the block of metal in front of me. Dimos huffed loudly and added his own weight to the machine. Gradually, it inched forward, painfully, slowly. I cried with relief as my legs finally outstretched.

'Don't lock them knees o' it's thwee more,' my tormentor commanded. I stopped suddenly, alarmed, angled and agonized. 'Now hold it there, hold it, hold it. OK. Now lock the machine.'

'How about the Trimthunder?' I asked hopefully, gasping, as I slid the restraining bolt back into place.

'No way, man. This is chest and abth, chest and abth. I ain't having you puthyin' around wid that toy on my watch.' His chiselled black face stared into the distance. Dimos MacGregor was squat and powerfully built, with permanently flexed arms, their veins swollen into distended pipes. His chest was a carved piece of mahogany and muscle mass. This was my personal trainer. I wanted an exercise rush to calm me for the meeting that night.

Dimos suspected that all his clients were 'puthyfooters', which was code for street runners, tennis players and others he considered soft and, by implication, irredeemably white. He'd been brought up on the streets of Harlem by a mother who had taken one look at her little baby and declared him 'de mos' beautiful' to hospital staff. A name was born. He was christened 'Dimos' and quickly learnt to defend it.

'You learned to be strong to survive there, my fwend,' he would say. I told him people named Quentin had the same problem in rougher parts of Britain.

He never mentioned the speech impediment that might have been the real spur to toughening up, and neither did anyone else. There was something about the firm jaw, covered by an angrily shaven goatee, which spoke a warning.

It was a beautiful, crisp morning when I walked to the gym, part of my mental preparation for the challenge ahead. Dog walkers were out with their herds of Labradors, terriers, retrievers and exotic mixes. They took over the sidewalks and dreamt of scripts they would sell, books they would write or parts they were up for.

I had slept deeply for the first time in days, and it was good to be hitting the Old Factory. I could hear the thumping work-out music as I approached its illuminated entrance-cum-coffee shop. I had planned to go straight to the Trimthunder. But Dimos was in and free and, as he reminded me, my 'puthyfootin'' to London meant I had missed a training session and also a chance to sign up for the first day of his jump-rope disco work-out. He seemed to be taking it personally.

'It's your body, man, know what I'm saying. But you got to do the time to get the shine.'

'I know, Dimos, I know,' I replied diffidently. 'It was a work thing. I had to go. I mean, I'll definitely come to the next, er, disco jump thing.'

'If I got a buck for every one o' my clients said that, ah'd be a rich man.' He glared at me accusingly. Dimos considered himself something of a fitness entrepreneur. The business plan was simple and unchanging, despite its failure yet to lead to videos or a slot on cable television. It worked on the principle of adding the word 'disco' to almost every conceivable form of strenuous motion. I had already, loyally, participated in his Six Pack of Abs Power Disco Stomach Punch course and his Disco Rollerblade Squat class, which left three people injured and was dropped rapidly amid a flurry of legal actions. Dimos was characteristically defiant. 'Ah mean, what kind of jackath come to a disco rollerblading jive who ain't never bin on rollerbladeth before? That what my attorney say anyway,' he added defensively.

I was stretched and bent for an hour, liberally cursed for my lack of flexibility and all-round puthyfootedness, before being released to the world of recovery.

I met Todd for lunch and final details. Our waitress skateboarded over. Todd ordered the turkey with mayonnaise, pickle and carrots on 73-grain wheat bread. I did the same, but asked to substitute with white. 'White?' she said, puckering her nose. 'I don't know if –'

'Yes, you do,' I broke in impatiently. 'Tell them it's for the Brit.'

'Okey dokey,' she replied happily, pushing off through double doors to the assembly line of Mexican kitchen staff, the invisible human engine of Manhattan life, who fill every restaurant whether it serves sandwiches or sauce Bernaise.

Todd was in charge, which would have been unsettling under typical circumstances. I was to meet my mob contact in Swanky's, a small Italian restaurant on Mulberry Street, the heart of Little Italy.

'He's called Sonny and he'll be sitting in a booth at the back. He'll be in a pinstripe suit and wearing a carnation in the button-hole. His grey fedora will be on the table in front of him. He may have a thin moustache,'

'Sonny? You're kidding, of course,' I said with disbelief. 'A grey suit and fedora? Hardly inconspicuous, is it?'

'He doesn't need to be, Ollie. That's the point, my man. This is his territory, and besides, he could be acting in a play, heading out for a fancy dress. The best disguise a mob guy can have these days is to look like one from the movies.'

I still never thought to question how Todd, seller of second-hand furniture of dubious provenance and repairer of Yosemite's damaged fauna, had acquired this connection with the brutal underworld of New York. My emotion was simply blind, desperate gratitude.

'Well, I suppose so. They did all seem to wear shell suits in *The Sopranos*,' I conceded, chomping through a two-foot flood defence of food. The waitress, I noticed, had worn rubber gloves to deliver my white bread, presumably a protection against toxic shock.

'Exactermento. Now, Sonny is a member of the Tavarese family. They run the docks in Miami and Jersey, but they're also into the sex industry in a big way. Word is they control the chat-line companies. Sonny's a captain in the family, very senior, not to be messed with.'

Todd stared at me seriously, holding his sandwich, a meal for Afghanistan. 'I mean it, dude. These guys are tough.'

I told him to relax. I could believe it. I'd seen the films, written about them. I knew about contracts and not messing with 'dem guys'. It was a straightforward meeting, I told myself, make a connection and go, pass on the name, leave it to London. I was really grateful and said so. 'I owe you, Todd. Really I do.'

Our waitress glided back. 'Everything OK?'

'Horrible, thanks,' I replied equably.

'That's so great,' she said, smiling brightly and disappearing with the payment.

Gina was out when I got back home, so I was left – worryingly – to choose between my selection of two ties. The suit choice was easier. I had only one, a grey Armani bought five years ago in a sale, with now unfashionably narrow lapels. I settled for the dark grey tie with a spider's-web pattern and just a hint of beer stain. Somehow the downward-pointed arrow motif below the word 'Paradise' with just a hint of beer stain failed to hit the right note.

Little Italy is not what it was when Joseph 'Joe Bananas' Bonanno and Anthony 'Fat Tony' Galerno ruled its streets; when kids and hoodlums hung out on metal fire escapes or sat idle and insolent on stoops. There were no Neapolitan tarantellas mingling with jazz from a dozen dance halls. Apart from its geography, which was gradually being devoured by the expanding mass of squid, fish eyes, species suspended in strange juices and improbable vegetables collectively known as Chinatown, Little Italy was not unlike the rest of Manhattan, and its street sounds were the usual homogenized noises of impatient taxi horns, sirens. I weaved through the early-evening crush of tourists, passed the Parisi Bakery on Mott Street, which is where Frank Sinatra bought his bread, and on to Mulberry, past the plate-glass window of Mare Chiaro, where ol' Blue Eyes sank vino in the back room. Swanky's was near by and easy to find. It had an extravagantly red canopy hanging over a clutch of outside tables and chairs. Waiters in white aprons hovered haughtily.

Through the gloom I could just make out the bar on the right, opposite rows of high-backed banquettes. A maître d' appeared at my ear.

'Signor?'

'Hi. I'm meeting someone, um, pinstripe suit, fedora hat, carnation.' This felt ridiculous.

'Ah, sì, the gentleman is here already. Please to follow me.'

I breathed deeply with relief.

He walked to the back of the restaurant towards a figure whose hooded eyes fixed mine as I approached. He stood tall and about as inconspicuous as a cardinal in Studio 54 during the hottest, most decadent nights of Disco.

'Mr Gibbon?'

'Er, Sonny?'

He reached out a hand. We shook.

'Pleased to meet you,' I said.

I slid opposite over the worn plastic of the banquette. Sonny poured me a glass of red wine from a bottle at his side.

'I take the liberty of ordering for both of us. Is OK?' he asked in accented English.

What could I say? 'Fine, absolutely fine,' I replied, praying silently for nothing involving calamari, which revolted me more than any other food, with the possible exception of live yogurt.

'What?'

'I said: "that's fine".'

'You have to speak up. I am little deaf. An accident on water-front when I was younger. Capisce.'

'Oh, yes. Completely capisce. Bloody dangerous places, water-fronts. I once fell into the Thames, pretty shocking experience.'

'Salute,' he said, raising his glass solemnly.

His face was almost round, olive toned and firmly plunged into a thick neck. A navy-blue shirt was offset by a violet tie. The carnation was present, as billed.

'Enough of small talk,' he said suddenly, and before I was aware that any had taken place. 'What can I do for you?' he asked loudly. Grief, he really was deaf. Why hadn't Todd warned me? I was going to have to try to arrange a murder shouting across a crammed restaurant.

The food arrived as I began to speak: a plate of steaming rubber hoops I instantly identified as the Devil's Starter, calamari.

'Eat,' Sonny commanded just as I was about to launch into my awkward request. I looked downwards and felt my stomach pitch and roil. 'These are finest calamari in America. A man who don't eat them is no man,' he said, staring at me pointedly. Sonny slurped and sucked his way through a pile, head bowed to the point where all I could see was the crown. I seized the opportunity, emptying my plate into a napkin and sliding the folded linen into my suit jacket pocket. By the time Sonny resurfaced, my plate was as empty as his.

He nodded approvingly. 'Is good, eh?'

'Marvellous. Absolutely delicious,' I replied enthusiastically.

A waiter arrived and whisked away our plates with an unnecessary flourish. The pasta arrived. I was pleased to notice that the sauce was, indeed, a bland pomodoro. At least that part of my article was right, I told myself approvingly.

I coughed after we ate, again in silence, clearing my throat to make sure my words emerged precisely and quietly. I took out my notebook and began asking general questions about the Mafia, how it operated, the structure. Sonny answered politely and quite fully.

After forty-five minutes I decided to try to edge towards my real purpose. I had been listening distractedly to his answers, feeling more tense as the evening wore on. I could still hardly believe what I was bracing myself to ask. Had I sunk so low?

'Sonny,' I finally said, as we sipped coffees. 'What would happen, for the sake of argument, if somebody asked you, purely hypothetically, to arrange a hit?' I laughed casually as if the idea, ludicrous of course, had just flashed through my mind.

'Speak louder. I no hear you. What you say?'

Bloody hell. I took a deep breath and looked around furtively.

I took another deep breath. 'DO YOU KNOW ANYONE WHO MIGHT ACCEPT A CONTRACT TO KILL SOMEBODY?'

I paused, aware of a sudden silence in the restaurant. I turned and faced heads peering around banquettes and chairs. Families, probably my friends from the customs desk at JFK, looked on curiously.

'Sorry, sorry,' I mouthed before turning back. 'It's a rehearsal.'

It seemed to work. I leant over towards Sonny. He had scrunched his eyes and was staring angrily at me, reaching suddenly into an inside pocket. Oh, my God. I prepared to fly out of my seat. Instead, he pulled out a small black box and hit it hard against the table. There was a loud high-pitched whine, followed by the sound of popping from each of his ears. Sonny smiled.

'Ah, better. I hear good now.'

'Great, great,' I said, relieved, lowering my voice to somewhere between auctioneer and carnival barker. 'Look, I was just wondering if this rubbing-out business was open to outside commissions.' He seemed to be assessing me. That was fine, reassuring almost. I quickly spread out a handful of the magazines Decca had given me, my calling card. 'I work for the guy who publishes these,' I said softly.

I quickly glanced around. No waiters about, thank goodness. I spread the display of flesh and crotches and animals across the table. He picked up a copy of *Doctor's Surgery*. The summer enema issue, I noted. He flipped through, pausing briefly at alternative uses for a stethoscope and blonde assistant.

'Might be better to lower it a bit,' I said nervously. Immigration and Naturalization could be anywhere.

He suddenly reached over and pinched my cheeks. 'I like you, Mr Oliver Gibbon. Now drink. Let us raise our glasses to business.'

That was it? I smiled as the pain subsided. The reference to business was a hopeful sign. I felt relieved, and raised my glass. He had understood. It was over and fairly effortlessly. I could get back to my life. Hand over a few telephone numbers, make it all up with Gina. Do something about Hughgrant's hair, keep churning out investigative features. I felt as if I'd been trepanned.

'Fantastic. I'm really thrilled, Sonny. I can't tell you how happy this makes me. Great weight off my mind.'

He nodded. I noticed something odd at that moment. Sonny was wearing make-up. There was no doubt about it. His cheeks had some sort of Mrs Romstein rouge on them and matter was caked underneath his eyes. I could see the point of disguising yourself in plain sight to avoid attracting attention. But this seemed a little extreme. There was something unnaturally black about the hair as well. I let it pass. What did I know? Maybe the Mafia always wore make-up in public.

'How do you know Todd?' I asked, sidetracking myself.

He smiled. 'Todd is family,' he answered.

'He is?' I could barely hide my surprise.

'He only has to pick up telephone,' Sonny added, nodding enigmatically. I was impressed. Who would have thought such a cheery lug would be family with a best-seat-in-the-house capital F? I made a note to treat Todd with more respect in future. Maybe even buy the odd bit of junk from his store, perhaps that potted plastic rose 'as seen in *The War of the Roses* starring Michael Douglas and Kathleen Turner', which he kept suggesting I purchase for Gina.

'So, what happens now?' I asked.

Sonny looked quickly around him, bringing his finger to his lips. 'I talk to people and they contact you. I have your number. Now

I must leave. No names. I don't want no names. Capisce? You tell them when they call.'

'There was just one other thing, if it's not too much trouble. I wondered if we could have a codeword.' I cringed inwardly. 'They chose one in London, it's not mine, I hasten to add. Bit of a cliché, in fact. But would whoever calls mind saying "badabing" to identify themselves. No offence, of course. Nothing racial or anything, just help avoid any confusions.'

Sonny nodded sagely and rose slowly. 'You'll take care of this,' he said, sweeping his arm nonchalantly over the remains of our meal.

'Of course, of course,' I insisted eagerly.

We shook hands. He draped a long coat over his shoulders. 'Badabing, my friend.' There was an adjustment to the fedora and out he strode, disappearing conspicuously into the crowds of Little Italy. One day he would be in all the guides.

I was beside myself with happiness. Everything was perfect. I slumped back in the banquette, paid the bill and swigged back the rest of the Chianti, finally leaving a 20 per cent tip to round off the perfect evening. Pasta, wine, a contract and a receipt amenable to having an extra zero added into the total box. Thank you, God.

I swayed out and was halfway down Mulberry when I heard the shout. 'Signor Geebon, Signor Geebon.' I turned, as did the late-night crowd. It was our waiter hurrying towards me, frantically waving a magazine. 'You leeve *Naked Slutty Housewives* behind,' he yelled, as a centrepage spread unfolded to reveal Miss Pert November. All eyes looked at the face turning a deepening shade of Chianti red.

11

'Come on, man. Where's your sense of humour?' Todd was pained, but mainly from laughing. So was Gina. They were doubled up and barely able to talk as they pointed at me, looked at each other, squirmed and giggled.

I had made a special effort to be quiet when I reached home, pausing only at an all-night deli to buy enough stamps to send *Shaved Crack*, unwrapped and anonymously, to Fishlove. Gina hated to be woken up and it was after 11.30 on a weeknight.

I was surprised to see all the lights on, even more surprised to find Todd and Gina sitting at the kitchen table, a wine bottle – nearly empty – between them. I had no idea he was coming around.

'So, how'd it go?' Gina asked, a smile playing disconcertingly on her lips.

'Fine, fine,' I replied cautiously. 'In fact, I think I may have everything sorted.'

'And how was Sonny?' asked Todd.

'He was, was –'

'Convincing?' he broke in.

'Well, certainly that.' Some inner antenna started to twitch. It was picking something up. I couldn't quite place it. I began feeding calamari to Hughgrant. 'Why do you ask?'

'Oh, I was just worried about the make-up, but he was fitting you in after some improv,' said Todd nonchalantly. 'The suit was fine. But I thought the hair was a little over the top and he seemed too brown to me. But I let it pass. I mean, he's the expert.'

My mouth drained of fluid, leaving the jaw to struggle through a lubricant of sand. 'What do you mean "he's the expert"?' I asked slowly, confused and uncertain where this conversation was going.

'I mean, he's the actor, the professional.'

'I don't think I follow . . .'

Gina suddenly guffawed, spitting wine out of her mouth. I stared at her. Suddenly, like the dead weight of a hammer to the back of my skull, it hit me. I had been set up.

'You met Sean Simmons tonight,' she said gleefully.

At that moment I wanted to lash out, but my body crumpled. 'What? What are you talking about?' I heard myself say.

'He's a thesp. Good one too,' said Todd casually. 'Been resting a lot recently. Said he was glad of the practice.'

'Glad of the practice. Glad of the practice. How could you?' I yelled at them. 'How the bloody hell could you set me up like that?'

'Oh, come on, Ollie. Lighten up,' said Gina. 'It was just a laugh. We thought it would be funny. I mean, I did give you a hint, telling you how odd it was that Todd might do something for you. But you were so determined to meet your great Mafia contact. You didn't listen.'

'Come off it, I trusted you,' I spluttered to both of them. 'God. I feel utterly betrayed, especially by you, Todd. I consider, considered, you my friend.'

'Hey, Ollie, cool it,' said Todd, still grinning widely. 'No need to burn the farm. We just wanted you to see sense. Man, you can't stumble around New York looking for hitmen. Anyway, what I did was no different to what you do with your phoney reports from New York.'

Todd continued before I could respond. 'Sean said you were very good, by the way. He called just after he left. What's the big deal? I mean, you would have made it up anyway, right? This way you get an actual guy talking. He was really impressed when you tried to pin him down to an actual hit. Great improv for him.'

I was hardly listening, firmly and miserably caught between all my lies, between not wanting to involve Gina or Todd and a desperation to have them, my fraternity house, share my peril.

'Yeah, right. OK. But look, this is serious. I could lose my job for reasons I can't explain. And anyway, the Mafia series was completely different. We're talking about my keeping a livelihood here and that means I have to find a real hitman. It's a test of my credibility with the new owner.'

'Well, I don't think it's so different,' insisted Todd. 'Anyway, how come you're getting all ethical on us all of a sudden?'

'Yes, how come, Ollie?' added Gina, proving once again that college bonds were thicker than water. Thicker, even, than lantern-jawed Todd, I thought savagely.

'You're in bloody public relations, so you get no vote on any issue relating to ethics,' I snapped. 'I've just decided no more faking it, that's all. You were both right, as it happens. I have been sailing close to the wind and was bound to get found out. I took the call back to London as a warning, that's all.'

A huge tuna floated into my mind, mocking. Another lie. We sat in awkward silence: Jokers and Joked Upon. Liars and Lied To. I was suddenly and pitiably aware of being back somewhere behind square one, alone, a full three days wasted. I felt such a fool. How could I have been so dumb? What kind of reporter was I anyway? I'd fallen into a simple deception, hadn't even questioned it. I was so desperate to believe Todd and his wretched, rouged friend. My only hope was that there wasn't a recording.

'At least we can laugh at the video,' Todd suddenly said, breaking the silence.

'You didn't?' I said, aghast at this final humiliation.

'No, don't worry,' he replied, laughing. 'We couldn't get the equipment in time. But I bet you thought he was reaching for a gun when he pulled out the hearing aid, didn't you?'

'My God. He even rehearsed?'

'He did that whole deaf routine in an off-Broadway show once. Brought the house down. He's good, isn't he? Met him in the store. He buys a lot of stuff. I mean for a guy from Des Moines, he totally kicks ass playing hoods. Listen, man, you gotta chill up over this thing. It'll work out. I mean, look at me. I don't let anyone rent space in my head, man.'

I grunted. 'Still a vacant lot, some might say.'

A Todd Moment then followed as he moved, characteristically, to change the subject, to end the discomfort. 'How about those murders in London, Ollie?' he asked suddenly.

'What murders?'

'That guy wandering around the East Und.'

'You must mean the East End,' I suggested.

'That's right, the East End, killing all those hookers.'

I was stumped. 'Killing prostitutes?' Had I missed some major story? I'd only just been over there.

'Yeah. Jack the Nipper.'

I was hooked. 'I'm guessing here. Could be wrong of course. But I assume you mean Jack the Ripper. Yes, what about him?' I replied carefully.

'That's him. Well, how about that?'

I decided on some more exploratory surgery. 'Jack the Ripper. Now, let's see, dead more than a hundred years? Foggy Whitechapel scenes? Verminous old hags? Eviscerations? Top hats?'

'That's it, that's it,' said Todd, sounding amazed. 'I've just seen the movie. It had Johnny Depp in it.'

And so we chatted. I explained how much England had moved on since he last checked in. Jack the Ripper? Unsolved but certainly dead by now. I recommended a selection of alternatives for a more contemporary look.

But I was still angry.

'Pour me a glass, Todd. It'll distract me from plans A through to Z, which involved beating your head into a pulp and then disposing of you in the Hudson under cover of night.' He thought I was joking.

The car made lazy, concentric circles as it prepared to land on the back of a moving elephant, which was smoking an enormous cigar. Gina was at the wheel and Colonel Gaddafi was in the back wearing an old Armani suit and medals. We weren't going to make it, I registered with alarm. I noticed Fishlove was there already interviewing the owl. Damn him. The elephant's back was too short. There was a sponge cake in the way. The Roads and Footpaths Subcommittee was voting to extend its meeting by another fifteen hours. There was also a loud ringing. I opened my eyes. There was still a loud ringing. I reached out an arm and grabbed the receiver.

'Hello?'

'Bleaker here.'

I sat bolt upright and looked at the clock. It was 5.30 a.m.

'We just wondered how badabing was progressing.'

'Fine, fine, really well, actually,' I said, scrambling to find some reassuring words to cover my abject lack of progress. 'I've got a couple of very positive leads to work up, and I'm pretty confident of having something within the next couple of days.'

'Good. Sir Derek is very keen to get this moving. It's an absolute priority. You do understand that, don't you, Oliver?'

'Call me Ollie. Yes, completely. Like I said, I have actually made contact with a couple of key players. I'm just waiting for them to, er, get back to me after they've had a chance to speak, to speak . . .' I grasped for an impressive, knowing sort of word, '. . . to speak with their principals and check schedules.'

'Call me as soon as you get something. Any time. Day or night. Incidentally, features were mentioning the Whitney Houston interview at the news conference this morning. We're very keen on that as well. Goodbye – Oliver.'

I slumped back on to the sheets, vibrating the bed enough to partially waken Gina, my driver. She uttered a complaining grunt before falling silent. Hope she made it on to Nellie. I lay wide awake, fretful.

Later in my office I glanced half-heartedly through the morning newspapers. Liza Minnelli was marrying again. Was that the fifth time this week? The Duchess of York was speaking for Royal Watchers, a group dedicated to helping Windsor addicts channel their cravings into more worthwhile activities.

I had an idea and called Bernie Bowker, the head librarian. There was a long, insulting delay before the receiver was picked up. 'Library,' said a suspicious voice.

'Hi, Bernie. It's Ollie Gibbon in New York. How are you?'

There was a sigh. 'Not so good, mate. Not so good. You've 'eard, I suppose.'

I feigned ignorance.

'Well, you wouldn't believe it. We're being made redundant, replaced by some online computer something or other running a cuttings service out of the Galapagos Islands.'

'No.' I sounded suitably shocked.

'Yeah. No explanation, not a word from management, just a little weasel from some department called Business Development. I mean, I'm fifty, Ollie, third generation at this place. It's beyond shockin'. Disgustin'. Bleedin' new technology.'

'You're absolutely right. Unbelievable. Still, I'm sure once they've thought it through and realized the chaos this could bring, nothing will happen.' Fewer things can have been said with less confidence, I thought.

I paused out of decency, a moment of mourning before pressing on. The end of a library was one thing. The end of my job quite another.

'Listen, Bernie. I really need your help and it's a tough one. I need to find some living and out-of-jail mobsters in the New York area pretty urgently. They're no good to me sprawled in a puddle on the pavement or stuck on Rikers Island staring at thirty feet of razor wire. What do you think?'

'Well, I'll certainly try. Can't promise anything. But there should be something.'

There was hope. Not much. But some. If anybody could find me connections, it was Bowker. He ran the acres of snipped stories filed in the bowels of the newspaper building. It was said to be one of the best libraries in Fleet Street, turning up those lost interviews given by mass murderers to stamp-collecting magazines before their infamy, careless chats by stars to fanzines. Nobody wanted to be on the wrong side of Bowker. His empire of faded newsprint worked to a unique system devised by his grandfather, Aubrey Bowker, its secrets passed on from one generation of

Bowkers to the next, its precise logic more jealously guarded than the recipe for Coca-Cola.

Most libraries file by theme or name. The *Herald* filed by association. Aubrey Bowker, who had begun his service during the First World War, decided that anything to do with Germany should be placed under 'Enemy', a practice that continued through the generations, each arriving Bowker adding his own particular filing refinement, encrusting the library with even more idiosyncracies.

The 'Enemy' was divided into a family tree of subsets. German military, for example, was under 'Boche', because Aubrey had served in the trenches in 1916 when the word was a common insult. 'Australia' also found itself uprooted and consigned there following a rude encounter between his eldest granddaughter, Maisie, and a backpacker in an Earls Court pub.

Bernie, the current heir, had a particular loathing for celebrity chefs. They were filed under 'Poison' or, as a further complication, 'Thick'. Oddly, football players were filed sanely in alphabetical order and by team. This may just have been a ruse to throw any possible code breakers off the scent. Except, of course, for Chelsea. They were under 'Gods' whilst 'Greek Gods' were to be found under 'Restaurant Names, Various'.

Bowker terrified people, especially young reporters who wandered – rashly – behind the desk at the front of the library to find assistance, only to see a frightening figure emerge from the gloom. 'I work this side. You the other,' it would say from the Stygian half-light. Bowker was paralysed down one side: his left arm hung withered, one foot dragged behind the other, a Phantom of the Library, pale from hours spent in its unnatural subterraneanea. The paralysis was the result of an office-party wound. He had fallen down a lift shaft, drunk, according to legend. The company was found liable. Rather than accept a payment, Bowker opted shrewdly for the promise of a job for life. He was Unsackable Man, fiercely independent, secure and scornful of each wave of new management.

Heartened and hopeful that I had at last found a reliable ally, I needed to commune with St Trimthunder and headed down to the Old Factory. Inside, there was no sign of Our Lady, but I went ahead anyway: forty minutes at Level Sixteen, powering my legs forward and backward as the digital display commanded, slowing down, speeding up, covering swathes of Lapland.

'Puthyfootin' again, Ollie,' commented Dimos, rather ruining my moment of glorious synchronicity between man and machine.

'Just doing a spot of cardio, Dimos. Good for the soul and trouser size.' I was feeling breezily confident.

'Bro, you learnin' nuttin' from me.' He went away in disgust, stalking the health-club work-out floor, a drill sergeant hunting for someone eager to lift weights, lots of them and often.

My mobile went off. Tiffanie Savage, the features editor, wanted a Whitney moment. 'No, sorry. No word yet. She's getting ready to tour.' I decided to increase the dosage of lowered expectations. 'I've heard from my source that she's been ill, nothing serious, just some stomach bug. But it's thrown the schedule, apparently. He thinks we're still in with a chance. I'll keep pushing, obviously. But it could be tight.'

'Good, Ollie. Keep at it. We're very keen to get this.' Then came the blow. 'I know the *Sentinel* are on to it as well. Apparently, their New York guy has met her publicist already and she seemed keen, so I'm told. They hit it off. We do need to get in there. Especially as you've been working on this for so long,' she added with just a hint of sarcasm. Bloody Fishlove.

I parried. 'Oh, I'm sure we'll get it.' I wondered about calling my bête noir to find out what he was up to. But why? I did not, absolutely not, need to stoop to the point where my own insecurities, paranoia even, made me hostage to what my rivals were doing. I had pride. I was successful. I was from the *Herald*. I dialled.

'Hey. How's it going? . . . You have? . . . Really? . . . Not much, chasing a few things. Nothing serious . . . Listen, I just wondered if you were getting anywhere with Whitney's people, heard you were on the case . . . Really? Well done . . . No, we're not interested, apparently . . . Yeah, amazing, isn't it? She'd be a great interview. What can I tell you . . . Yeah, we must have lunch. Definitely soon. Cheers.'

12

'Sorry, Ollie. No joy. I've tried everything,' said Bowker sadly. 'I looked under "Godfather", "Singers". Nothing. Lots of dead blokes, of course. But no live ones who are actually out there doing the business.'

'Damn. Really? Is there anywhere else it might be?'

'Truthfully, no. There aren't going to be any city profiles, businessman-of-the-year things. I'm very disappointed. It's definitely one to look into. Can't believe we've done nuffink on this. Most depressing.'

The slough of despond he found himself paddling in was nothing compared to mine. I had hoped Bowker was a short-cut to keeping the job, protection from local government and immersion in council-tax payments.

I slumped back in my chair, demoralized, and dropped my feet on the desk. Hughgrant came trotting in. 'Disappear,' I ordered. He turned obediently and scuttled out. The vile discharge of calamari at the foot of the bed was still unforgiven.

Three days to go. I needed something to take my mind off things. I was going to have to call Whitney's people again. I had tried several times. The calls were never returned, and I kept doing what I always did when something awkward came up: found distractions. I pressed the TV remote idly, aiming at the television. Nothing. Again. Nothing. Just the dead noisy storm of signal failure.

'Unbloodybelievable.' It was the last straw.

I knew the cable company number by heart. One of the mysteries of Manhattan is the unfathomable complexity of its television service. Aside from the profligate 600 channels, covering everything from cookery to line dancing, sometimes the system just packed up entirely.

'You have reached Go Bright Cable,' intoned a firm, electronic voice. 'We are committed to customer service, and for that reason your call may be monitored or recorded for training purposes.'

'Yeah, yeah,' I said impatiently.

'To make a bill payment, press one. To subscribe to Go Bright Movie Classic, press two. To subscribe to Go Bright Music Plus, press three. To subscribe to Go Bright Movie Classic and Go Bright Music Plus, press four. To report a problem with Go Bright Movie Classic, press five; to report a problem with Go Bright Music Plus, press six . . .'

I went to make some coffee, to ponder my problems. A murder and trying to interview Whitney Houston were just too much.

The water boiled. Downstairs the builders were busy destroying the apartment one small hammer-blow at a time. I poured the water into the coffee maker, savouring the smell. I placed the plunger, reached for a cup. Diversions were good. I went to the bedroom and picked up laundry that needed doing, thinking, thinking, thinking.

It was a slow walk piled high with sheets to the communal laundry room. But I was back within a couple of minutes. I thought I would see Eddie, firmly remonstrate about the strange smell, a sort of rotten eggs with a dead-rat twist, that had recently begun to fill the kitchen. He was nowhere to be seen. Back in the apartment, I plunged the coffee and went back to the office.

'. . . press twenty-three; to subscribe to the Go Bright Sports Plus and Music Plus Party Stars service, press twenty-four; to report a fault with Go Bright Sports Plus and Music Plus Party Stars service, press twenty-five . . .'

The other line went. Typical. This was now a delicate operation. How to keep holding on to my precious place in the queue for a real-live voice at Go Bright, a human to whom I could explain my problem, person to person, pulse to pulse, whilst reaching for this next call. Sweat broke out on my brow as I put on my safe-breaking face and carefully punched in the code.

It was Gina.

'I was just wondering how you were.'

'Fine, fine,' I lied enthusiastically.

'I've learned that whenever a Brit says that, they mean "bad, bad". Talk to me. What's the problem, hon?'

'You know the problem,' I said. 'I've got to somehow hook up with people I have not one whit of a connection with. If I tell Stanley that, he'll realize everything I've been writing has been a huge fake and sack me. Otherwise everything's fine.'

'You're worrying too much. Just call. Explain. Say you can't get hold of anyone. If he's unreasonable, tell him you'll go to the cops; there's got to be some law against getting employees to fix you up with hoodlums.'

'Right. Guess who they'll believe? A multimillionaire businessman who has tea with the prime minister, or the employee stopped by immig –' I hastily stopped mid word. 'Or his employee. Anyway, I've already told them that I've made contact. He's read my pieces. I'm Mr Mob as far as Stanley is concerned. If he knew I'd made them all up, he'd dump me for certain. It's a bloody mess.'

I felt miserable, fouled, corrupt, crushed, but there was nothing Gina could do. 'Look, I've got to go. I'll call you back. I'm trying to get the cable fixed.' I pressed the other line button.

'. . . press forty-one. Thank you. Please wait on the line and an operator will be with you shortly.' At last. What timing.

'The office is now closed. To repeat the automatic option choice, press star or call back between 8 a.m. and 6 p.m., Monday to Friday, when a customer representative will be glad to take your call.'

'It is bloody Monday to Friday!' I screamed. Suddenly, a miracle more amazing than the parting of the Red Sea. A human voice.

'Go Bright Cable, the-greatest-name-in-home-entertainment. This is Corinna. How may I direct your call?'

'At last. Hi. Are you real?'

'Excuse me, sir?'

'Nothing. Look, my cable isn't working, for some reason. I can't get any channels. The screen's just blank.'

'It will be an honour to transfer you to technical support. Now you have a nice day. Thank you for calling Go Bright Cable, the-place-to-be.'

'Thank you. Thank you. Thank you. I can't tell you how much that means to me. Thank you so much.'

There was a long pause, some clicks. 'You have reached Go Bright Cable. We are committed to customer service, and for that reason . . .'

Time was running out, so was my professional life. I could feel it draining away. The cable collapse was the last straw, and the absence of a human voice at the company that supplied it seemed symbolic. I felt utterly isolated.

I had promised a news feature on the Missouri town devastated by a tornado. They wanted a thousand words filled with first-hand accounts of facing the worst that Nature could offer and losing everything. I flew down there. Apparently.

'Myra Bleaker looked at the wreckage of her shattered home yesterday and wept as a pipe dripped,' I wrote mechanically, staring across the Hudson. '"I got no job. We've lost everything. I'm done devastated,"' she said, clutching her six-year-old daughter, Mary-Lou. 'One person was killed, a retired electrician, when hurricane-force winds struck Fingered Butte early on Saturday morning. Neighbours said James D. Resin was a quiet, Christian single man who got on particularly well with young girls. "He kept himself to himself," recalled one.'

The telephone rang. It was Fishlove. He suggested lunch. Sometimes you feel so sorry for yourself that even the company you most avoid seems attractive. 'Great, see you in Florent at 1.30,' I heard myself saying with what sounded like pleasure.

Florent was across the street, a camp French bistro of plastic laminated tables and chrome bar stools. The walls were lined, inex-plicably, with prints of exotic, seedy foreign ports. Hamburg and Dieppe featured prominently. Fishlove was waiting.

He was completely bald and completely tall, over six foot. A thin smile worked its limited emotional display on a polished, unlined face. There was something of the camp commandant about him. His shirts were always white and immaculately pressed. He wore plain ties. It was quite disturbing.

'Hi, Fishlove, great to see you,' I said, conjuring up a smile to signal sincerity and preparing for the game. The game required that each of us pretends to like the other, to commiserate fulsomely over past failures and thwarted story ideas as if we actually cared. At the same time, the idea was to pick up as much either damaging or repeatable gossip as possible, and the Holy Grail, the absolute Saddam of All Things, was to find out what the other was working on: the big features, exclusive interviews, anything that might be embarrassing to miss.

'How's it going?' he asked, staring at me intently. 'Saw your Mafia stuff got a good spread. Who is that Rosselli guy, by the way? Couldn't find him in cuts.'

'Oh, just a contact. Doesn't get written about much,' I said quickly.

'Really? Only I'm thinking of doing a follow. Interesting line about him going to Britain.'

'Wasn't it?' I felt a rising panic.

'Yes, wondered if you might give me his contact details.' He was looking at me carefully, questing. I saw my own flushed reflection in his metal-framed glasses.

'Well, the thing of it is, I had to promise not to give out his number. I mean, don't want to piss off the mob,' I said, my dismissal sounding strangulated.

'Odd he should have talked to you at all if he's worried about publicity. Very peculiar. But it's not a problem. I'll ring my mate in the FBI. I'm sure he'll be able to help. He knows everybody.'

That was all I needed, Fishlove sniffing around and discovering my fraud. I'd be finished.

'Listen,' I said hastily, 'let me have a word with my contact. See what I can do. I mean, I'd love to help you out, of course.'

'That'd be great, Ollie. You know, it had crossed my mind that you'd made the whole thing up.'

'Good grief, Fishlove,' I said, laughing hysterically. 'Made it up? Gosh. That's a low blow.'

He nodded his head, staring at me with that unnerving stillness. 'I heard you were under a bit of pressure to deliver, that's all. Not that you deserve to be,' he added diplomatically. 'I gather your editor liked my feature on that rainbow-worshipping cult up in the Catskills.'

I felt myself stiffen. 'Is that so? Nobody said anything to me.'

'Don't suppose they would,' he said, smiling knowingly to himself. Bloody Fishlove.

It was time to change tack. I had, of course, been roasted for not finding out that some faded seventies Brit pop star was running a glorified brothel two hours from Manhattan. Why aren't they all just put down after the Greatest Hits album?

'Everything else OK?' he asked.

Else, I thought, annoyed by the implication. 'Everything, absolutely everything is fine, fine. Steady. You know. You?'

'Yeah, can't grumble. Got a few things on the go.'

'Anything interesting?'

'No. You?

'Same.'

A waiter hovered. We ordered steak sandwiches and beers.

'You bothering much with Whitney Houston?' I asked as casually as possible.

'Don't talk to me about Whitney. Can't get her publicist off my back at the moment.'

First round to Fishlove, I thought.

'You're very quiet,' he said.

'Sorry, just a bit distracted.'

We ate in silence. I wondered in a moment of insanity whether to tell him the problem. But I could just see it appearing in the *Sentinel* as an anonymous diary item.

'Any gossip?' he asked.

'No, not really. Everyone's hanging on. Just the usual promise of massive investment cunningly disguised as sackings. The library seems to be for the axe.'

'Is that so?' Fishlove seemed interested, which worried me. I composed myself whilst the sandwiches were manoeuvred to the table.

'Excuse me,' I said to the waiter, 'this is sprouted wheat. I wanted just the regular white.'

'I am so sorry. Now we have wheat and oat, wheat with folic.'

'Do you have just a regular wheat on its own?'

He sucked in his breath at this daring suggestion, leaning his chin on the cup of a manicured left hand. 'Well, there you have me. I just don't know. I can check for you.'

'Don't bother. It's fine. I'll stick with this.'

'You were saying about the library,' said Fishlove. I told him. He nodded sympathetically, a sign of extreme pleasure.

'I feel for you, mate,' he went on with a plausible stab at sincerity. 'They're adding staff to our library, I heard the other day.'

Christ, round two to Fishlove.

We moaned for about an hour: hopeless newsdesks, impossible requests, ludicrous deadlines, lousy subeditors screwing up brilliant prose. The usual chatter.

'I'd better be getting back. I've got to call Whitney's people,' he said. 'They keep pestering.'

I felt queasy. 'Really? Are you going for an interview, then?' I asked gingerly, a silent scream forming somewhere in my bowels.

'Don't know. I've got a few other things on the go. We'll see. They seem very keen. She's got the new album to promote, the tour coming up. There's talk she'll be playing at the next Buckingham Palace gig.'

'I'd heard,' I lied, glancing at my watch. This amount of competence was debilitating. 'Well, better get back,' I said.

'Yes, me too. White House are calling me back at 3.30.' The White House? We walked out together. 'Nice seeing you, Ollie. I'll probably catch you at the party tonight.'

The trick I had learnt with Fishlove involved never saying 'What party?' but always 'Which party?'

'The one for the launch of that film *Chocolat Paradiso*. Whitney may be there, I hear. You know she's done the soundtrack?'

Had she? 'Oh, that party. Yes, I'll definitely be there. It clashes with something else. But, hell, a free drink is a free drink,' I said. Whitney Houston. Fantastic. I could probably snatch a word with her publicist, maybe even with her.

We parted outside. Fishlove strode purposefully towards his apartment, which I knew was in an anonymous midtown co-op building, probably to work, play solitary chess or something equally threatening.

I went back home and called the Silver Films public relations people and spoke with a publicist named, as they usually were, Lisa. She told me all the invitations for the *Chocolat Paradiso* party had been sent out. Could I fax over a letter stating why I wanted to attend the party, include a few examples of my work and offer a credible new theory for the origin of Man? I said I was out of the office, but that I was proposing to write a long piece about the film. It worked.

Some of the depression lifted. At least I could get wasted at someone else's expense and give Fishlove a run for his money on Whitney, even if I were no nearer to solving my real problem. If only I could get to her. I needed an edge. I spent the afternoon memorizing lyrics.

13

A large figure stood at the door dressed in pink knickerbockers, curled sandals and bejewelled turban, a scimitar thrust into his thick green waistband. From inside came the steady thump of Euro-trance. 'Ticket, sir?' he said.

'Gibbon,' I said confidently. 'Called this afternoon and spoke to Lisa in public relations. She said I'd be on some sort of list.'

'So, you got a ticket or what?' he replied, bored. 'Can't let nobody in without one.'

I put on my children-under-six-and-bouncers voice and smiled encouragingly.

'As I just explained. No, I don't have an actual ticket, but I am on the list. Perhaps it would help to think of it as a virtual ticket.'

He looked at me blankly.

'Where's Lisa?' I said, barely disguising my exasperation. 'You can check with her.'

'Don't know no Lisa,' the Sheikh of Fifth Avenue said stubbornly, moving on to scrutinize the real tickets being thrust at him. I had already, humiliatingly, ceased to exist.

'There must be somebody you can check with,' I said with some determination. 'Look, here's my press card.' I held it in front of his eyes. 'Can't I just go in? Or could you go in and find Lisa?' I stared as he processed these two options, each clearly suspect.

'Look, sir. I don't know no Lisa and I ain't allowed from here. Nobody said nothing about no list or virtue ticket. You gonna have to stand aside, there are other folks trying to get in. Folks with tickets,' he added pointedly.

Suddenly, out of the door came one of those creatures of the New York night. At first it seemed nervous to be so exposed, poking its head, sniffing the night air, glancing from left to right. It was a Person With Clipboard and I seized the moment.

It looked startled when addressed. 'Hi, I'm Ollie Gibbon from the *Herald*, a British newspaper. I spoke to Lisa this afternoon and she said to just show up.'

It stopped, surprised, and looked down its list, flipping pages, occasionally glancing up at me. Was this some kind of retinal eye scan? 'Gibson, Gibson . . .'

'No, no. It's Gibbon.'

'I'm so sorry, Gibbon. I still don't see it, I'm afraid. Wait here, please.'

It turned busily and disappeared inside, emerging a few minutes later with a small family group of People With Clipboards. They looked at me as if enjoying some peculiar, fascinating and rarely seen morbidity.

'Hello, my name is Gary. I'm the assistant to the event publicist synchronizator,' said one. 'Can I help you?'

I breathed deeply. 'I hope so. I'm here to cover the party for my newspaper, the *Daily Herald*, which is the, well, a leading British daily, and was told by Lisa in the Silver Films press office to show up because my name would be on a list for those not sent an invitation.'

He clicked his tongue loudly, running his eyes down a list attached to his clipboard. Others did the same.

'Well, we do have a list. But I don't see a Gerbons anywhere, do you, Haley, Kelly?' Gary asked, looking around at the group. They all nodded gravely. I plunged on.

'Look, for a start it's Gibbon. G. I. B. B. O. N., not Gerbons or Gibson. Gibbon, like the historian.'

'Like the ape, you mean. Oh. I am so sorry.' His eyes knitted as he read the list. 'Well, I do not see that either,' Gary said, blond highlights caught in some reflection. 'Try again. Just kidding. Oh, well, I'm sure it's fine if you know Lisa. Just give me your business card.' I handed it over and he walked over to the door sultan. 'It's OK, Antonio. You can let him in.'

'Thank you,' I said, finding that all I had, in fact, joined was the line for a blue stamp on my wrist. Could it be harder to get into the Pentagon? Roswell Alien Research Center? Inside I could see, good heavens, yes it was. Whitney Houston, beautiful, shimmering, radiant with a glass in her hand. Then I saw Fishlove. He was heading towards her.

There were five people in front of me waiting for stamps. The line had stalled. A woman was complaining. 'Come on, come on,' I muttered. God, she was still talking. Bloody hell. 'I've got allergies. I'll get a reaction,' I heard.

'I'm sorry, ma'am, those are the rules. Everybody's got to get a stamp.'

'This is quite intolerable. There must be someone in authority I can speak with. Please get me your supervisor.'

I started to panic. Whitney had disappeared from view. I knotted my hands, felt my pulse start to race. It was Person With Clipboard again. He listened and nodded sympathetically to the over-dressed old trout with her ludicrous earrings, a constellation of crescents and orbs hanging from each lobe. I half expected to see the space shuttle navigating between them. Or the Hubble Telescope.

She went on and on, allergies this, allergies that, readers in Wisconsin. I'd heard of Wisconsin, but nobody had ever adequately explained why it was necessary. Eventually, incredibly, she was just waved through, unstamped. I sighed audibly.

There was still time. I held out my wrist for the stamp and rushed through the huge, draped entrance and then began to skid alarmingly, uncontrollably.

I twisted sharply as my feet seemed to develop a life of their own, unable to grip the surface. I glanced down and mouthed a silent scream. Falling backwards, I just had time to register fine crystals of sand. Why? I lunged out hopelessly, grabbing a length of turquoise canopy-draping in the hope of steadying myself against gravity. There was the long, loud crack of ice breaking to the prow of a trawler, slowly but with growing speed. I was aware of a hush. Out of my eye I saw Whitney, her mouth open, staring at me. I tried to smile back encouragingly. Hundreds of eyes were staring. Everything just slowed as I pirouetted, grasping higher up the ripping curtain only to hasten its destruction before finally twisting and plunging to the floor, draped in some sort of heavy, musty muslin that came tumbling around me.

Through the muffling fabric I heard voices. 'It's not in the programme, I'm sure.' 'Is he drunk?' 'Are we insured?'

'Quite an entrance.' The last one I recognized as full-focus consciousness returned. It was Fishlove, droll as ever. I thrashed around, felt hands grasp me and was eventually on my feet, surrounded by a sea of faces. If I had been American, I would have threatened to sue. But I turned on the usual apology soundtrack.

'Sorry, so sorry. Excuse me. Please, carry on. Perfectly OK. Can't think. Slipped. Fine. Thanks. Sorry.' I headed quickly to the bar, limping and in some pain.

Fishlove smiled thinly. 'You all right, old chap? Great entrance. Scared off Whitney anyway. Well done.'

'No? Really? Damn it. Shit, shit. Sorry. Bloody sand. I mean, why do they bother with all this bloody theme stuff?' I said, brushing the Sahara off my suit.

'She rushed out just after you brought the house down. There were bodyguards all over her,' said Fishlove. 'Shame, I was hoping to grab a word.'

I secretly thanked God for that small mercy of prevention and ordered a vodka tonic.

The room was awash with fashionably undressed women of such jaw-dropping brilliance that their faces carried no expression whatsoever. Only truly gorgeous women have bland countenances. They don't need to look interesting.

'Why do we come to these things?' I grumbled to Fishlove.

'Free drink, girls, canapés and girls. And you never know, maybe the odd tale. Both spellings of the word,' he said, eyeing the crowd, a periscope on legs. I grunted.

'Did the White House get back to you?'

'Yes, thanks.'

Not even a clue. Bastard. Fishlove was scouring the room for a possible story, the never-resting shark. Soon he'd be calling London to check in. Sure enough. There he was, holding the mobile surreptitiously to his ear, cupping his hand over the mouthpiece so I couldn't hear. Hear what at this time of night? At the third stroke, the time sponsored by Accurist will be ... I thought savagely. I was jealous. Jealous of Fishlove. I was mulling over life, the universe and the Mafia when I spotted Danny Mehan, legendary, hard-bitten and grizzled reporter from the *New York Metro*.

He certainly looked the part. His thin, long, folded face was pitted and poorly shaven; his eyes were framed behind red rims; his skin was a pallid white from years of smoking and dive bars, places of dark, secret lives.

We had met once before, outside the FAO Schwarz toy store on Fifth Avenue one midnight when a new range of *Star Wars* products was released. Every newspaper editor in the northern hemisphere had the same original idea of interviewing people who had stood in line for eight hours to buy a plastic Darth Vader with breakable light sabre. It had been an improbable sighting. Mehan usually covered the New York City Police Department. The toy assignment, he explained, was punishment for bad-mouthing his news editor.

'Whydya want this crummy toy?' he asked one startled, fat teenager, a Marlboro bobbing on his lips. As the youth garbled some half answer, Mehan butt in. 'Aren'tcha too old for this kind of thing? I mean, what are you? Sixteen? Seventeen? Ever tried dating? Bet you were in the choir,' he said accusingly, shaking his head and wandering off in disgust. I watched, fascinated.

An eight-year-old girl was next to be caught in the rheumy, bloodshot sights. She was carrying a small cage containing a pet hamster. 'Whydya want one of those, missy?'

'They're cool,' she replied with conviction.

'My ass,' said Mehan. 'D'you know that in Ecuador they deep-fry living hamsters in three different temperatures of oil to stop the flesh getting too tough?'

He moved further up the line as the girl collapsed in tears. It was mesmerizing watching the emotional carnage being wreaked. He bumped into me. Only I apologized. We shook hands.

'Mehan. *Metro*.'

'Gibbon, Ollie. *Daily Herald*.' I noticed the empty pages of his notepad. 'Got anyone interesting?'

'Nah. Bunch of arrested development no-hopers. I'm off. Fancy a quickie at O'Malley's?'

It was the last sentence I would ever recall from our encounter. I remember only the hangover with chilling clarity. The night itself was erased from my mental hard drive. There was beer, of course. There were whiskey chasers. Towards the end of the evening there was a small bottle of sticky brown liquid that tasted combustible. Then there was some sort of oblivion, followed by dawn on the doorstep of a restaurant a mile away from home. I never did find out how I got there. But I had steered clear of Mehan and O'Malley's ever since.

What was he doing here?

'Hi, Danny,' I said. He looked across and raised a hand in greeting. 'How are you?' He looked at me blankly. 'Ollie Gibbon. Remember? We met at the *Star Wars* thing last year.' There was still no reaction. 'You know, the line of people waiting for toys outside FAO Schwarz?' Blank.

'Sorry, don't recall. Still, pleased to re-meet you, pal, and at least this way you can bore me with whatever you bored me with last time, 'cos it'll all be new to me.'

I laughed merrily. Ha, ha, ha. Why couldn't I think up a line like that? We sipped our drinks in companionable indifference, watching the cavalcade of mannequins and hangers-on on the other side of the rope. Waiters passed around chocolate in the shape of body parts.

'You seen this movie?' Mehan asked suddenly, biting into a knuckle filled with strawberry conserve.

'No. You?'

'Nah. It's got subtitles and French actors. Why would I? I'll wait for the Hollywood remake.'

I was confused. 'This is the Hollywood remake, I think.'

'It is? And they've used French actors.' He seemed genuinely surprised.

'I think so, yes. But they speak English. I haven't heard anything about subtitles.'

'French actors, you say. Went to France once. Didn't like it. Pointless little place. Hang on, no, that's Luxembourg. France was OK, decent grog, thin women. Another stiffie?'

I said yes. That, in a nutshell, is the measure of how much willpower I have. As we walked back to the press bar, I had a brainwave.

'Danny, you cover the crime beat, right?'

'You got it. Twenty-three years, almost a life sentence,' he added, coughing up phlegm and laughing grimly.

'Could you help me with something, just a small thing? Well, actually, probably quite a big thing.' I paused. 'I need to connect with someone, well, connected.'

'As in mob connected, I take it. What for?'

'It's for a feature I'm doing on organized crime,' I lied. 'I need to interview someone involved in contract killings, hits, I guess.'

Danny roared with laughter as I glanced around nervously. 'I'd love to help you, friend, but every made guy I ever knew is in Sing Sing or retired to a golf buggy down in Florida. But good luck to you. Let's drink to it anyway. Tell you what, gimme your card. If I come up with anything, I'll call. Here's to swimming with fishes.'

And did we drink to aquatic sports. I have a half-focused reel in my memory; the rest lies trashed in some dark alley, shredded by rats and peed on by vagrants. I do recall Mehan arguing ferociously with a waiter over the size of a chocolate spleen and with the 'politically correct shit' who thought melon-jam-filled breasts were acceptable to serve, 'but not the male member that makes it all fucking possible'.

Fishlove left early, mouthing something in my direction and looking at his watch as he disappeared. But by this time I was seeing two of him anyway, so I waved back and gave it no thought.

At some point I was ejected with Mehan, and bundled noisily and inelegantly out on to the street. I made it a point of honour to get home. But halfway there I was prepared to compromise. I would settle for anybody's home.

14

The first one hit me just above the eye. The second bounced off my shoulder. 'You are so disgusting,' Gina yelled. 'How could you? You know how I feel about this stuff and you bring it into the house. And where were you last night?'

'Wait, wait. Listen, I can explain.'

'Explain? This doesn't need any explanation. And you stink of drains.' A volley of three magazines headed my way. One was *Collar*, I noticed shortly before impact.

By the time I had uncovered my hungover eyes ('It's all right, Scotty. The Klingons have stopped firing, lower the defence shield'), she had disappeared into the bedroom, slamming the door. I cursed myself. Most people realize at the age of about ten, eleven tops, that putting stuff under the mattress is really no place to hide anything. You might as well hang a blinking neon sign above the bed: 'Mum, look here.' I limped to the kitchen and put the kettle on for some tea, my birthright, which I resorted to in times of crisis. The night had been uncomfortable, much of it spent in a road builder's pipe due to be laid three streets away. I was fed up and poisoned. There was nothing for it. I was going to have to apologize, come clean, admit everything and plead for mercy. She would understand.

I poured the water on to my unhappily sanitized American brand of Earl Grey, decaffeinated with added calcium and lecithin. The bedroom door opened. Gina emerged carrying two suitcases.

'What are they for?' I asked.

'What do you think? I'm leaving, Ollie. I can't take this for one second longer. You have got to get your life together. All that pornography you brought into our home is just part of the problem. What does that say? Tell me, Ollie. Does that say "I'm well balanced, happy and fulfilled with a good relationship" or does it say "I'm a sick fantasist who gets his kicks watching women screw a mastiff"?'

'Great Dane, actually,' I corrected weakly.

'You need help. You need therapy, you really do. What kind of reporter, even for a British tabloid, makes things up anyway? Tell me. What kind of reporter agrees to help his boss make a criminal connection? You know your problem? You have no principles, no core. There is no you to you. It's all a big fucking fantasy.' She paused. 'Even us.'

I opened my mouth to protest, badly wanting to say something that might explain everything. But nothing emanated from my deadened, shattered, stiffie-riddled brain.

'You should read Daddy's books, you know, instead of sneering at them. You might actually learn about yourself. What's happened to you?'

Oh, grief, not the bloody cubes. I counted to three and a tuna swam past my eyes. She carried on: 'He understands people. He says that reporters are frustrated, the square sides of their beings don't connect. He says you're all caught up in other people's lives because you can't cope with your own.'

So that was it. 'Oh, really. And just who the hell does he think it is who gives his geometrical twaddle publicity? Who does he think he's talking to when he goes on book tours? Who got Richard Nixon out of the White House?'

All reporters use Richard Nixon when things get tough; it was that rare moment when a good story happened to trip across public interest. Gina snorted. 'My father, for your information, is a best-selling author who cares about people and someone who real journalists want to interview. And as for Richard Nixon, jeez, that was a frigging generation ago. Got a newer model?'

'Bill Clinton and Monica Lewinsky,' I said instantly.

'Oh, right. You guys were only ever interested in Clinton from the waist down,' Gina shot back. 'It was a sex story and you know it. Nobody gave a shit about the Constitution or lying to

Congress. It was all about blow-jobs and a stained dress. Give me a break.'

'Listen, miss high and bloody mighty. Has it occurred to you that there might be another explanation for those magazines? Has it? Of course not. You've just leapt to the first conclusion that presented itself.'

I could feel myself entering barrister-mode ('Is that wise, captain?'), puffing up to sardonic speed warp two. 'Mercifully, you work in public relations, that faultless bastion of ethics and principle. Who could doubt your right to chastise a fallen mortal engaged in the ungodly sin of journalism?' I raised my arms heavenwards, a debauched Southern preacher discharging to a muddled flock of dirt farmers. 'Was it not Moses himself who said, as the tablets were cast down, "And let no man writeth for newspapers"?'

There was a silence. We stared at each other, two spent forces. 'Have you quite finished?' she said quietly, lifting the cases and heading towards the front door. 'Because I really think we may be. I'm leaving right now, Ollie. And not to stay with Grace. I'm going home. To the ranch. And don't expect me back, even if you lose your keys. You can come to me this time, when you've actually thought honestly about what's going on.' She smiled, but it was forced. There was a tear in her eye. 'I loved you, I really did. But not like this. Something's happened and you're not letting me in.'

'Listen,' I said feverishly. 'Look, I can explain everything.' I took a deep breath. This was it, the moment. 'Stanley called me over because he wants me to arrange a hit, a murder, for him. He gave me all those magazines just so that I could prove I wasn't with the cops or anything.'

I stared expectantly, waiting for a melting of the angry features set in front of me into sympathy. The cases were on the floor, which I took as an encouraging sign.

'Obviously, I don't actually have to do the killing as such,' I added for amplification.

The lull seemed unnaturally long. 'Oh, very good, Ollie,' she said, clapping her hands slowly. 'You really haven't been listening to a thing I've been saying, have you?' She nodded her head. 'And the other thing that's really disappointing is just how lame that is. I think you could have come up with something a little better. Especially with your experience of faking.'

She lifted her bags and headed for the door. I rushed over, grabbed her shoulders.

'But it's true,' I yelled. 'Honestly. Do you think I'd make up something like that?'

There was a silence before she replied, quietly, 'But that's just it, Ollie. You make everything up, don't you? I think you just made me up, your token girlfriend.'

I opened my mouth. It was too late, she was out the door. I erupted crazedly. 'And you're bloody wrong about tuna,' I shouted down the stairs. 'Wrong, wrong, wrong. And I was with a hooker last night. She was great. I had sex with a chocolate pancreas.'

I went back into the apartment, slamming the door shut behind me, then rushed out again. 'It had marzipan inside,' I shouted into the empty stairwell. By now I was that baffled bull elephant on the Serengeti, suddenly realizing that the bastard with a gun does have a licence. There was nothing to lose. 'And another thing. Yes, you were right, the Carpenters CD *is* mine,' I bellowed. 'Hey, hey, wait a minute, Mr Postman . . .'

I felt raw, vulnerable, angry and combustible as I slumped into an armchair. It was a two dead gerbils moment. I'd even forgotten to make sure she took Hughgrant, who had assumed an accusatory position by the door and begun to whine. 'Stop snivelling,' I shouted. It seemed to work, on me anyway.

I picked up my telephone to see if there were any salvations waiting. There was one message. It was from Bleaker.

'Hello, Oliver. I just wanted to check how the research for our little project was going. Sir Derek is particularly keen to keep to the timetable and have this resolved before the next board meeting. The local government correspondent job is still available. Badabing.'

I deleted the message and headed for the vodka, which I mixed with cranberry juice, reversing the usually accepted proportions. I felt terrible.

And there was something else, dimly recalled from the party. What was it Fishlove had said? See you in Chelsea? Meet me in St Louis? See you in church? Yes, that was it. See you in church. Church? What did he mean. Church? I put it out of my mind. Fishlove was the least of my problems, for once, in a crowded field. ('And they're off. It's Mafia Hit by a head, leading Gina's Buggering Back to California and, trailing, Fishlove's Church. As they approach the final furlong, it's . . .')

I slid further into the chair, abandoned by my girlfriend as a lying, possibly bestial pervert and harassed by employers menacing me with return and a lousy demotion unless I put them in touch with a hit man. 'Cheers,' I said to Hughgrant. He ignored me, and carried on with his crap.

15

'It's Danny Mehan. I've got a name for you,' said the gravelly voice.

'You have? That's fantastic, Danny, absolutely fantastic,' I replied into the receiver through another in the rolling programme of thick hangovers.

'Yeah, stroke of luck really. There's this guy who used to muscle for the Treviso family down on the fish market. He's called Frank Scarpesi, runs his own crew now. Smart fellow, by all accounts. A contact in the Feds was mentioning him the other day. Said he was on the up. Even got his own publicist, apparently.'

'Great.' I was due some good news.

'He might talk, but who knows. He could just be some blowhard. Anyway, I've got a number. Listen, pal, do me a favour. If you get anything interesting from this guy, fill me in will you? Fair trade?'

'Absolutely. Of course. I'll meet him, have a chat and if anything comes of it I'll let you know.' I suddenly felt much better. 'Up to much?' I said instinctively.

'Nah, quiet as a nun's whatsit, if you catch my drift. I'm doing a profile of that cop who beat up the immigrant woman, broke her arms and legs.'

I remembered the story, an appalling and flagrant example of police brutality, shocking even by the swaggering standards of those who are supposed to protect and serve. 'That really was bad,' I said with some feeling.

'Too right. Another example of political correctness, pansy liberals going after those who risk their lives to keep the mean streets safe. Anyway, here's the number. Gotta go.'

After I put down the receiver, I felt like dancing. All I needed to do was make a call, set up a meeting, hand over some money.

I would contact Gina, tell her I was sorry, that all my problems were over, suggest a holiday somewhere hot.

Outside, a pale autumn sun broke through the clouds. God's little nod of approval. I wondered who the patron saint of hits was. I offered up a small prayer of appreciation to St Magnum, just in case. 'You've made my day,' I said to the heavens.

It was time to take Hughgrant for a walk, although the mess on the carpet seemed to make that redundant. The exercise would at least clear my head. We went north up the cycle path between the West Side Highway and the river. I needed time to think about what I would say, to compose an introduction. Did I come clean over the telephone? Probably not. Maybe just a hint? That sounded better.

'Ah, he's so sweeeeeeet.' I turned. She was tall and blonde and being pulled by a Swiss mountain dog, a heavily built beast with dopey eyes and lolling tongue that looked as if it might have trained by pulling Switzerland.

'Thank you,' I replied. 'He's called Hughgrant. I'm trying to persuade him to shit outdoors.'

'Hi, hughiepums,' she said, leaning down deeply to reveal a mass of barely corralled breast, the only sensible reason for heterosexual men to buy small dogs. 'I just love the colour. Where did you get it done?'

'Magnificent, isn't it? A neighbour, actually. She's just starting out on dog perms. Got the idea from some magazine out West. They're all the rage, apparently. Maybe something in *InStyle* next issue. And how old is your wonderful friend?'

'Freddy is two now,' she said with pride.

'Well, I must say he looks smashing,' I said silkily, wondering how many steps it would decently take before her home telephone number could be requested.

'Thank you. We're heading off for an audition, aren't we, Fweddyweddy?' she said.

'An audition?'

'He's been called back for the new Homespace Real Estate commercial. We're so excited. He's up against a French poodle and

99

a cockatoo for the part of the family pet. But I'm very hopeful. We've beaten the cockatoo before and poodles. Well, you know, they're very last season.'

I nodded sagely. 'You're right. He should walk it. Listen, we should –' Before I could finish my sentence there was an agonized bass noise from the mountain dog. Hughgrant seemed to have half an upper jaw in Freddy's mouth and, despite being raised bodily from the ground as the far bigger beast tried to shake him off, was hanging on for all he was worth.

'OHMYGOD,' screamed the woman. 'GET HIM OFF. GET HIM OFF.' I reached down and pulled at Hughgrant's collar, ordering him to let go. Eventually, he relaxed his bloodied jaws and fell into my hands, squirming angrily.

The other dog was pulling his owner around in circles as it yelped in agony. She fell on to the hard sidewalk. I reached to help her up.

'Get away from me. Look at what you've done,' she screamed. 'Freddy's nose is bleeding and he's filthy. I can't possibly present him in this condition. That disgusting little monster should be destroyed. DESTROYED.'

'I'm really sorry. I've no idea what came over him. Hughgrant's in therapy and until now has been fantastic with other dogs, quite deferential, actually. Look, can I help you home? Let me pay for the veterinary treatment.'

She was sitting on a wall by now, sobbing gently. Freddy had actually perked up. It seemed that Hughgrant's bite really wasn't up to his bark. Freddy's owner was the one who needed help, I decided hopefully.

'Can I call a cab?'

She nodded a negative, shoulders heaving.

'Would you like some water? I live near by.'

No again. She looked at me. 'This was our big break. We've been working for this for months, grooming, discussing the role. I even had him watch old *Lassie* videos.'

I bent down and examined Freddy closely. 'Listen, I've had a look and it's not that bad. A bit of water and he'll be fine. You can make the audition.'

She looked at me coldly. 'Have you no feelings? He's been traumatized, assaulted. Don't you understand? He can't possibly be expected to perform after being being mugged like that. Let's just say you ruined his big chance and leave it at that, shall we?' she said coldly. 'I hope your conscience can deal with it.'

'Don't you think you're making rather a meal of this?'

'Listen, whatever your name is. Just count your lucky stars I have no idea who you are, otherwise I'd sue your sorry ass, OK? Now just leave us.'

'I suppose a telephone number is out of the question?'

'GOD,' she shouted.

I walked away, secretly relieved that no introductions had been made. The Trimthunder experience was still fresh in my bank balance.

Back home I decided to make the big call and dialled. I was strangely calm, relieved to have got off so easily and made a note to mention the incident to Dr Kleinman.

'Yes,' said a deep voice after the telephone had rung just once.

'Er, is Mr Scarpesi available, please?'

'Who wants to know?'

'Well, I do. That is, he has been recommended to me for some, er, unusual work.'

'He don't take commissions from strangers.'

I hurried on. 'Listen, it's a very well-paid piece of work. We're talking $50,000. Would that be of any interest?'

There was a long pause. Then another voice came on the telephone. It sounded younger, even amused. 'Frank Scarpesi. Fifty thousand dollars for some plumbing? Where did you hear about me?' he asked. 'Let me guess. Was it the piece in the *Wall Street Journal*? No, I'll bet it was *Vanity Fair*. You know I'm not really that handsome,' he said. 'But what can I say.'

What was he talking about? 'Yes, yes. That was it.' It was a relief not to have to lie about my true source.

'I knew I shouldn't have done that interview. But, you know, when someone says they're doing a Crime and Criminals issue and do you want to be in it, what do you do?'

'Quite, quite.' It was coming back to me, a dim memory. Of course. Scarpesi was tipped as a coming man. New Mafia, I think the writer called it. I'd assumed it was all made up.

'Well, it clearly pays to advertise,' he laughed. 'Sure we can meet. I like the outdoors myself. You know Swanky's in the Village?'

'Yes,' I said, hardly able to believe that Todd had chosen a place that actual mob guys chose themselves. Maybe his furniture was genuine too.

'Meet me outside at six. Come alone.'

'How will I recognize you?' I asked.

'You won't. I'll find you. You sound British to me. Wear one of those, what are they called, bowler hats.'

'I don't have one, I'm afraid. They're not compulsory any more,' I added stiffly. It was one thing to be arranging a hit with a cold-blooded mobster, it was quite another to be laughed at.

'Tell you what, buy a copy of *Make Me an Offer*, it's a book about my business. Carry it under your arm. I'm on page sixty-three, by the way. They've still got it at Barnes and Noble on Union Square. I checked over the weekend.'

That was fine, even easy, and I put the handset down. Excitement and apprehension flowed through me. I felt dizzy. This was real.

'You know, this was where they filmed the christening scene in the original *Godfather* movie when Michael Corleone was getting all his rivals whacked.' Frank Scarpesi was staring reverently at the unprepossessing, rendered exterior of Old St Patrick's Cathedral, across the street from Swanky's. We were well away from the early-evening crowds. He had chosen carefully, I thought. The church-yard was supposed to be locked. Somehow he had a key. But then this was Little Italy. His father probably had the key before him and his grandfather probably killed the person who actually owned the key.

'Now, what can I do for you?' he said, looking directly into my eyes. Scarpesi was about thirty-five with wavy, dark hair. There was already a fleshiness to his saturnine, handsome features, a heaviness to the jaws. But he was hardly conspicuous. I would have to tell Todd when this was over. The real thing looks alarmingly ordinary. He was wearing designer jeans and a grey, hooded sweatshirt over an elegant but casual shirt. If he was carrying a weapon, it must have been in his ear. He had searched me for any sign of a wire and insisted we talk facing the church wall. 'Lip readers,' he said. 'You can never be too careful. Now, speak to me.'

'I was wondering if you might be able to help me,' I said, sounding surprisingly calm, given the circumstances.

He looked at me, a smile playing on his lips.

'Look, before I go on, I just want to say this has absolutely nothing to do with me.'

'What doesn't?'

'What I'm about to ask.'

'What is it you're about to ask?' He was playing with me.

I was at a crossroads. The signs directed me towards Sensible, Exciting, Your Parents Would Approve and Unfathomably Lunatic. I ignored the first three options.

'I want you to get rid of someone. Murder them, I suppose. As I said, I can offer $50,000,' I blurted out quickly, swallowing hard.

He looked at me for what seemed an age. 'There, that wasn't so bad, was it?' Scarpesi said eventually, emollient, putting a consoling arm around my shoulder. 'This is your first. Am I right?'

'Yes, yes, it is,' I said gratefully.

He patted my shoulder. 'There, there. Don't worry. The next one will be easier.'

Scarpesi had a fantastic bedside manner. 'No, I don't think you understand. There won't be a next time. Really.'

'Of course. Now, I want you to write the name down for me,' he said, handing over a piece of paper and a Mont Blanc pen.

'I'd rather just say it, if it's all the same to you.'

'I'm afraid it isn't. You see, this is my security. I don't know anything about you, but I do know the laws of entrapment. If you're a cop, handwriting analysis will prove you asked me to do this illegal thing with an inducement. It's just insurance, you understand. A legal thing my lawyer insists on. Nothing more. We don't know each other, after all.'

I did what he asked. He read the name and whistled. 'You've selected a ripe fruit to pick,' he said. 'The biggest skin trader on the East Coast. But that's cool. You're paying enough for some pretty classy wet work.'

I was relieved. 'Listen,' he said. 'There is one thing. I gotta check out whether this guy's got protection and from whom. I'll let you know. Just a formality. I'll tell you about payment then as well. I'll require a deposit, naturally.'

I told him I could offer 20 per cent. He nodded in approval. We got up. He asked how I was feeling. 'Much better. Thanks for asking,' I stammered.

'I know it's hard,' he said soothingly. 'But the way I see it is that you gone to all this trouble, you must want it. Now I'm no brain doctor, but I bet you sleep sounder in your bed tonight now that you got all this off your chest. I don't know what your grouse is with this guy, but it won't be there for much longer. You understand me?'

He was right, I thought guiltily, stopping in the Tavern for a swift three on the way home.

Bowker had news from the library, he said in a message I picked up later. 'There's some geezer called Frank Scarpesi. Found him under "Italian Food: Cold Dishes", as it happens. Must've been one of those my old man set up. Anyway, this Scarpesi seems to be out there. There was a piece in *Vanity Fair*. They talked to some FBI guy who says that he's a modernizer, wants to make the family legitimate, that he's really sharp, got his business degree and all that.' Bowker was relishing this chance to prove the power of Mind over Windows. 'Anyway, the piece is all about how he'd been set up and so on. So he sounds just what you're after. Give us a call if I can help any more.' I was about to walk away. But Bowker hadn't quite finished. 'One thing, he sounds bloody vicious. He knifed some guy in a fight. Hope that helps. Cheers.'

It ought to have felt like good news, but somehow felt otherwise. I wished Gina was there. I wished she believed me. I wished I told the truth except when it was inconvenient to lie.

I needed cheering up. I tried to call Todd. There was no reply. He must have been off on one of his bizarre buying trips. 'Out West,' as he would say, a euphemism for scavenging from film sets in Los Angeles. He was actually quite charming with women and employed this skill to great effect. The trick, he once explained, was persuading set designers to part with stuff, which wasn't that easy in an age of sequels. On more than one occasion, Todd would say with a wink, he had had to perform 'a studly act' to procure a particular item. It was certainly an arresting image. Todd in full erotic flight dreaming of an armoire seen in *Jaws*. Each to his own, I thought. At least nobody died at the end of his working day. I tried his mobile. No reply. Undoubtedly left behind as usual. I was suddenly feeling very alone. I tried to call the Cube Ranch. It was on answerphone, or cubephone.

16

We had arranged to meet in Central Park, on the west side near the 72nd Street entrance. I carried the deposit money in an old gym bag. It was surprisingly heavy. I got out of the C Train, which had lumbered up from 14th, and walked across to the park entrance, past Strawberry Fields, the memorial to John Lennon that was surrounded, as usual, by solemn votives. Imagine, I said to myself, there's no Stanley, no Bleaker too, it's easy if you try.

A voice had spoken of picking up the 'first instalment'. It had already arrived in my bank account from London. I was to go to the public toilets a few yards into the park. Guy Armitage would have been quite at home. Scarpesi probably thought that was a British thing as well. I walked in. It was extraordinarily dark. The air was filled with fetid, primal smells. A man stood at the row of eight urinals. He was in a suit. I stood next to him and coughed.

'I've got something for you,' I whispered, leaning over.

'Say what?' he replied.

'I've got a thing for you. You know.' I looked at him. Meaningful. 'A package.'

The man stared at me, startled. He frowned. 'You got the wrong guy, pal,' he said.

'What? No, I haven't,' I said impatiently. What was wrong with him?

'Yes, you have,' he said, pushing me away from the urinal. 'I gotta wife and three kids. I didn't come here looking for no "package". You mistook me for some other sicko. Now go screw yourself.'

Shit. 'Christ. Look, I'm really, truly sorry. There's been a mis-understanding. I was supposed to meet someone here, a business meeting.' The man stared at me as my excuse trailed off. He began backing towards the exit.

'Don't come near me, OK, or I'm calling the cops.'

'No, really, don't do that.' That was all I needed. 'It was a mistake.'

'It sure was,' he said angrily, turning and stomping out. Several people came and went as I stood at the urinals, making eye contact with each one. I felt the warm breath of immigration officials. I could just imagine Lt James D. Resin demanding to know whether loitering in lavatories was also part of my job.

A slim, delicate Asian man came in. He was wearing a tight yellow t-shirt and red shorts and seemed to walk on the toes of his feet. He peered at the world through the darkest glasses I had ever seen.

'I been watching you,' he said to me. 'This my place. I never seen you work here. You a cop?' His face darted around nervously.

'No, certainly not.'

He brightened. 'You looking for action, maybe? Special discount.'

'Wrong again,' I said indignantly. 'I've just arranged to meet someone here for a discussion.'

He opened his eyes wide and laughed pitilessly. 'Tell that to judge. That oldest one in books.'

'Really? Well, in this case it happens to be true.'

'Listen,' he said. 'I no got time, understand. This place mine between three, five. You cannot be here. I ask you real nice. Go.' He waved a small hand towards the park.

'I've got every right to be here, just as much as you.' I was being unusually defiant, confident. Gina would have been proud.

Then suddenly his swagger collapsed. Deflated, he broke down and began weeping inconsolably, shoulders shuddering. Hell, not again. All I seemed to do these days was make people cry. I felt suddenly awkward.

'This not fair. I need this, man. I got bills to pay. Why you take my pitch? This calamity. This is calamity for Asian entrepreneur.' He looked at me. Moody, defiant. 'What you think? We should all work tables in Chinatown? You racist pig.'

'Calm down. I'm not here to –' I reached for a suitable phrase – 'offer any services. In fact, I will be out –' I looked at my watch and sighed – 'exactly 14 minutes ago.' Where was this contact? Meanwhile, the sobbing continued, oblivious to what I had said. I thought about putting my arm around him, to protect this suddenly blossomed fragility. But it seemed inappropriate. He might ask for money.

'You got something for Frankie?' said a deep, level voice.

I scrambled to my feet. 'Yes, I have,' I said, relieved.

'Then tell your lady friend here to beat it.'

'Actually, he's not my friend. We've just met. Not that it matters, of course.'

'No, it don't. Tell him to get out of here.'

'This worse kind of exploitation. You white guys ganging up to stop Chinese make living. You both disgrace.'

'Hey, get out of here, sweetie pie.' A gun suddenly appeared.

'Wooo. Just making point. This still a democracy, you know.' He disappeared. 'We all on same buses now. This not Tiananmen Square,' he shouted defiantly when prudently out of sight.

'Gimme the money,' said the heavy-set man, clicking his fingers. So much for pleasantries. I handed it over, $10,000.

'How will I know when it's been done?' I asked as the man flipped through the notes.

'You'll see it on the news, same as everybody else.' There was a pause as the checking continued.

'We want the rest in cash, here, exactly twenty-four hours after you receive a message on your cellphone. It will be "Call your Uncle Johnny." Remember that.' Without a further word, he left. I followed after a minute. A figure emerged from behind a bush.

'You done business?' he asked.

'Yes,' I replied jauntily. 'Elvis has left the building. It's all yours. Good luck.' Then I had a thought. 'Listen, I'd like to do some business with you myself.'

'You would?' He suddenly cheered and immediately began his pitch. 'Good afternoon. My name Leopold, pleased meet you.' He reached into a small holdall and produced what appeared to be a laminated menu. 'Here. Take look.'

I examined the illustrated sexual options, each described in Chinese, English and German. There were numbers to help the ordering process.

'Hand-job, ten dollar, very special price for you,' he said. 'Dutch – that number fifty-three – Puerto Rican, Amazon Fish Dance. All on early-bird special before 5 p.m. You want Icelandic Dog? No problem. But you got give one day for me get ready. You want house call? No problem. Just small service charge. Visa? No problem. American Express? No problem. Sometime possible to combine items. Complimentary fortune cookie. You want hear today's specials?'

'No, that's fine. This all looks terrific, Leopold. Let me give you my name and telephone number. Let's meet up. Call any time. Day or night. Here, I'll write it down.'

I took out a pen and scribbled on an old business card: 'Fishlove, 212 691 9368.'

It was late afternoon by the time I reached home and the sun was starting to set over Hoboken, splashing the horizon like broken yolk. It was the only time the Jersey shore, with its graph lines of nondescript skyscrapers, had any beauty. I took the brilliance as a good sign, a purging. I was calm, despite embarking on an unspeakable act. Scarpesi was right. I did feel better.

Curiously, my block seemed to be pulsating, the walls pushing outward as I approached. I squinted. Surely a trick of the light. Things gradually became clear. Rhythm, it seems, travels faster than sound. There was a party taking place in the apartment below mine. Reggae pulsed out. The communal front door, I noticed with annoyance, was open. I walked through and adjusted to the aural assault. A thin, sweet smoke hung above the stairs. A man was kissing a woman passionately, a seabird disgorging fish into the beak of its mate.

'Excuse me,' I said politely, easing past.

'Hey, Dogman, come on in, have a drink dis fine night,' a voice ahead of me said. It was Eddie, clutching a bottle of Red Stripe. Through the open door I saw dozens of dancing bodies, strobes flashing. 'You lookin' tight as a spring. You need some chillin'.'

'No, thanks, Eddie. I really must get back. It's been a very long day. What's the celebration for, by the way?'

He looked mystified.

'The party,' I clarified.

'Oh, dis not a party. Dis just a little break, man. We don't have a party until when we finish.'

'Really? I'll try to still be alive for that great day. Do you really think you might squeeze that in before the end of time? Who are all these people, then?'

He laughed generously. 'Dese jus' frens com around help us wit some o' de heavier work, de painting windows gloss ting.'

I somehow found myself being drawn into the reek, relaxing with each inward, seductive breath of marijuana. Soon there was a beer in my hand.

'How's the plumbing work going?' I asked. 'I'm still getting some very strange coloured water in the shower.'

'Dis my good fren Sylvia from Montego Bay,' Eddie said, hastily changing the subject by grabbing a beautiful, tall woman who looked half my age and twice my fantasy.

'Hello,' she said in one of those silky voices that often persuaded me to buy expensive perfumes. 'How you know the man here?'

'Well, I don't know Eddie very well. But since he's been working on this place, we've got to say hi to each other. We, I mean I, live just above.'

'You the man with the coloured dog?' she said. 'Eddie told me about you.'

'He did? All good, I hope.'

'Well, a little strange, I think,' she said, smiling. 'He say you got your dog dyed a diffren' colour while you away.'

I frowned, wondering how exactly Eddie had explained the Hughgrant incident. 'What else did he say?'

'Nuttin' too much, just that this old woman claimin' she was your special fren' com aroun' and say she want to surprise you by givin' your dog a special makeover.'

'Oh, she did, did she.' I felt my stomach knot. 'Firstly, she is not my girlfriend, on account of a tragically unbridgeable age gap. Mrs Romstein, the woman in question, is my occasional dog minder. I make it á rule never to go out with anyone who can remember personally the fuss when Moses parted the seas.'

'So you're not dating her, then?' Sylvia said, a look of surprise crossing her gorgeous face. 'Eddie, that lady we got next door with the spliff, is that a differen' one?'

Eddie separated from the knot he was talking with.

'Dogman say he ain't datin' that woman you invited,' said Sylvia.

'You not?' said Eddie, looking at me surprised.

'Eddie, of course I'm not dating Mrs Romstein. She's two millennia old, for Christ's sake,' I said, appalled. 'She's not here, is she?'

I turned as a querulous voice spoke my name. I spun around. 'Mrs Romstein. How lovely to see you.'

'Well, we'll leave you two alone for a while,' said Sylvia. 'I guess you got some talkin' to do, some explainin'.'

'No, I haven't. Don't go,' I protested. Too late. Sylvia had shimmied away, attached to Eddie. There was a tug at my arm. I sighed, looked down. Mrs Romstein was dressed, if that was the word, in a tight pink Spandex tank top, her aged dugs hanging like wizened aubergines. A constricting pair of Earl brand jeans finished the grotesquerie. The whole creation rested perilously on a pair of two-inch high heels.

'You're looking, looking . . .' I struggled to find the right words, the lexicon to do full justice to what was being paraded. 'You're looking very, very. You're looking very different tonight, Mrs Romstein.'

'Thank you,' she said, mewing softly, the gratitude fuzzed by tokes. 'And how is little Highgrab?'

'Little Hughgrant is fine, thank you,' I replied. 'We went for a walk this afternoon and he actually took a shit outdoors.' I was braced to rebuff some serious flirting and really didn't mind what I said.

A tall, equally old figure emerged from the flashing illuminations and smoke. It was Mr Kapachutski. He and Mrs Romstein embraced. We introduced ourselves for the ninth time in three years.

'How are you enjoying the party?' I asked him politely.

'In my country we never had party. Each winter when wind blow off mountains so hard it strip skin off, we sit and tell stories of old days.'

'So, reggae, Red Stripe and marijuana is a step up, I would imagine?' I said with what I hoped was just the right degree of levity, anything to head off regime stories and possibly a cabbage-shortage incident recollection.

For a moment it seemed to work, deflecting him in the way small sheets of tin dropped behind a bomber can sometimes distract even a determined ground-to-air missile. 'Yes, yes. This very good,' he said raising his bottle. 'Very, very good.' Then a tear welled in his eye. Soon he was crying, roaring his sadness. People turned. Mrs Romstein put her arms around his quivering shoulders. Eddie came over.

'What's happening, man? What you say?' Eddie asked, looking at me accusingly.

'Me? I didn't say anything, nothing at all. I just mentioned what a great party this was and how it must have been an improvement on his early life.'

'How could you? He hates to be reminded of those days, everybody knows that,' said Mrs Romstein.

'Hates to be reminded,' I said, aggrieved and panicked. 'What days? He brought it up. I was trying to get him away from thinking about all that, whatever all that is.'

Both Eddie and Mrs Romstein looked daggers at me. Over their shoulder, Sylvia was laughing. Glad someone was finding this funny, I thought.

'I think you bringin' bad vibes in here with all dis war talk,' said Eddie.

'War talk? I never mentioned any war.'

'Mr Kapachutski is very sensitive about his past,' said Mrs Romstein. 'He doesn't like to talk about it. He was found innocent. There was a tribunal. They were all liars. He was tortured, you know.'

'I didn't know, which is why I didn't mention it,' I said, eyes wide.

I heard a voice over my shoulder. 'He come in, started flirtin' wit de old woman. Her man come over. He turned on him, started talkin' about de war or somesuchting, said he was some evil torturing kinda person.'

I spun around to stare at my accusers and defend myself. But I could see it was pointless. I pushed my way to the door, savage and confused as I climbed the stairs. The snogging couple had now, somehow, levitated to a position outside my door, still exchanging fluids intravenously.

'EXCUSE ME,' I shouted, weaving past. They were so startled that they actually unlocked flesh, probably for the first time since daybreak, and stared at me. 'You seem to have progressed your tongues up two levels. Congratulations,' I said. They looked unconcerned. I opened my front door and thought I heard the word 'uptight asshole' before slamming it shut on my day.

Congratulations to me too, I thought bitterly. I'd just arranged to have a stranger killed and reduced two blameless old people to tears.

'Sssssssssh!' said Fishlove.

He was peering through binoculars at the white clapboard church across the street. I scrambled across the shingled roof and lay down next to him.

'Anything happening?' I whispered. Distracted by minor things, such as murder and crumbling relationships, I had completely missed the story that 'much loved' Sefton Timble, the British comic actor, had died of some unspellable disease in New Jersey.

'Yes, I'm on my way to the funeral now,' I had lied, scrambling to gather a notepad and pen, when I got the call from the foreign desk the next morning. So, that's what Fishlove meant the other night, I thought. Damn. Thank God he answered his mobile, which I called from my hire car.

'Hi, Fishlove. Just wondered –'

'It's in Edison, New Jersey. Church of Faint Hope. Go through the Lincoln Tunnel and follow signs off the turnpike,' he said humiliatingly, before I even asked. Needless to say, he had also found the prime vantage point. We kept low behind the small parapet. Across the road, police scanned the horizon for interlopers; Alsatians strained at leashes, presumably trained to pick up the scent of British reporters.

'Did you get a snapper in the church?' I asked idly.

'Chrimo's somewhere in the cemetery,' he replied.

Big, burly Chrimo, a Geordie transplanted to New York. He worked exclusively for the *Sentinel* and had a reputation for getting the first photos, the topless starlet with the man she wasn't marrying next weekend, the first steps of a famous paraplegic.

Nothing was moving at the church. A small cortège, including a hearse, waited outside its large oak doors. I looked anxiously at my watch. 'Come on, come on,' I urged. 'I'm going to have to file something.'

'You are, aren't you. I filed about half an hour ago,' said Fishlove.

'Really? I mean, what was there to say?'

He kept staring ahead. 'Talked to some of the relatives, the cops. Got the order of service, songs, that kind of thing. Sent over about 800 words.'

I felt something icy grip my lower intestines. 'Get much?'

He looked at me and smiled. 'Yes, thanks.' He then went back to peering through his binoculars.

And thanks for the help, I thought bitterly. There was nothing for it. I left the roof area and began to write madly:

Comic genius Sefton Timble was buried yesterday after a moving ceremony in New Jersey.

Friends and family gathered to pay their last respects to the man who helped shape British comedy. Timble died tragically of [subs: plse insert] disease. He was 61.

A close friend, who asked not to be identified, said: 'A few people cried, but there was laughter as well. It was a very moving. It was a good send-off. Just what he would have wanted.'

Fans arrived from across America to bid their own farewell. 'He was lovely, tragic, wonderful,' said James D. Resin, a fashion photographer from Rhode Island. 'He was a great star. I was devastated to hear he'd finally fallen to [subs: plse insert] disease. It was terrible. I just had to come here to say goodbye.'

Timble was part of the legendary 'This Was The This That Is' comedy team. The 6'6" comedian became an unlikely Hollywood star. Married nine [subs: plse check] times, he starred in *Ogle*, playing a tall British comedian who falls in love with a beautiful blonde, played by Mo Clive. They went on to star together in four sequels – *Stare*, *Racked*, *Dressed*, *Undressed* – and a lighthearted reworking of 'The Last Supper' set in a small New England town.

This was good, really flowing. Across the street, the church doors opened. 'Fishlove, they're coming out,' I whispered loudly.

He reached for his binoculars, scouring the sea of black clothing and vibrantly blonde hair. 'Is that Mo Clive?' he asked. 'She's laughing with that tall guy.'

'Well, it is now,' I said.

I carried on writing: 'Mo Clive, weeping uncontrollably, was one of the first to emerge from the church. She held the arm of a male friend for support.'

'I'm off,' Fishlove said. 'I bet they're heading for the local cemetery. Chrimo checked it out yesterday. There was a long open grave there. Must be for Timble.'

We rushed to our cars as the cortège pulled out from the church. My mobile rang. It was the foreign editor.

'Hi. On its way. Tell the picture desk that Mo Clive was here. What? No. I don't think he knew Jordan. But Mo was crying, obviously devastated. Still stunning to look at, of course.'

We snaked through the tree-lined suburbs, mourners pursued by reporters. Fishlove was first off. An elderly driver pulled his Buick out in front of him, moving so slowly that even the stately paced black convoy was pulling ahead.

'Shit,' I swore explosively.

Thankfully, the Buick driver realized he was being chased by Hacks of the Apocalypse and pulled over. Fishlove roared past, expertly ignoring the car heading at him from the opposite direction with outraged horn honking. Where did he learn to drive like that?

We managed to catch up with the line of stretch limousines, reaching it just as the last funeral car pulled into the cemetery. There was just one entrance and a high black fence. A security guard in peaked cap put his hand up as Fishlove drove in. There was a brief exchange. Fishlove reversed, turned around his car and pulled off to the side of the road. My turn to try.

I saw a badge stitched on to his shirt above a quilt of military campaign ribbons: ETERNAL REST SECURITY. ARMED RESPONSE UNIT.

'Can I help, sir?'

'I'm here to visit the grave of Ernest Hockengarden.'

'Proceed.'

He waved me through with an imperious sweep of his gloved hand. 'Yes,' I said, pumping the air some yards in. Ahead, I could still make out the rear of the cortège. It had stopped. I drove quietly up and parked about a hundred yards away. Ahead I could make out burly men scanning the road. They wore headsets and sunglasses.

I got out of the car as the first big shaven-head reached me. 'Excuse me, sir. May I help?' Help sounded suspiciously like hinder.

'I'm here to visit the grave of my uncle, Ernest Hockengarden.'

They looked at each other and then at me, the notebook, the mobile, the pen. It wasn't rocket science. But I could see they were unsure.

'We'll be glad to walk with you, sir,' he said.

'No, that's OK. I can get there on my own.'

'It's no trouble,' he said determinedly. 'We'd be pleased to.'

I closed the car door and headed towards the Timble gathering.

'It won't be that way, sir,' he said. 'You said your uncle's name was Hockenbird, right?'

'Hockengarden, yes.'

'Well, sir, you need to be way over there where the *h*s are. This is *s* and *t* only.'

Hell.

'Really?'

'Yes, sir.' They looked at each other. 'Now, if you don't mind, we'd like to ask you to turn around and head back out. There's a private interment taking place.'

There was nothing for it. Lunch with Fishlove, who was waiting outside. Chrimo was with him and looking sullen. His left eye was swollen.

'What happened to you?' I asked.

'Bloody bouncers. They spotted the camera I'd hidden in the handle.' He held up a shovel, where a rather large hole was clearly visible and rather crudely carved.

'Bit of a give-away, I suppose.'

'Yeah, well, I had problems with the electronics.'

'What happened?'

'Bloody flash only started to go off, didn't it? There was all this light coming out. The goons grabbed me, ripped the camera out of the shovel and we had a bit of a set-to. I nearly fell in the bloody grave. Good mind to sue.'

'I wouldn't bother, Chrimo,' said Fishlove. 'Not worth it. Did you see Mo Clive, by the way?'

'Nah, she wasn't there.'

Fishlove and I looked at each other. Nothing needed to be said. We would be keeping that particular fact to ourselves. A picture of Mo Clive in the paper was likely to get our stories more prominence than one of a coffin.

We found a diner on the way back to New York. 'Well, that was pretty painless,' I said.

'Yes. Quite,' Fishlove agreed. 'You haven't forgotten the number for Salvatore Rosselli, have you?' he suddenly said as we left the table.

'Damn, should have brought it with me. Sorry. I'll e-mail it over when I get back.'

'Excellent. I was starting to think he was the Invisible Man.'

How we laughed. 'Shit, shit shit,' I said in my hired car.

17

'Call me most urgently,' said the message. It was Bleaker sounding rattled. I was pleased. 'It is imperative that you contact me immediately regarding badabing.'

Let him sweat, I thought. I wanted to savour the moments until I made the call. Caesar's text message to the Senate: 'Cnqrd Gaul. Gt garlands rdy.'

It was going to be wonderful. Meanwhile, work went on and Tom Harman wanted an update. 'We've heard Whitney's people have been talking to Fishlove at the *Sentinel*.' His voice was cracked with worry. 'Can you give them a call again? We're definitely interested. We can guarantee them two pages, copy and picture approval, basically anything. The owner's very keen.'

'Sure, Tom,' I said to the machine. 'I'll call for the umpteenth time and for the umpteenth time they won't be interested because we're a piss-anty paper nobody reads.' Bugger Fishlove.

Harman could sweat it out as well. I tracked down Todd. He was back in town, he said, and thought it would be just great to meet up for a bite. He had heard from Gina.

Of course he had, I thought.

'She's fine,' he said breezily over coffee at the Brew Bar. 'I spoke with her yesterday.'

'Did she say anything about me?' I asked.

'Mostly we talked about the weather and the redwoods in California. She said the riding was great, and it was wonderful to be out of the city in the fresh air. She's managing to work as well, using her dad's home office system. Did you know he has his own TV studio there? Isn't that something?'

'No, I didn't,' I said impatiently. 'Did she say anything about me? About us? Anything at all. I mean she must have been giving our relationship some thought in between pondering the ancient beauty of the redwood and the timeless calm of a Californian autumn.'

'Well, let me see now,' said Todd, pausing to mine for what was clearly going to be an insultingly small nugget. 'She asked how Hughgrant was doing. So I said I'd find out.'

'Is that it? She wanted to know about the bloody dog but not about me?'

'Sorry, man. She didn't go into specifics, but I got to tell you, that porn. I don't even want to go there with you. But she said you kept lying to her and even when she was walking out the door, you came up with some monster misspoke that just blew her over the edge. That was it.'

I wanted to tell him everything and probably should have done. Misspoke? Where do they learn these words? But there was something about what Bowker had said that made me keep quiet. The last thing I needed was my friends knowing what was really going on, being drawn into the evidently volatile world of Frank Scarpesi. Todd and all that goofy good nature would be overwhelmed. This was not a hole a character actor could pull me out of. I was secretly relieved that Gina thought my confession was just another hideous untruth, a 'misspoke' to taunt her with the flaws in our relationship.

But I did tell Todd about the porn and how it had been given to me, what happened at the airport and how incredibly lucky I had been even to get past immigration on the last trip.

He loved the story, of course. 'That's wild, man, I am absolutely going to build a script around that one,' he said. 'That is just the funniest thing I ever heard. There's a screenwriter comes into the store. He'd love it, dude. You crack me up. Can I tell him?'

'It wasn't very funny at the time,' I replied frostily. 'And I don't want any publicity, thank you very much.'

He looked downcast. 'She always hated that shit. Even back in college. One of her first boyfriends had a stack of *Playboys* under his mattress and she found them. That was it. She went off the scale ballistic. Left him just like that. In fact, that's how we met, kind of on the rebound.'

I didn't want to go there. Todd and I had an unspoken pact that we never discussed how he came to lose her and I ended up with the prize.

I looked at him, still laughing to himself. I wondered whether he was secretly moving in already. Perhaps he and Gina were talking regularly, reconnecting the dead electrical points of their relationship and finding an energy still there.

Could I trust my best friend in the city any more? It was troubling. I really needed him, probably more than I needed Gina at that moment. He was all that passed for normal, all that remained unchanged. That was how bad things had become: Todd had become the most balanced thing in my life. I wanted to tell him everything. But I knew it would hardly be doing him any favours. The fewer people who knew the better.

'I've known Gina a long while,' he said soothingly. 'You gotta give it time. She's probably working it all through, talking to her folks, that kind of stuff. She loves being out there. It's so peaceful. It's got a great vibe. She can think. You've just got to be patient.'

He was right. I wanted to move on to less painful things anyway.

'I know she loves you, it's just gone missing,' he said, slapping my shoulder encouragingly. 'You're peas in a pod, man.'

'Really? I seem to be the only one being shelled.'

We talked about the store. It was touch and go, despite his inherited money. It was a basic problem with business acumen, one that had first reared its head with the inaugural promotion poster he unveiled proudly as Gina and I clapped expectantly, champagne glasses raised: GRAND OPENING: ONE FOR THE PRICE OF TWO. Gina and I had looked at each other and shrugged before calmly taking it down.

Todd was on a high. He was excited about getting some cushions spotted in a market just outside Chicago. They resembled the ones featured in *Austin Powers*. He planned to label them as items 'reserved' for use in the film.

'I know it's kind of unethical, but they are so cool and sixties. I had to get them for the store. What do you think?'

Unethical? He was sitting opposite someone working towards a doctorate in the subject, followed by a full concert tour. I told him that it sounded a fine and honourable marketing initiative. I was sure Gina would approve and she was in public relations.

'You know what, you should write a book,' he said, sensing my bleak mood and doing his subject-changing thing to remove the difficult vibe.

All reporters live to be told they should write a book, a suggestion replete with implications of imagination and talent, of a creativity beyond joining up the dots of other, preferably torn, lives. I had, in fact, been thinking for some time that I should do something, anything to escape the orbit of Derek Stanley. My research into the bestseller lists of the *New York Times* had yielded a theory: books about cookery, cats or Nazis always seemed to sell well. But I didn't know much about any of them, as I explained to Todd.

'I got it. I got it,' he said, scrunching his face in concentration. 'Wait, wait, any second.' There was a pause, and an expression of elation spread across his features. 'Meals for Nazi Cats.'

I stared. Dumbfounded. 'Bring them all together, dudesman, it's a cert. Hey, and you could bring out regional editions, establish a whole brand. You could do "Meals for Nazi Cats – South-Western Home Style". It's a sure-fire hit, man. Let's do it. I'm psyched.'

'I don't know,' I said doubtfully. 'Sounds a bit off-the-wall to me.' But he was undeterred, manically scribbling cat recipes with a Bavarian twist, as if, suddenly, the secret of life was within sight. The Brew Bar thoughtfully provided coloured crayons for patrons to access their inner child and doodle on its white-paper table coverings. Todd, I was disturbed to note, pulled a crayon out of his jacket pocket. 'How about tuna with sauerkraut? Turkey breast and Pilsner? Hey, this is even cooler: bratwurst and milk biscuits?'

Here was the difference between our two cultures – again. One was about drive and dynamism; the other – mine – was about doubt and disappointment. 'I definitely don't want any tuna meals.'

It was late in the afternoon by the time Todd and I had finished feeding Third Reich delicacies to felines. I would call Bleaker to reward myself with a truly delicious moment.

I thought six my time, 11 p.m. his, would set just the right dramatic note for a link across the Atlantic. I called the mobile telephone number that I had been given in London. It rang just once before being answered.

'Hello?'

'It's Ollie Gibbon.' I wanted him to go first, to reveal his anxieties for a change.

'Thank God. Where have you been? I've been trying to get hold of you all day,' he said, sounding flustered and accusatory.

'I was out meeting some PR guy to try to persuade him to give us the Whitney Houston interview,' I lied effortlessly. 'It's not looking too good, I'm afraid.'

'Well, that can wait. The important thing is that badabing is off. Do you understand? Off?'

I felt punched momentarily senseless. 'What do you mean "it's off"?' I asked, feeling the blood drain from my face. 'I've just made all the arrangements.'

'Sir Derek and Mr Goldblam have reached a very amicable agreement, one that is beneficial to both parties, over the future of their respective businesses in the United Kingdom. Mr Goldblam has given us assurances that he does not intend to come over here and has never heard of anybody called Rosselli. There is no need now for, what shall we say, a more permanent solution.'

I struggled to regain composure. 'Well, that's all well and good. But I delivered the deposit money today to a man who is now under contract to do the business we discussed.'

There was a gasp in Purley. 'What! Then you must stop him immediately. Immediately.' Bleaker sounded hysterical and I started to feel it.

'There is absolutely no way that what we discussed can happen,' he went on. 'It could seriously jeopardize Sir Derek's business interests. He needs to work with Mr Goldblam to open up the American market, to keep everything, including the *Herald*, afloat. Circulation has not been too good, as you know. But the other titles are showing great promise. Keeping everything going includes your job, I might add.'

I felt myself beginning to explode as Bleaker, in his terror, flooded me with information that he should have kept to himself. Not that I had time to enjoy the refreshment of corporate gossip or the promising future for *Collar* and Co.

'Well, I might add that the whole badabing business was set up by you for your bloody business interests. I went through several hells to find the right person for the job.'

'That's as may be. I haven't got time to argue with you, and, as you know, we have no knowledge of what you've been getting up to out there. We never discussed anything, if you recall from the meeting.'

My mobile began ringing. 'Look, that's my mobile going. I'll call my guy and get the job stopped. I'll call you back.'

'Let me know straight away,' said Bleaker. I interrupted the fifth ring of 'Ode to Joy'.

'Gibbon,' I said.

'Call your Uncle Johnny.'

I turned on New York One, the city news channel, in a trance. The wait was no more than twenty minutes.

Now this breaking news. Prominent publisher and Democratic fundraiser Sol Goldblam has been killed this evening following an apparent accident at his Brooklyn printing works. Initial reports say that the man behind a string of erotic magazine titles died after shelving collapsed at his warehouse.

Emergency crews battled for fifteen minutes to rescue the sixty-year-old publisher. They were hampered by fire breaking out in a building next door. Police said there were no witnesses, and that Mr Goldblam appeared to be in the warehouse alone. A senior fire officer told New York One that it was a million-to-one accident. Mr Goldblam, a controversial figure implicated in a number of unsolved homicides, was walking under the shelving when it fell, said the officer. He was crushed by several tons of magazines.

At least it resembled an accident. Death by porn was a neat touch, I had to admit. I wondered what I was going to say to Bleaker. Perhaps he might be pleased after all. Maybe it was, as Frank Scarpesi said, easy once it happened. I would soon find out, but if I was going to have a sleepless night, so was that creepy git in London. I decided not to call him back for a while.

I slept badly and, in my dreams, was trying to develop fins so I could keep up with all the other fish: the cod and sea bass, the swordfish, redfin, northern pike and rock bass, the pan-fried tuna and sticklebacks that were pulling ahead, leaving me behind as I struggled not to sink; the sharks in dark glasses were gaining . . .

Outside a storm blew through, rattling the windows. I sat watching it and drinking tea. The skies were a rage of mauves and reds. Clouds rolled over the city, disgorging rain in tropical torrents. On the horizon, lightning sheets lit the sky, crackling the air.

I wondered what to do next. If only I had picked up the message earlier instead of feeding my vanity, Sol Goldblam would probably still be alive. I might even have extracted some reward from Stanley for nimbly saving the day, I thought bitterly. Instead, I would have to call Bleaker and demand that he hand over the balance. It would be an awful conversation, I knew. There would be anger and demands. Eventually, a fitful slumber came. I dreamt of Grimsby Council Public Works Subcommittee.

'You wilfully ignored my calls,' hissed Bleaker. 'Let me make this clear. You alone are responsible for this disaster and you alone are going to have to get yourself out of it. Sir Derek is incandescent.'

I felt the blood rush to my head. My pulse was racing, heart thumping. 'Listen, Trevor, there isn't time for all this, OK? What's done is done, and we both know why it was done. I need to have the balance, the $40,000, wired to my account today or we're in deep shit. I have to pay off the guy who did the badabloodybing by 5 p.m. my time.'

I could hear fear in my voice, which sounded unusually shrill.

'That is quite simply out of the question,' replied Bleaker. 'You'll just have to tell them that you made a mistake, you wanted to call off the deal but it was too late. It was all a misunderstanding. Tell them we want the deposit back, less, say, $2,000 for out-of-pocket expenses they may have incurred.' My brain started to throb. I was struggling to believe what I was hearing.

'Listen. You don't just not pay these people. It's not like arguing with the electrician over a bill. We had an agreement to dispose of someone and they're going to hold us to it.'

There was a pause. 'No,' said Bleaker quietly. '*You* had an agreement. I have no idea what you thought you were doing. But as far as Sir Derek is concerned, you were given a sum of money to make contacts for us in New York to help with a business venture. Everything else is either your wild imagination or a fraud. Get this mess sorted out. We'll be calling you about the future of the New York office shortly.'

'I need that money,' I said loudly, hysterically.

'Goodbye, Oliver,' said Bleaker, breaking the connection.

I felt like putting a gun to my head. Then I thought, why bother, people would soon be queuing for that privilege.

I looked at my watch. I had four hours. I wondered what to do. Hughgrant came over and pawed my leg. Empires fall, nations flood. But one thing remains constant: Yorkshire terriers need to be walked or they pee on your Persian. I put on his lead and we went outside.

It was grim. My life was in ruins for doing everything my employer had expected, for being honest – for once – with my girl-friend. It was better when I did nothing that was expected. Now

I was living my own news story, and it was wilder and more real than anything my imagination had ever conjured up.

When I returned, the Rastas were hard at no work, sitting around playing cards intently. They ignored me these days. I was still unforgiven from the party. Was it my flirting cruelly with Mrs Romstein? Was it turning proud old Mr Kapachutski into a blubbing wreck?

They faced away from the door. Eddie glanced up, but quickly let his eyes fall to his cards without a word or a smile. I was alone, I realized. Even the builders had turned their back on me. I thought about calling the cops, telling them everything, but then saw how outlandish it would seem. I imagined some blank, bovine desk clerk chewing gum as I told him what had happened over the past few days. There was nothing I could prove. Detectives would find my story risible and who could blame them? If they read it in the *Herald*, they would probably believe it.

The storms had cleared the air and a bright sun shone down, but it did little to lift my mood. I thought about going to the gym. But even the prospect of prayer at that secular temple failed to help me. Lethargy and resignation took over. I would have to do what Bleaker suggested: appeal to Scarpesi's better nature. The very idea seemed ridiculous. But I had no choice. Again.

18

'Hey, watch it,' he screamed. I stepped back sharply. The last thing I needed to be responsible for was the death of a middle-aged rollerblader in Central Park. I could see the headline: KILLER WIPING OUT LOW LIFES: NOW CLAIMS INVESTMENT BANKER.

Misery was my new friend, and distraction a consequence of the relationship. The park is always beautiful in the autumn, a fiery show of red and ochre leaves, but I scarcely noticed. Even the squirrels, aggressive enough to all but tap your shoulder for handouts, stayed away. They knew a dead man when they saw one.

I headed towards the lavatories. What a place to have my fate decided, I thought. I might have hoped for something grander, perhaps the Roman steps at Grand Central or a roof-top bar with sensational views over the city.

I went inside. Scarpesi was already there with two other men. One of them moved to the entrance and put out a CLOSED FOR CLEANING sign.

Scarpesi smiled. 'You see the news?' he asked enthusiastically, eyes wide with pleasure. 'I thought the team was inspired, inspired. It was such a perfect way to go, don't you think? I'm sure that's what Goldblam would have wanted, to die surrounded by breasts.' They all laughed. 'It wasn't so hard, you know,' Scarpesi said. Here was the artist unable to resist boasting about his work, the touches, the skills. 'His place was old, run down and quiet. He always went up there the night before distribution. It was some sort of luck thing with him. He worried the warehouse would burn down or something and he'd lose everything. Actually, the shelves were good. Solid, you know. We got him when he came in, broke his neck. Then we pushed a pallet of magazines on top of him and snapped the shelving above with our feet. I mean, if we'd used a saw, that would have been kinda obvious to the firemen, right?'

I was nodding but barely taking it all in, as Scarpesi strode his stage between the urinals and the sink, a latter-day Olivier. I heard a pipe drip. For once, I really did.

Finally, the self-adulation ended. I didn't know whether to applaud. Scarpesi beamed at me. 'So, you see, I deliver. Reliability is the core of good business, I truly believe that. Anyway, now it is time for you.'

He looked at me and at my hands, noticing for the first time that they were empty. I was carrying nothing. 'Maybe you got the money somewhere safe?'

I grimaced and stared at him. 'I'm afraid there's a slight problem.' My lips had dried. 'I can't pay you. The people I work for changed their mind about the deal. In fact, they tried to get hold of me yesterday to call the whole thing off. Unfortunately, I didn't get the message until too late.' Scarpesi watched me intent, impassive. 'Obviously, they're keen to get the deposit back. However, the good news is that they say you can keep a couple of grand, for expenses and no receipt required, which is amazing for them, let me tell you,' I said brightly. 'That should more than compensate you for your trouble.'

There was a silence. Scarpesi walked over, standing close enough for me to see the pores on his nose. He twisted his head to one side. 'I don't think I heard you right. Say that again.'

I repeated everything, adding, 'Look, Frank, if I may call you that, it was a great piece of work. True artistry. Something you can be really proud of. I mean, money isn't everything. Van Gogh died penniless, but look how the world admires his art today. I'm sure the same will be true when they look back on the death of Sol Goldblam.'

I wasn't ready for the blow when it came, straight to my belly. I doubled over, fell to the floor, the air rushed out of me. I coughed, gasped and hardly felt the foot kick my kidneys. Pairs of hands lifted me roughly to my feet. Scarpesi punched my left ear.

'You want the money back. Is this a joke? Listen, nobody walks out of a deal with me. Do you understand? I want that $40,000.'

'I haven't got it,' I spluttered, sagging.

'Let's go,' said Scarpesi, suddenly cold and businesslike. 'Stand up. I don't want trouble. We're just gonna walk outta here. You got it?'

I nodded and started to walk to the entrance. The hoods stood on each side of me. There was nobody outside and I was in no fit state to make a run for it.

'Mr Fishlove?' said a bush.

'Beat it,' said one of the goons as Leopold emerged. He obviously had a nose for self-preservation and started to back away.

'Call me in an hour,' I shouted. 'I'd like to arrange a meeting.'

Scarpesi laughed. 'Yeah, call him at home, that's what you should do. Our friend here was taken a little ill, we're looking after him.'

'Was it Icelandic Dog?' said Leopold, concerned. 'It very hard if you not ready. I call you one hour, Mr Fishlove. I bring towels.' He disappeared into the lavatory to prepare or to warm up.

I had hoped we might seem strange. But I realized we were just four guys walking through the park. Why didn't they wear dark suits any more? I wondered. There was nothing to draw the eye. Why would anyone even register the three smiling men and their glum friend? Scarpesi was dressed in khakis and a plaid shirt. His cohorts wore the same, except for the jackets, which, presumably, hid guns. I had no idea the mob went in for dress-down days as well. They really were keeping up with the times, modernizing, as *Vanity Fair* had put it.

There was a BMW waiting on 76th, a few blocks up on Central Park West. The windows were tinted black. A door opened as we approached. I was invited into the back seat by my escort, one shielding me from onlookers, the other twisting my arm up my back in persuasion. It worked.

Scarpesi climbed in the front. The driver pulled away. I would remember the route, I said to myself. No, I wouldn't, it soon became clear. I hardly had time to see the cloth forced over my nose and mouth. I tried not to breathe in the acrid ether, but in the end succumbed to whatever oblivion awaited me, the eternal aquatic sleep.

My degree in hangover headaches covered most varieties known to science, including the consequences of Greek wine. But nothing prepared me for how I felt when, gradually, consciousness asserted itself in a struggle against the death gene. I tried to resist because the groggy pain was unbearable, the worst headache of my life.

My eyes opened slowly, one lid unpicking itself delicately from the other as the pupils fought for focus. Eventually, the surroundings became clearer. I was in a basement, that much was certain. Light came through a small window at roof height, too high for me to see outside. The room was bare apart from a jug of water and one glass on a small side table by the bed on which I lay. Beside the glass was a single packet of Advil. I reached for it.

I swallowed the two pills before attempting what they do in all the films, which was to try the door handle. It turned uselessly. I heard a cough. Locked in and guarded. At this point, dejected, our hero sits on the bed, head in his arms, preparing for someone to come, the sort of person who gets nominated for best supporting actor Oscar. I decided to wait for my co-star in a horizontal position.

I looked at my watch. I must have been wherever I was for a very long time. It was daylight outside.

Scarpesi eventually came, alone. 'How you feeling?' he asked personably, the family doctor making a house call. 'I know that knock-out stuff kicks ass. The guys used it on me at my stag night. But you got the painkillers, right?'

'Yes. Thanks. Very thoughtful.'

'Not at all. Not at all. Sorry about the rough stuff back in the park. But you know how it is. Reputations and everything. The team hate to see me go down to a double cross, Mr Gibbon, or may I call you Oliver? It's bad for business. Word gets around and you look weak and out of control. Next thing, everyone wants to get out of paying their debts and then where would we be?

'Now, the tough thing is, I got to get that money off you.' He said it with what sounded like regret. 'What do you think?'

'Look, firstly, it's Ollie and secondly, nothing would give me greater pleasure. But the problem here is that the people I work for in London are just determined not to pay. They can be quite tight.'

'I was so afraid you were going to say that.' He clapped his hands together and frowned. 'Here's the deal and it's not negotiable. I want you to call them, tell them the situation here. The thing of it is this, and here's your ace.' He stopped for a moment and looked straight into my eyes. 'You're going to die unless they send the money.'

My knees buckled and I sat heavily on the bed as random thoughts flashed unbidden through my mind. Gina, cricket, Hughgrant, the Derbyshire Dales, a pint of bitter.

'Sorry to spring it on you,' said Scarpesi gently. 'But there it is. I couldn't let you live. Truth is that Goldblam was slime. Truly. But there's gonna be some cop heat because of all the media interest and I need payment to take it. I mean, aside from the principle of the thing, you'll understand that you are the only person who could link me to Goldblam's death and you're a journalist, which means you talk a lot, no disrespect.'

'None taken,' I said dully.

'I'm going to get Fat Angie, the guy watching the door, to take you to a pay phone near by. This is your chance to save yourself, Mr Gibbon – Ollie. He'll be watching, so no funny stuff, OK? You won't be coming back here, so don't bother telling anyone where you are, even if you do work it out.' He smiled.

'You laugh a lot, you know.'

'You're right. I do. I think it's because I enjoy my work. It's challenging, stimulating. That's the key to a happy life. I love all this shit. You know, being a made man, a boss. I get a rush every time I don't get a bill in a neighbourhood restaurant, which is every time I go into a neighbourhood restaurant,' he said, and winked.

'Sounds like my job.'

'I have a lot of respect for your business. Really I do. You keep the myths alive, you know. I like that. People revile you, fear you. It's just the same with us. But we both do it anyway and you know why? Because it doesn't feel like work, that's why,' he said with a note of satisfaction. 'Of course, I've had to do a lot of stream-lining to make my operation profitable, bring it into the twenty-first century, so to speak. Still a long way to go. We need to go legitimate, which is where all the profitable, risk-free corruption is these days. That's where my business degree has really helped, looking for opportunities.'

I remembered the cutting Bowker had dug out.

'I've got rid of a whole load of buttons.' I must have looked surprised. 'I'm sorry, slipping into jargon there. How rude of me. They're basically the soldati, the soldiers. We have far fewer than other families. They work longer hours, but make more.

'We also have fewer caporegime, the middle managers. They're not very productive, you see. They just take off the top of what comes to me from the buttons. You need to be lean to survive in this market. The Russians, Koreans and Chinese are all organized in the five boroughs now. It's tough, believe me. But, like they teach you in business school, competition improves the product.'

I looked up when the lecture was over. 'Forgive me, but I don't think there's any comparison between what I do for a living and being a murderous thug. No disrespect.'

Scarpesi laughed. 'You found me, Ollie, not the other way around.' He rose to leave. 'I'd love to carry on with our chat. Regrettably, time is pressing and I have another engagement. Angie, you can come in now.'

A lumbering fridge came through the door. His head was shaved to the scalp. Where a beard might have been were thin ribbons of hair, a helter-skelter of dark, drawn lines.

'Angie, say hello to Mr Gibbon here.'

'Hello to Mr Gibbon here,' the hulk said sullenly, looking coldly at me.

'Angie is much faster than he looks, by the way, so don't try anything stupid. He's also armed. But what he really likes to do is break kneecaps with a heavy rubber instrument he always carries now that the sharp ones can't get through security at airports any more. Do everything he says and you won't get hurt.'

'Yet,' I added, watching Angie hold up a small rubber truncheon.

The man with the MBA and a special interest in mob finances smiled again.

''Erald,' barked a receptionist.

'Sir Derek Stanley, please.'

Travelled Trish came on the line. 'Is Sir Derek available? It's Ollie Gibbon in New York.'

'Hello, there. I'll see if he's free. He was having his kick-boxing class and meeting advertising. But they should be done by now.' She sounded uninterested in my call, oblivious to what was going on. There was a pause, time for most of a Kinks medley to play through.

Fat Angie had brought me outside to a corner public phone booth, just to make sure nothing could be traced.

'You've got a bloody nerve,' Stanley spat down the telephone, breaking into 'Lazy Sunday Afternoon' abruptly. 'I 'ope you've sorted out that business you created.'

'Not exactly, I'm afraid.'

'What do you mean?'

'The people I've been dealing with are demanding the rest of their money or they're going to kill me.'

'Well, whose bloody fault is that, then?' Stanley shouted. 'We tried to get hold of you all day yesterday. But you was nowhere to be found, was you? Far as I'm concerned, this is your problem.'

I caught sight of Fat Angie on the corner, staring intently at me, his blank eyes an invisible leash. The prospect of death is a surprising stimulant to action. Forget Scarpesi's ace, I had a card of my own to play.

'Well, the thing of it is this, Sir Derek. So far they don't know who I'm working for.' I paused for dramatic effect. 'But that could change.'

Stanley barely caught his breath. 'If you want a pay cheque or your expenses next month, don't even go there. I haven't forgotten about those Whitney Houston CDs,' he countered. 'You're hanging on to that job of yours by a fred, my son, a fucking fred. Whoever said you could claim for them anyway?'

'You don't seem to get this, do you? There won't be a next month for me unless you pay up what was agreed to these people,' I said.

There were at least two people waiting behind me and some accusing stares. 'Sorry, sorry,' I mouthed. 'Long distance. Bad line.'

'What was that?'

'Not you. I'm out on a street corner being watched by a heavily armed man with people waiting to use the telephone.'

I felt a small tap on my shoulder. 'Say, mister. You gonna be long?' asked a worn, middle-aged woman. She was carrying piles of laundry, which on closer inspection turned out to include at least three young children who clutched and weaved around her legs. 'I ain't got all day.' There was a pleading look in her eyes.

I nodded, cupping my hand over the mouthpiece. 'Just a couple more minutes,' I said. She sighed hard.

In my ear, Stanley was relieving himself of some colourful language. I wondered whether it was a condition. Perhaps he had to get the words drained off every month in some invasive, hopefully painful, surgical procedure ('now this might hurt a fraction, but there's a particularly foul "fuck" down there I want to get out before it multiplies. Forceps, nurse. The sharp ones').

There were nuggets of demands and requests blasted, randomly it seemed, amidst the sea of filth. I caught at least one 'reputation', the odd 'do what you're told' and 'scrounging lazy hacks', a clutch of 'bastards', two 'Whitney CDs' and an Indian summer of 'fucks' in the spewing mess.

'So, you see if you do anything that embarrasses me, I'll see your career is ruined, fucking ruined. There ain't going to be no more money. Furthermore, like the poet said, "You'll never work in this town again", got it? Now listen and listen good. I'm about to have tea with the prime minister, he wants me to head up some

Better Business Ethics task force bollocks he's setting up. I do not expect to hear from you again. When this has been sorted, I want you on the next plane back to London, where I can keep an eye on you.'

The tapping on my back was becoming insistent. I turned. There were at least five people waiting, pointing at me. In the distance I could just make out Fat Angie. He appeared to be arguing with a street vendor over the price of a hotdog. At that moment I saw a squad car draw into the street and inspiration paid a welcome call.

'And another thing, I want to know who that Salvatore Rosselli bloke is. We can't find any trace of him and I'm starting to wonder . . . Hello? Hello?'

I had dropped the receiver, turned and pushed the woman at my shoulder hard. She reeled backwards and screamed, stunned. 'He hit me. He hit me,' she yelled. I then pushed, with the flat of my hand, a pale youth with tri-coloured hair. 'Hey, watch it, man,' he said, pushing back tamely. I fell theatrically hard against a trolley full of food that careered into the street. Then I heard the siren winding up.

The car pulled up. Fat Angie was staring at me and then at the cops, wondering what to do.

'This guy started fighting with everyone, officer,' said a woman. 'He gone plain loco. I saw everything. He a menace. You gotta book him. He just pushed this poor lady for no reason at all. We was just waiting in line.'

My first target nodded in agreement. 'I only asked him how long he'd be,' she said sullenly.

A ruddy-faced officer looked at me through a face mottled with a fury of vein lines. He was holding his nightstick. 'Is this true?' he said, looking at me through narrowed, make-my-day eyes.

'Yes, and I'd do it again,' I said defiantly. The crowd gasped. I could see Fat Angie talking into his mobile.

'Oh, would you?' he asked, turning to his partner. 'Get contact details from these people, Kenny.' He turned to me. 'OK, buddy,

I'm booking you for assault. You have the right to remain silent. Anything you say can and will be used against you in a court of law. You have the right to speak to an attorney, and to have an attorney present during any questioning. If you cannot afford a lawyer, one will be provided for you at government expense. Got it?' he said, attaching handcuffs to my wrists.

'I certainly do, officer,' I replied, relief washing over me. He put his hand on my head, guiding me into the rear of the squad car. Fat Angie was nowhere to be seen.

It turned out that I was in a part of the Bronx that was a grim urban smear of dereliction and decay. The car took me to the local police station, speeding past tall red-brick tenements, high towers of anonymity and despair. The worst of New York. The bit they never put in the tourist brochures.

'Tell me what a white British guy was even doing on 145th,' said Officer O'Toole, pausing from the slow, painstaking, one-finger typing of his report.

'Well, I'm a reporter for a newspaper and I was just calling my office in London,' I said. 'They want me to do a piece about how crime is falling across New York thanks to police cracking down on street thugs.'

I felt another plan, of sorts, emerge and pulled out my press card. 'In fact, I was very impressed with how quickly you guys turned up. Incredible. I'll be putting that in my article, of course.'

'You will?' said O'Toole.

'Definitely. In fact, I'm probably going to be interviewing the police commissioner next week and I'll be telling him too.'

O'Toole stopped typing. He scratched his head for a moment and looked around. 'Let me get this straight. You're saying you pushed that lady just to see how quickly we would respond.'

'That's about the size of it. I mean, I hardly hit her at all, just a little push with the flat of my hand.' I demonstrated on his shoulder.

'Watch it,' he warned.

'Sorry,' I said quickly. 'But you guys were fantastic, very polite, I thought. And the way you controlled the crowd, kept people back and stopped the whole thing from getting ugly. Masterful.'

'Yeah, well, I've got a few years under my belt,' said O'Toole, puffing up. 'I could tell you some stories, about how things really are. They give you all that falling crime bull back at headquarters.' He glanced around to make sure nobody was within earshot. 'It's crap. Out here on the front line, it's fit to bust wide open.'

He stopped typing altogether and concentrated on venting his pent-up rage. 'I got thirty years with the force coming up next June,' he said. 'Then I'm getting out, taking my pension and heading into private consultancy work. That's where the money is.'

'They probably don't know what to do with a really experienced officer like yourself,' I encouraged.

'Damn right. Bunch of college snots down in Police Plaza. What do they know? They ain't never broken up a riot, stopped a shop lifter or faced down some crazy with a gun. Me, I've been shot at eleven times. Imagine that. I'm lucky to be here.'

After another forty minutes, O'Toole and I parted the best of friends. I promised not to quote him, but definitely to stick it to the guys down at Number One Police Plaza. The charges were dropped, naturally. I was just about to walk out of the station, when O'Toole called me over. 'Hey, you might like to know that a couple of guys were here asking after you. Said they were friends of yours. They're waiting outside in the Beamer with the dark windows across the street.'

Time for some fast work. 'You know, officer, the one thing I've never done since I came to this city was go in a squad car. I know it's a bit irregular, but if you're heading out again, could I hitch a ride for a few blocks? It would definitely help my piece.'

'Sure, glad to help a gentleman of the press,' he replied with courtly charm. 'It'd be my pleasure. We're parked out back.'

They dropped me at 34th and Park Avenue in Manhattan, anonymous, affluent, businesslike and far from the Bronx, not just in miles. I glanced occasionally out of the back as we drove downtown. We were not followed. The BMW with the tinted windows was, I hoped, still sitting outside the front of the station, its occupants waiting to pick up their 'friend'.

Scarpesi had left my wallet with me, which was either stupid or showed considerable confidence in Fat Angie's ability to keep me under control. I disappeared into the subway on Park. It would soon be dark and the bowels of Manhattan, filled with commuters heading home, seemed the safest place to be whilst I thought what to do next.

It was a mess. Scarpesi's hoods would certainly be in the Village by now, hoping I would be stupid enough to head home. I looked into my wallet. It was all there, about $20, the credit cards, driver's licence. At least there was something to help my survival chances.

I travelled around for about forty minutes before deciding it was safe to surface. I chose Christopher Street, knowing it would be packed with tourists experiencing the cradle of gay activism in the city. More importantly, there were plenty of cash machines.

I punched in my pin number. Nothing. I tried again. A telephone next to the machine promised to connect me with an operator twenty-four hours a day. Incredibly, a human voice responded within moments.

'Hi, I can't seem to get any money out,' I said.

The voice asked for the number of my card. 'That was reported stolen about two hours ago, sir. It's been cancelled.'

'But that's ridiculous. It hasn't been stolen, I've got it here. I'm obviously me because you've just asked me for the security details.'

'I'm sorry, sir. It's bank policy. You can just call the office during business hours tomorrow. They'll be able to arrange for a new card to be sent out to you immediately.'

'But you don't understand. Tomorrow is too late. I need the money now.'

'I'm sorry, sir. There really isn't anything I can do this late.'

'OK, OK. I guess I can use my Visa card.'

'That's coming up on my screen as cancelled too.'

Bastard, I thought. Scarpesi was smarter than I'd thought. I was stuck with a useless credit card, no mobile and less than $20 in my wallet. He had hobbled me, made sure that I wasn't going to get far in a hurry. I slumped against the wall, watching the family pods of Midwesterners wander past, camcorders flopping against loose bellies and, for the first time in my life, wished I was one of them. I needed a friend.

Todd was still in the store when I arrived at about 8 p.m. He was talking to a pale, thin Goth with red streaks in her hair. She stood on large platforms, head tilted to one side.

'I can't guarantee that this particular headstone ended up in *The Blair Witch Project*,' I heard him say, 'but it was definitely on the reserve list, according to my supplier, which is almost as good. It got past the audition, if you know what I mean. That's why it's such a sensational price.'

She looked about nineteen and uncertain. 'Look, you go away and think about it. I'll hold it for you until tomorrow evening. You just let me know. Deal?'

She nodded and walked off. Now here was a genuine beamer, I thought, as Todd, smiling broadly, loped over.

'Yo, man. How's it hanging?' He punched my shoulder. 'Good to see you. Wondered where you'd been. Brewski?'

'Not right now, thanks. Look, I need your help and I mean really need it,' I said. Something in my tone took away his smile. He looked serious, an unnatural contortion that took time for his facial muscles to adjust to.

'I'm in deep, deep trouble. You don't need to know anything about it. In fact, it's better if you don't. But I've got to get out of the city tonight and I need money. That's it.'

He barely missed a beat. 'So, do you think I could be an investment banker, handling portfolios of stock for wealthy people, helping them navigate the treacherous world of Wall Street like that guy in *American Psycho*?'

'No. Now, if we could just get back to the deep, life-threatening trouble you may recall me mentioning a moment ago.'

'Oh, sure. Absolutely. Go for it.'

'Well, it's a long, complicated story.' I looked at the expectant, open face in front of me. No, it would be too cruel. 'The short version is that some guys are on my tail and they've already had me banged up in the Bronx. I got away, but they're tracking me. They've cancelled all my cards and I can't get any money out of the bank until tomorrow. But I can't hang around until then.'

Todd stood open-jawed, trying to digest a sentence with more than the preferred one fact in it, and then narrowed his eyes. 'This isn't some kind of wind-up for a piece you're writing, is it?' he asked. 'You're not still pissed over that Swanky's deal?'

'No, no. I swear. On my mother's grave. It's all true. A story got a bit out of control, and the last forty-eight hours have been a nightmare. That's all I can say.'

'That is so intense.' He seemed persuaded and we headed off to a cash machine. The most he would be allowed to take out was going to be $1,000, but that would be enough to get me on a plane and far away tonight.

I watched as he put in his card, punching in numbers and password. 'Man,' he said, disappointed.

'What is it?'

'Bummer, dude. I'm a little light. I've only got $320 in the account. I paid for a whole load of shit last week and haven't had anything to pay in yet. I'm sorry. I should have pressed that Goth for the headstone. If only I'd known. You should've called.'

He was right. It wasn't going to get me far. No last-minute departure to freedom. 'Don't worry. Some of that would be fine, Todd, if you can spare it. Anything.' I tried not to sound bitter or disappointed. It was hardly his fault I was running from a swim with the fishes. I took the cash and promised to call him the next day from wherever I found myself. I wondered what the area code was for the Hereafter.

19

Elton John found freedom in Philadelphia, so I decided to try the same. A train left from the bowels of Penn Station just before midnight. The concourse was surprisingly busy, even that late. Office workers, stumbling home after an unwise number of margaritas in downtown bars, wove around each other; couples after a night on Broadway clutched arms. Urgent, innocent lives filled with minor debasements, fleeting deceits. Sensible, decent people with sensible, decent jobs. I felt shameful and alone. The carapace of self-importance fractured by the hell of my last few days.

I stood drinking a vodka rocks in a station bar, waiting for the train to be called.

'Hey, may never happen,' said a voice. I turned. A hand reached out for shaking. 'Bill Scotter. Industrial Wall Mountings.'

'Gibbon – Ollie – fitted rose bushes, partly industrial.' Another lie. Easy. Second nature. Not that Scotter of Industrial Wall Mountings seemed to care.

'Pleased to meet you, Ollie Gibbon. You waiting for Philly?'

'Yes. You?'

'Am I waiting for Philly?' He slapped his sides with mirth as if he'd just heard the greatest joke. 'I'm so regular, they practically named the train after me. That's where we're based. Live there now, matter of fact. Kids love it.'

Not that I was feeling particularly sociable. But it seemed sensible to have an instant buddy, someone to deter any goon who might be passing by. Paranoia, I knew. But Scarpesi was certainly searching Manhattan.

'People often assume the alloy used is the same, which always cracks me up. Like a three by four quarter bit is going to have the same permutations as a two by six.' He roared with laughter, pulling on his beer. I smiled knowingly, but played my own sound-track.

What would I do if I were Scarpesi? Naturally, I would stake out my apartment, talk to neighbours. Thank goodness Gina wasn't there.

What else would I do? What happened in the movies? They covered the airports and train stations. 'A cornered rat sometimes runs when he hasn't got the guts to fight,' I could almost hear him telling his soldiers.

'. . . not that pre-moulded wall wasn't good for older buildings. Now don't get me wrong . . .'

They were probably here now, searching. I looked at my watch. Twenty minutes until the train left. The departure board had, to my horror, only three trains listed, each from a platform that was reached by single file down a narrow escalator. How hard was it going to be to watch each one? Maybe they had been there all evening, anonymous behind khaki trousers and plaid shirts. In the films, the dark-haired fugitive heads to the lavatory and dyes his hair or undergoes some quick plastic surgery to emerge as Cameron Diaz. I had neither the time nor the materials.

'. . . so I do the tricks at kids' parties, dress up, that kind of thing. My boys love it . . .'

'Sorry, what was that?'

'Just saying how I do this party thing, dress like a clown for the kids. You know, tell a few jokes, bend a balloon or two.'

'Really?'

'Sure. Wanna see? After the meeting I headed out to Abracadabra on 17th. Great gear. Look at this.'

Scotter reached below the bar to a bag. He pulled out a red skull-cap enriched with a slash of green Mohican-style nylon hair. He put it on. It looked atrocious. No, I certainly was not going to be wearing that. There was worse. Scotter seemed to take my aghast expression as some sort of encouragement.

'Wait, wait,' he continued merrily. 'Wait till you see this.'

I looked around nervously. 'Don't you think we should head for the train? I think it's been called.'

'Sure, sure. Hold on, hold on.' He rummaged enthusiastically, emerging victorious with an enormous black walrus moustache and a pair of fake glasses, the kind with eyeballs on springs that were hilarious in 1863.

A voice came over the public address system: 'The 11.37 Philadelphia service is now ready for boarding on Platform 23. All aboard for Philadelphia.'

'Da dum,' my new friend said, a vision of forced lunacy and body-shuddering laughs. Bloody hell, I couldn't have him anywhere near me, I realized. Talk about a magnet for anybody looking.

'Bill, look, I've got to dash. Good to meet you, it really was. Fascinating.' I reached to shake his hand. He reached back instinctively.

'Wait, wait. I'm right behind you.'

Not if I could help it. I hurried out of the bar, grabbing a newspaper to hold close to my head and left Scotter scrabbling with his bags. I was sure they did this in the movies. I also stole a scarf on impulse from a vendor, seizing the moment whilst his head was turned, staring into the bar at the clown vision.

I headed for the platform. There was a queue waiting for the escalator and two people studying each passenger. One of them was Fat Angie. I wrapped the scarf tightly around my face, to obscure all but my eyes, and glanced towards the floor.

'Ollie, Ollie Gibbon,' I heard Scotter shouting from somewhere behind me. 'Excuse me, excuse me. My friend's up ahead. Hey, up yours too, pal. Suck on it, why dontcha.'

He was heading towards me. The crowd was parting keenly to give the lunatic with the Mohican, bobbing eyes and walrus moustache easy passage.

'Hey, this case is heavy. Let me through. Please,' he said with confident, boozed-up entitlement.

There was no alternative. Any more of this and the enemy up ahead would start paying attention. Worse, they were going to hear my name being called.

'Bill, over here,' I said as quietly as possible. He puffed and heaved his way over. A disguise was supposed to make you invisible. I had somehow conspired to end up with the most visible being in the universe.

Fat Angie caught my eye. He had heard. A faint smile moved his fleshy lips.

My new best friend saved me anyway. In addition to an excess of clown gear, Bill Scotter was suffering from a surfeit of beer-induced bonhomie. He grabbed my arm to steady himself at the moment we approached the escalator, before Fat Angie could reach through to take it for himself.

I pretended not to notice my former captor, was determined not to catch his eye. I glanced back from the safety of the moving escalator. The plan must have been to snatch me before I boarded any train.

Fat Angie, I saw with satisfaction, clearly did not have a ticket. The collector refused to let him pass, despite some heated remonstrations. I watched him trundle away as a nearby policeman began to show interest. Three minutes to departure. I could just make it. The question was, could Fat Angie?

I headed with my clown to a row of seats near the front of the train. By this time, I was helping Scotter carry his extraordinarily heavy case. 'Samples of the new range,' he explained as I laboured.

I rushed back to one of the open doors and looked towards the escalator. There was no sign of Fat Angie. I looked at my watch. One minute. I felt relief pour over me as the conductor raised his red lollipop-shaped baton and uttered the life-saving words 'Waaaaall aboard' before blowing his whistle. I ducked in, pulling the door shut behind me, sliding the window down so that I could peer out. There was still no sign, I noted with satisfaction. Maybe he'd been distracted by a reasonably priced cinnamon roll.

The seventy-five minutes to Philadelphia would pass fast, I knew. I also realized that even Fat Angie would have the brains to arrange a reception committee for me. I glanced over at Scotter, already snoring in the corner, skull-cap askew, the bobbing specs stuffed into a top pocket. The sleep of the harmless. There was no sign of the walrus moustache. I felt a spasm of sadness. One outing in the spotlight and already destined for the rubbish heap.

I brooded. At least I had some time. I left my seat quietly, anxious not to awaken the slumbering party animal and unleash a spew of clown stories. I wanted very much to lose him before we reached Philly. I could see Scarpesi even now, roaring with laughter at his inept quarry trying to sneak on to a train with a human beacon attached to his arm.

He now knew where I was going and exactly what to look for. Sixty minutes to go. Reporters are good at chasing people, not being chased. Maybe I should have stayed in Manhattan? I had no idea how I was going to escape, without being seen when the train reached its destination.

I walked down a corridor and tested the doors. They were centrally locked. There was no question of leaping off as the engine slowed into the station. I thought about hiding on board, but they were bound to check.

Twenty minutes to go. The suburbs of Philadelphia came into view, illuminated streets of brick-built houses. The train began to slow and occasionally released a mournful whistle. I almost did the same. I had little money and no disguise. All I had was a comatose travelling companion.

He was still fast asleep, twisted awkwardly in his seat. Not surprisingly, there was nobody sitting beside us. I gently eased the already loose Mohican clown cap off his sweat-glistened scalp and pulled the glasses out of his top pocket. We were both wearing dark suits. I never wore a tie if I could help it. He clearly did and, by the look of it, always the same one. I removed it and tied it around my own shirt collar. Scotter had left a half-finished whiskey miniature on the table. I grabbed it, swigging the contents for a rush of confidence. The walrus moustache suddenly caught the corner of my eye, jammed down the back of the seat next to Scotter. I pulled it out gratefully.

Ten minutes. I rummaged quickly in the Abracadabra bag, recovering a joke nail-through-the-skull and some stink-bomb capsules. I shoved the stink-bombs into my jacket pocket. I left the nail-through-the-skull. No point in giving the mob any ideas. Scotter was stirring, some inner sensor telling him it was time to wake up. I stole away, hoping he would be too bleary to check his purchases let alone remember his friend from the platform bar, and headed quickly to the lavatory, locking myself inside.

I arranged the skull-cap and the moustache, adding the spectacles as the conductor announced that we would shortly be arriving in Philadelphia and to remember to take all our belongings with us. Poor Scotter. Little did he know that someone was taking most of his. But this was a matter of life and death. I was sure he would understand. At least I left his wallet. He might even see the funny side of it. At the very least, he might stop befriending strangers in bars. I glanced at myself in the lavatory mirror. Not bad.

There were three of them, obvious and preened. Dress-down mob days had not arrived in Philly. They wore snappy dark suits and had sunglasses perched on their heads. They stood carefully scanning every passenger entering the main concourse through the funnel of a narrow metal gate. I tried to steady my nerves. The alcohol had helped. It was showtime.

I chose my target and started reeling from side to side, singing a loud, tuneless la, la la. They spotted me at once, as I was exactly what they had been told to look for.

I twirled and edged closer to a thin, whippet-faced man about my own age and height. The heavies stared at me. The sea of heads in front dipped and crested, briefly obscuring me for just long enough to drape the lurid pink scarf gently over the shoulder of my walking companion. There was no chance of being able to edge away from the clown loony, I could see him thinking as he studiously and, helpfully, looked away. People were packed too tightly for him to escape my unwanted company. I saw him wince. I began singing.

'Who let the dogs out? Who, who who,' I whooped, jigging gently.

'Do you mind?' he said, still looking away from the shoulder on which rested the scarf, his nose twitching in disgust. Even the whiskey fumes were helping me.

I saw the goons staring at him, now completely focused. Fat Angie had, as anticipated, told them to watch out for a man in a clown costume and to snatch the person he was with, the one with the pink scarf.

It was frightening how efficiently and cleanly they extracted my nominated me. Nobody else seemed to notice as they surrounded him, one on each side taking an arm, the other walking closely right behind. There must have been a gun involved because the man made no protest as he was frogmarched away. They could have been a group of friends, purposeful for sure, but that was all. Eventually, of course, they would realize their mistake. But not before driving off. There would be no reason to check his identity, after all. He was clearly the guy with the pink scarf and the only one attached to a drunken clown. How many could there be on any one train? Even from New York. My double would be stunned, then protest, but they would tell him to shut up and, paralysed by fear, he probably would. They were just doing a favour for their friends in New York. He would be taken to some safe house and locked in a basement.

There would be a call, probably to Scarpesi. 'We got the mark,' their boss would say. Scarpesi would grin. Somebody would be sent by car to collect.

I wondered how much time I had really bought myself. Scarpesi might actually get them to check their prisoner's wallet, look at the driver's licence. He might ask about the accent.

What was absolutely certain was that they would realize their mistake, be embarrassed and angry. It was just a matter of time. I looked around the cavernous, elegant station with its huge vaulted ceilings. Despite its majesty, it was smaller than Penn Station, harder to find a corner in which to hide. I wondered about spending the night on one of its benches. Would they come back when the mistake became clear? Probably. Would they assume I had headed into town, found a hotel for the night? Probably.

I reached into my pocket. I had less than $150, including change, and no plan. It was barely enough for a night in this cradle of American freedom or for a ride anywhere else. What was more important, I said to myself, life or a good night's sleep? Easy.

'Welcome to the Holiday Inn, Mr . . .' the voice hovered expectantly.

'Monkey. That's M.O.N.K.E.I.G.H. The *g* and *h* are silent. Well, I say silent. Just shy, really. They're chatty once you get to know them.'

'I understand, Mr Monkeigh. We have a superdeluxeplus with king-sized bed, non-smoking room available for $130, including a full buffet breakfast and complimentary finger massage. Or I can supersize you for just $100 more to the John F. Kennedy Presidential Suite.'

'Good grief. What a stroke of luck,' I said.

'Excuse me?'

'That John Kennedy should be out of town the very night I arrive. What an incredible coincidence.'

'Oh, no, sir. Mr Kennedy's dead,' he said with a trace of bemusement. Hadn't I heard? 'It's really just named that way to honour his memory.'

I looked serious again, then smiled. 'I was joking.'

'Oh, right, I get it. Like the idea he would be staying here when there's the White House?'

'Well, something like that, yes. Listen, haven't you got anything costing less than a monthly mortgage repayment?' I asked.

He whisked his face into a semblance of regret. 'I'm sorry, sir. This is convention season, our busiest time of year. Prices go through the roof for the next couple of weeks.'

'The superdeluxeplus sounds fine,' I said, yawning and suddenly shattered.

'Excellent choice. How will you be paying for that? Cash or credit?'

'Cash,' I replied wearily.

'I'm afraid I will have to ask for full payment in advance,' he said, trying to sound apologetic.

'No problem at all. Quite understand.' I handed over $130. He watched me count it out. 'Sorry about the change,' I said. 'I'll have to hit an ATM in the morning.' Probably literally, I thought.

'There's one just outside the hotel, Mr Monkeigh,' he replied.

My room was on the eleventh floor. I flopped backwards on the bed. Exhaustion washed over me. But for the first time in a long time I felt safe. There was no chance on earth of Fat Angie's boys having the wit to search for a Mr Monkeigh. I could sleep safely. I wanted to enjoy the moment. It was nearly 1.30 in the morning.

That night John Wayne, Pamela Anderson, her breasts and I fought off a marauding band of Indians. They had completely encircled our Pepsi bottle. We would be lucky to get out alive. Mercifully, our marshmallow guns were fantastic, mowing down the Cheyenne and their allies, the hotdog sellers at Yankee Stadium. The breasts were magnificent too, firing off a rocket launcher, killing a tuna. Then Fishlove, of the Ways and Means Sub-committee, raised an objection and the meeting was adjourned so that my dead body could be carried out. I remember one of the councillors asking whether that meant the report on footpath clearances would get into the next edition of the paper. As I lay on the pavement, a Yorkshire terrier stabbed me with a bone.

I woke with a start, sweat sodden. The room was stiflingly hot. The air-conditioning had been switched off. I looked at my watch. It was 8.30 in the morning. I eased out of bed, one leg at a time, and headed to the shower, trying to plan my next move as I went through the morning ablutions.

There seemed to be so few choices. I would have to go to California, head for the Cube Ranch and make up with Gina, if she would let me. I would be safe there, behind what I imagined were enormous walls, fences, security guards and the other perquisites of great wealth. Maybe there were packs of trained cubes? I felt better as the water washed over me. At least I was clean. I felt a small pang of longing for my apartment, its plumbing, the erratic cable-television service. I even missed Hughgrant; I would have to call Mrs Romstein.

It hit me as I dressed and reached cautiously through my pockets, pulling out notes and change to lay on the executive table. I began to count: $17.23 and something from Venezuela. 'What bastard slipped me that?' I wondered aloud, angry and aggrieved.

Breakfast was in the Casablanca Room.

'Here's-looking-at-you, how may I help you today?' a bored young waitress asked. I ordered two eggs sunny-side up, Canadian bacon, rye toast, a side order of pancakes, hash browns and a large orange juice. It had been a long time since the last meal, a hastily snatched deli sandwich with Todd, and it could be a long time until the next one. Todd had urged me to go to the police, call the FBI, even contact the British Embassy if I were in trouble. Anything. But how? I was inviting arrest as an accessory to murder at the very least. Scarpesi had my handwriting to the name Sol Goldblam. I could be charged with actual murder.

I gorged myself on the food, washing everything down with strong, acrid coffee. What would Bogey have done? I asked myself, staring at a still of the *African Queen* navigating a swampy, tropical river somewhere. Sink, I answered gloomily. I ordered more toast, before finally easing myself out of the restaurant. I left a $5 tip. 'Here's-looking-at-you-have-a-nice-day,' said my waitress, as she scooped up the money. I was left with $12.23 and something from Venezuela. It wasn't much with which to save a life.

I went back to my room and called the bank. At least I could get some money out. 'First Amiable,' said the voice after a board game of digital prompts finally exposed the human.

'Hi, my card was cancelled yesterday, but not by me, and I urgently need to get some money out of my account. Can you help?'

'I first need to verify some details, sir.' I gave him my security number, my mother's maiden name, my favourite star sign. Everything.

'I'm sorry sir. But your utility with us is under fluid.'

'What?'

'There isn't enough money in your account.'

'What do you mean? That can't be right. My salary should have been paid in yesterday. It comes over every month.'

'I'm not showing any deposits at all this month, Mr Gibbon.'

'Does that mean I can't make a withdrawal?'

'You have no loan facility with First Amiable. If you want, I could arrange for you to speak with a Money Mountain builder ambassador.'

'How long does that take?'

'Usually about four working days for approval.' My heart sank again. What the hell had happened to my pay? I put down the receiver and called the *Herald* in London.

'Accounts, please.'

'It's Ollie Gibbon in New York . . . Fine, thanks . . . Look, I just wondered what had happened to this month's pay. It's just that nothing's arrived in my account yet and I'm kind of short . . . He did? . . . When? . . .'

The bastard. Stanley had stopped the transfer personally, said John Taylor, the chief cashier. No explanation was given and, of course, none requested. Taylor was very sorry, but what could he do? Nothing, I knew.

I tried the credit card company. They would send a replacement out, but only to my New York address. It would take at least two days. That was probably fast, in the scheme of things. But in my acceleration through hell, a day to wait for the means to get away from the Prince of Darkness was just too long. I sat, slumped on the bed. $12.23 and something from Venezuela. Maybe I could ask for the tip back?

By now, Scarpesi would know that the wrong person had been picked up at the station. Fat Angie would be livid, humiliated. He was probably on his way to Philly personally, seething and swearing all sorts of revenge with his rubber device. The mob outreach programme down here would also be furious. They would probably be searching the hotels, staking out the airport and, of course, the railway station to try to save face.

There was no point in hanging around, I realized, rubbing my hand across the two days of stubble. I hated not shaving. How dumb. Facial hair would help me, surely. Bogey would have grown a beard in this sort of situation. The director would have insisted.

20

'I'd string 'em all up. High an' slow,' he said affably. 'They're out to destroy what our forefathers got us all them years ago. They're takin' over, gittin' more and more pow'ful. They ain't accountable to no man, far as I can see.' He spat a thick thread of phlegm and chewing tobacco out of the truck window. 'Fucking phone companies.'

We were heading west on Interstate 76, towards Indiana and Nashville. Right-wing talk radio was turned up loud and the cab heater was on full. It was sweltering inside the tin cocoon, rank with overweight, underwashed trucker and casually discarded fast-food cartons. But it was a free ride out of Philadelphia and away from the indignity of not paying for my phone calls, which was all that mattered.

He had picked me up as I thumbed a lift at the highway entrance. It felt like being a teenager again. At least I was wearing a suit.

'Don't pick up strangers as a rule,' he had said, introducing himself as Clem. 'But it's a long trip this time.'

I told him my name.

'Pleased to meet you, Ollie. I reckon a guy wearing a fancy set of duds ain't gonna hijack a truck full of pork bellies, now is he? It'd be kinda messy work.' He roared with laughter. Clem was big and, it turned out, firm-minded on a wide range of subjects. 'The working man in this country is bein' squeezed from the left. The unions is a bunch of hoodlums, feathrin' their own nests, and the Democrats is in bed with 'em.'

I nodded at appropriate moments as the scenery drifted by, drab miniature pines and occasional raised signs. They promoted food, service stations and motels, and sprouted with lurid eagerness through the otherwise unchanging landscape. 'Howdy Doo Dee

Donuts, Take Exit 4F'; 'Chocfulla Additives Ice-Cream, Next Right.'

I suspected that Clem picked up hundreds of victims, a serial conversationalist using the freeway network to lure unsuspecting hitch-hikers into his uncompromising world views.

He just wanted to talk and talk and talk. I learnt about his early life in Louisiana, growing up on the family crocodile farm and helping in the attached crocnugget diner. 'Ma done make the finest croc chow in the whole of Whissum County,' he said proudly. His parents moving everyone north to a small farm when the bottom apparently fell out of the crocnugget market in Whissum County. 'Vietnam,' Clem said, by way of explanation. They moved to pigs, but apparently just subsisted, something that was covered in depth by Clem, who seemed to have an encyclopedic memory for hog prices. We sped along the unchanging blacktop.

'Subsidence farming ain't easy, boy. Let me tell you.' I learnt about the college years, which didn't happen, the early jobs, marriage to Mary Beth; the affair with Mary Beth's best friend, Louise, who hit on him one camping weekend; divorce from Mary Beth, the two kids with Sara Jane, who was a friend of Louise.

They were named Shania and Clem Junior. Somebody would need to put me on suicide watch, soon, I thought, as we roared through the vast, blank heartland. But at least I was getting away from my hunters with each completed reminiscence. That made me feel better.

I doubted, with some smug satisfaction, that Scarpesi, Fat Angie or their well-dressed heavies had worked out where I had stayed. Paying in cash was a masterstroke, I realized, even if I was now all but broke. There was no credit-card imprint anywhere in the city. There was no palm they could grease, no favour to pull. Find me now, you bastards. On the radio, a liberal was losing ground to a conservative, which was the American way.

'You ain't frum round here, is you?' Clem asked after about seven hours. 'No, no, don't tell me. Let me guess.' He rubbed his bristled, jowly chin with one hand, glanced over at me, scrunching his eyes as if trying to place a zoo exhibit against a memory from some distant school trip. 'Say summit.'

'The quick brown fox jumped over the white rabbit,' I replied crisply. There was much humphing. I tried not to groan. How hard could this be?

'Hah,' he said jubilantly. 'Blue Ridge Mountains, prob'ly Kentucky way.'

I gave him a look of regret. 'Sorry, Clem. Close. Actually, London, England.'

'Londonengland,' he repeated, awed by this revelation of some distant galaxy. 'Fancy. Londonengland. But I ain't ever bin to Arkansas, so I guess I never was gonna guess it, wus I,' he said.

We stopped at a roadside diner. I stretched my legs whilst Clem went to a pay phone. He said as we clambered back aboard that he had to detour to Filroys Stump 'for a collection'. I looked for it on his tattered road map. No sign.

'Where exactly is Filroys Stump?' I asked, curious.

'Oh, you won't find it on any map, boy. It ain't been incorporated. Is jus' a ragtaggle of houses off the interstate.'

I wondered what this 'collection' might be. We were now listening to country music.

'God's relaxative,' pronounced Clem happily as singer after singer paraded their achy, breaky hearts to the drear accompaniment of slide guitars.

'Lerve is lahk a praire rose, driftin' awayayay,' went one, or maybe all of them. 'Bert, jes lahk thayit fragile fler, serm dayayay ait'll cum mah wayayayay.' Clem sang along to the ones he knew, which was most. He pitched his contributions just a few notes off-key. It was a small but insistent torture.

Most of the time he talked, which gave me plenty of time to think. Was there anybody I could turn to? We stopped at a petrol station, a rare but welcome punctuation, and I tried to call the Cube Ranch. A prerecorded voice told me that it was 'in retreat' until the following weekend. What on earth did that mean? I wondered furiously. In retreat? 'Like Napoleon from Moscow? Like polio?' I screamed at the receiver, blowing a loud raspberry before replacing the receiver.

I had made Todd promise not to call Gina. I don't know why. I wanted to think it was because I worried for her, was acting to protect her from the extraordinary mess in which I found myself. The truth was probably self-preservation. If she knew I was coming, pursued by Mafia, that might just be the final straw and I could end on the outside of the Cube Ranch, no way to get in. And heaven only knew what mangled story Todd would come up with.

Clem seemed hugely happy to discover that Londonengland was, in fact, way over yonder, in 'Ewerope', a place he had seen on the Discovery Channel, which he liked to tune into 'of an evening' before turning in after a few beers with the boys. I said he should go to visit.

'We done better'n that already,' he said smugly. 'I'm takin' the whole family to the Old Country Park this year. They got Ewerope ready and waitin' fer us in Alabama. We can do France, England, Wolf's Screaminator roller coaster and Germany. They even got us a med'eval banquet with crawfish gumby followed by Key Lime Pie. Now how about that! God, I love this country,' he said enthusiastically.

On the radio, a preacher was warning against the sin of some unspecified excess, punctuating each sentence with a toll free number. 'Call 1 800 AVARICE, my friends, for your video and booklet, which will change your life for just $19.99. That's right, folks, $19.99. And for just $10 more, you get completely free, the Good Folk Christian Choir CD, featuring fifteen of those old-time religion songs you love.' On and on and on.

Eventually, we swung off the interstate and roared down a narrower but equally nondescript blacktopped highway for thirty miles, bobbing up and down in the poorly sprung seats. It struck me that Clem never asked me what I did or why a man with a rumpled suit and no luggage would be thumbing a lift to Nashville. When he unwrapped his sandwiches, a heart-stopping, pungent combination of meats, pickles and mayonnaise, I unfolded a medley of muffins, scrambled egg, cold bacon and fruits stolen from the Casablanca Restaurant without drawing more than a 'I got some spare mayo in back there. Hep yerself.'

He was like most Americans, with his interest in strangers, especially foreign ones, only partial. Everyone was just busy, chasing ambitions, lost loves, recognition. Too busy to notice.

'I thought you said this place was close to the interstate,' I said.

'Yep, jus' another three mile about and we're there.'

Forty minutes later we made another turning. It was starting to get dark. I noted with some alarm that we had not passed a house or any obviously human structure for at least twenty-five minutes.

'Where are we?' I asked uneasily. 'Roughly, give or take a continent or two.'

'We're right on the edge of the Kumskwatchi Mountains, jus' south of the Mohash River,' he replied. I found neither on the map. I sighed and gave up. I might as well continue trusting fate.

Clem pulled to a halt suddenly and I pitched forward as valves and pistons exhaled noisily and the rig settled down with a final judder. It was pitch-black. Silent. There was not a light to be seen. Not a house. Not a person. 'We're here,' he announced confidently, opening the cab door and leaping out. I followed, walking around the vast polished grille to join him. Where on earth were we? I expected to hear duelling banjos.

Then I leapt off the ground in shock and yelped.

I started to relax after the second glass of clear liquid, which tasted faintly of blueberries. On the other side of the room, Clem was in animated conversation with a group of men and women. Beside me sat a waif-like young woman of exquisite beauty. More importantly, she seemed to like me.

It had only been about an hour since the Big Leap Upward. I was standing next to Clem, contemplating how national cartographers armed with satellites and goodness knows what technology had somehow managed to miss a bit, when I felt the tap on my shoulder. I spun around and yelped to find myself staring into her iridescent blue and green eyes.

'Hey, cool down. Damn near give me a heart attack,' said Clem. 'Hi, Destiny. Your Pa around?'

'Sure, he's waiting back at the place. We thought you was comin' yesterday.'

'Always come on the weekend, you knows that,' Clem chided gently as we walked through a wooded copse. Destiny led the way with practised ease and without a torch. I brushed undergrowth, caught my foot in a branch and was roundly thwacked by face-high branches. Annoyingly, Clem managed to navigate the deranged, unkempt landscape without difficulty. In an ideal world, a coyote would have howled. But nothing seemed to stir in the thick underbrush except the steady chirrup of crickets. We walked for about ten minutes before emerging into a clearing. Ahead I could make out what looked like a wooden farmhouse. There were people on a veranda, opaque figures resembling Victorian silhouette portraits and textured by a dim wattage from the house.

'Hey, Cody,' shouted Clem. 'How ya'all doing? Destiny says you was expectin' me yes'day.'

'Surely wus,' a deeper voice replied. 'Then I looked at the calendar, realized we was a day out. But you know how it gets roun' here. Come on in.'

'Wait here a moment,' Clem said to me, as he headed towards Cody.

There was some heated discussion between Clem and the deeper voice, punctuated by stares in my direction. Great, I thought, this is where I get told to squeal like a pig before being sodomized by a grunting, toothless yokel.

'Hey, Ollie, come on in, meet Cody and the folks,' Clem shouted. I walked nervously to the house and shook hands solemnly with about fifteen people filling a dark entrance hall. It was a blur of introductions. 'This here's great-grammy Louella. She jus' celebrate her one hunneth birthday.'

'Really? Congratulations. How do you do.' I shook a withered hand as she smiled a gummy rip, her watery eyes appearing to be somewhere else entirely. 'She don't say much,' Cody explained. 'Lot of dribbling mess, usually, so we don' encourage her.'

'And this here is my cousins Davey, Claw, Claw Jr and Phetus.' They were sullen, like feral outlaws from a different, primitive age. Each had a long black beard and dark, deep eyes. They looked at me slowly. None of them shook my outstretched hand. I pulled it back.

'Hi,' I said anyway.

'Don't pay no mind to the boys. They're careful roun' strangers on account of their thing.'

A tall, blond man towered above the clan. 'That's Horst. He ain't kin. Been with us a couple years since Phetus found him in the woods. Says he got sep'rated from his tour group.'

Horst nodded. 'Guten tag,' he said.

I was finally properly introduced to Destiny. She looked about twenty-three. Dark, wavy hair hung down her shoulders. But it was her eyes, humorous and intelligent, knowing and inviting. She would look magnificent on the Trimthunder, I thought.

'Hello,' she had said, a brilliant smile opening her face. 'Come and sit with me while Pa talks about the collection over there.'

She had taken my arm and led me away from the fire to a wood-backed bench on the other side of the large, open sitting room. A huge shape shifted in the half-light. It was a wolf, I noticed with alarm, as fiery yellow eyes slashed with black stared out. There was a growl.

'Hush, Mighty. Don't you mind him, he's jus' mythy with new folks in the house, thasall. He'll settle down. Just sit beside him there.'

She patted the bench. Mighty stared at me, daring me to try.

'Tell you what,' I said, 'why don't you sit by him and I'll perch on the other side of you? Would that work?'

'Well, I guess,' she said, sounding doubtful. There was no way on this earth I was sitting next to that thing. I might want children one day.

Destiny was extraordinarily beautiful, her small oval face a translucent white jewel set in luxuriant, raven locks. Full red lips completed the vision of perfection. What was she doing here? Wherever here might be.

'We always been in this place since I was borned,' she said matter-of-factly, anticipating my unspoken question. 'We never leave.' There was a sadness, I thought. She had never watched television. Heard talk about it, she said, but the family had never seen the need. Sometimes they made a trip down to the store to pick up supplies in the old station wagon. But mostly she stayed home and cooked.

'Somebody had to keep house after Ma died,' she explained.

'Oh, I'm sorry to hear that,' I said.

'It don' matter. I was still a baby when it happen.'

'What?'

'When the sproat got her that night.'

'The sproat?'

'You know, what live in the hills. Normally they don't come down till after the geezenberries are in. But this one was mean as hell and grabbed Ma right off the front steps. Leastaways, that's what Pa says.'

Her eyes had widened. I stole an anxious glance out the window to the porch. Suddenly, I could see why Mighty was welcomed indoors.

Clem and the others were laughing, oblivious to us. They talked loudly, but it was almost impossible to understand the meaning of the dialect. Crazed packages of words flew into the air to gales of appreciation. Cody embarked on an incomprehensible mime to illustrate a story he was telling. It ended with him sticking his middle finger in his mouth and barking. His audience roared appreciatively. Even Destiny smiled.

'I heard that one a million times,' she said. 'It gets a little rusty after a while. You want another shine?'

I nodded yes. The hooch I had been given was mellowing and unknotting.

'Is you married?' she asked suddenly.

161

'No.'

'Why not, Oily?'

'Ollie,' I corrected gently. 'It's not quite the same thing.'

''Scuse me,' she said, giggling and hiccuping. 'I guess I've had me too much tonight as well. So, how come y'all still alone?' she persisted.

'Well, I'm not exactly alone,' I said. 'It is possible to be with someone but not in wedlock.' But even as I said it, I felt a sadness envelop me. Even at the best of times there was something unformed, unspoken about my relationship with Gina. The current mayhem had brought it into full focus. It was true. I was alone: deserted by my girlfriend, abandoned by my employer and forced to flee from people I barely knew.

'Things just haven't worked out for me,' I said. 'I have, well had, a girlfriend in New York. But she left me a few days ago.'

'Sorry to hear that,' said Destiny, stroking my arm delicately. 'It's hard to find the right one, I guess, when you got all that choice.'

'Oh, she was the right choice,' I found myself saying. 'We just drifted apart, the way you do. We were one of those couples who get trapped in a loving relationship.'

I looked across at the expectant, innocent face. 'You don't know what I'm talking about, do you? And I hope you never do. You'll find some guy called Todd and live happily ever after in a small house with a white fence, two happy children, a cat that never sheds and a virtuous job.'

She looked at me serenely.

'Oh, I know some things, mister. I know you got to be true to yourself and those you love. Truth is all.'

I felt her comments like a small sting. God, she was so right. The shine was having a curiously erotic effect on me, warming my blood in strange, remote and sensual places.

'I really miss her, as a matter of fact. I've been an idiot. Stupid, vain, weak. She's fantastic.' I stared at the concerned and beautiful face in front of me. 'I hope I can win her back.' I took a long swig.

'Like the knights of old,' said Destiny.

'Yes, something like that,' I replied, smiling feebly.

I tried to fight off an urge to lean over and kiss the vision in front of me. Then something startling happened. She leant over and kissed me, forcing her tongue urgently through my lips. Without thinking, I wrapped my arms around her and we locked. Destiny eventually pulled away and stared into my eyes. I was embarrassed. Thrilled. Charged. Nobody else in the room seemed to notice.

'Feel like walking? It's a beautiful night,' she said, touching my hand lightly.

I would have given up a limb at that moment, had she asked. I was entranced, enraptured.

She led me out. I saw Clem briefly note my departure, before turning back to the group around the vast, crackling fire. They seemed deep in conversation, heads bowed into the circle. I was the outsider, welcome company on the long road, but not to be included in the discussion, which presumably involved the mysterious 'collection'. I felt hurt.

We walked outside. It was clear, cloudless. The stars made a sparkling canvas out of the eternal and unknown.

'What you do for a livin'?' Destiny asked suddenly. I said I was a newspaper reporter.

'Exciting work, I'll bet,' she said. Everyone makes that mistake, I thought. 'You can really make a difference, cain't you?' she continued. And that one.

She was a believer. People were. They thought we exposed badness for some sort of public good rather than to salve our, and their, butterfly minds. I wanted to tell her that it was mainly about doing the minimum amount of work for the maximum size of byline, more W. C. Fields than Jimmy Stewart; that newspapers filled their pages with harmless, publicist-driven celebrity drivel to avoid having to spend money on any real research.

I wanted to tell her that, sometimes, newspaper owners asked their employees to arrange hits because the only people more venal than reporters were those they worked for. I was definitely feeling sorry for myself, but also debauched and disgusting by any comparison with Destiny, who seemed to live a blameless, saner life deep in the woods worrying about sproats.

I asked about her own ambitions, which seemed an odd choice of word. She hoped to marry Beau Turner. He lived up the valley, she said. They went bareback riding together. Bareback riding. It was like an advertisement for goodliness, I thought, or Ralph Lauren.

'I think you're a good man in a hard place,' Destiny said determinedly. 'I really do. You just needs to tell her that. You needs to start feeling strong about yourself.'

If only it were that simple, I thought. We reached a barn. Destiny opened it and walked inside. 'Come on in,' she beckoned with her hand, smiling. I followed. In the far corner was a pile of hay on to which she fell. I watched. 'Come on, it's so soft,' she said.

The sweet scent was as intoxicating as shine. I let myself tumble and rolled into the hay, feeling relaxed for the first time in days. 'Wow,' I said, laughing. She did the same and rolled over on top of me. Soon, we were pawing, tugging, kissing, groping, stripping and grunting with the abandonment of lust. It was delicious, moist, thrilling and all my dreams made pliant flesh.

This never happened to me, not in London and not in New York, a city whose rituals of dating had turned sex into an agenda item, and one further down the list than most men would want. We made love for hours, it seemed, waking up in each other's arms and continuing where we left off. Outside, the crickets scolded us for falling asleep, but in the end I plunged into a delicious unconsciousness.

I woke to the sensation of a licking on my chest and smiled. I had some energy left. I reached out my arm and puckered my lips expectantly.

'God, bugger off!' I shouted, outrage overpowering the instinctive caution I felt towards Mighty, who slunk into the shadows, growling in complaint. There was no sign of Destiny.

I scrambled up, dressed and walked over to the house. The family group was sitting at a long trestle table. Nobody looked at me. Someone I vaguely recalled being introduced to as Claw's Woman pointed me towards a seat.

I sat down apprehensively between Claw and Phetus. Neither looked up from their rhythmic spooning of a grey liquid from plain, white china bowls. Each had a mug of coffee, which reminded me that I had a hangover resembling Celine Dion: mild, persistent and strangely annoying.

Flies buzzed around the table. At the head sat great-grammy Louella, sucking the contents of her bowl noisily through a straw. Clem and Cody were on either side of her. I was suddenly struck by how similar they were. Cody was a thinner, leaner version of Clem. Claw nodded in my direction, smiling sparely and without warmth.

'Sleep good?' he asked.

'Like a log, thanks.'

Claw and Phetus grunted, a sound that might have passed for a knowing laugh.

'Anything keep you up all night?' Phetus suddenly challenged, staring at me. I felt myself blushing to the murmur of quiet laughs around the table.

'No,' I said cautiously. 'Nothing.'

'No problem with the flies,' Claw suddenly chimed in, emphasizing the last word. The laughter was more overt.

'Thas nuff, you hear,' said Cody sternly. 'Let the man eat his grits in peace.'

So, that was the mush passed down the table and now in front of me. I took my spoon and began eating, cautiously at first. The Southern corn pulp was heavily salted, but I was ravenous and took it in hungrily, wiping the plate with hunks of bread piled in the middle of the table. Nobody paid me any more attention. It was almost as if the sight of an Englishman in a suit was too commonplace in Filroys Stump for anyone to pass comment.

There was still no sign of Destiny. Something in the questions from Claw and Phetus stopped me from asking where she was. I thought about last night, her passion and her expertise. She seemed to know perfectly when to raise and lower the tactile temperature, like some sexual sprite. Neither of us had talked during our marathon. I could not remember when I had last fallen into such a deep, sated slumber.

I asked if I could wash and was pointed towards a back room. Inside was a basin and a single, cold tap. I turned it on. There was a minor juddering as it groaned into life, sending a jet of cold water into a scratched metal bowl. I thought guiltily of Gina and my unfaithfulness. She left me, I told myself. What could she expect?

I shaved the growing stubble, now more beard, with a cut-throat razor that hung by a stretch of cord from the wall. There was not a toothbrush to be found. I used a piece of cloth hanging by the sink, rubbing soap on to a corner and then cleaning my teeth as best as I could without retching. I might have emerged cleaner than when I entered, but it was a close call.

The cousins, I was pleased to notice, had left the dining room by the time I returned. Great-grammy Louella sat alone, drooling lightly, and smiled warmly as I passed. 'Git choppin' the wood, boy, or I'll cut your balls off,' she suddenly exclaimed, eyes ablaze with venomous hostility.

'Absolutely,' I said, shaken, quickening my pace towards the sitting room. I heard the unmistakable sound of goodbyes on the veranda. It was Clem and Cody, locked in a back-slapping embrace. They then shook hands.

Clem started to walk off. Appalled, I realized he had either completely forgotten about my existence or intended to leave me here. I hurried outside. 'Clem,' I shouted. He turned, looked surprised.

'You need a ride?' he asked.

'What? Of course I do,' I replied, stunned at the suggestion that I might have found my destination in Filroys Stump.

'You got it,' he said cheerfully. 'Rig's this way.' He pointed at some indeterminate point in the dense underbrush that ringed the wooden house, a protective perimeter from the twenty-first century, make that from the twentieth and nineteenth centuries as well. I looked back as we approached the woods. The house, neat and surrounded by barns and ancient, rusting farm equipment mired in the earth, seemed a perfect, permanent part of the landscape.

I saw a curtain twitch in a top-floor window. I suddenly remembered Destiny and felt sad. Was she looking out and imagining a world of opportunities, gadgets, choices, new people? I stopped on an impulse and just waved blindly at the house, hoping she would notice and know it was just for her. It was lechery and love, I realized. I would have to ask Clem for a telephone number, an address, anything so that we could stay in touch.

The engine heaved into life, shuddering the cabin as Clem took his truck into a wide circle and pointed it back, away. We had barely exchanged a word walking through the woods. He whistled tunelessly.

I looked across, thinking I should thank him for the ride and roof. Not that he knew why I should be so grateful. It was extraordinary how I was just accepted.

'Did you manage to get your collection business done?'

'Yep,' he replied firmly.

'Great.' I waited expectantly. Nothing. 'You do a lot of collecting here?' I ventured.

'Some.'

Clem stared at the road ahead. There was clearly not going to be any explanation about the mysterious activity that had taken us off the highway into a place that, technically, did not exist.

We pounded along in silence. The shine had done little to burnish my day as I bounced in the passenger seat. Nashville was still several hours away. Clem found a country-music station. The singer said the world had 'gorn cray azee'. I knew what she meant. My own life was certainly tipping towards insanity despite the balm of Destiny's pale, silken arms.

'How'd you like Destiny?' Clem asked suddenly. I looked over.

He was still staring fixedly ahead, concentrating on the flat, straight ribbon of bitumen.

'A lovely person. Great company,' I answered cautiously.

'Ain't she,' replied Clem. 'Hard to believe she'll soon be fifteen.'

21

I was still flushing when we pulled into Rayon, a hamlet just off the interstate. Conspiracy to murder and now sex with a minor. Have mercy, your honour.

Clem said he always had lunch at Rosie's, a diner off Main Street, when he was this way. He waited obediently for the traffic lights to change at the town's single intersection, despite the fact that not a single vehicle was anywhere in sight. Up ahead I saw Rosie's, with its glistening chrome frontage and a sign that proudly boasted BEST MEATLOAF SOUTH OF THE MASQUATACH.

We sat by the picture window, which had views of bare, distant mountains. There was nobody else there, although it was barely 1 p.m. 'You had Rosie's meatloaf before?' Clem inquired.

'No, is it good?' I asked, marvelling at what incalculable odds would need to have been defied to bring me to this bleak, nondescript place on any earlier occasion.

'Best ever,' he said with passion.

'Sold,' I replied, slapping the table. Clem was nothing if not a keen student of instant stomach pleasers, I had decided. A large woman made her way over at a nod from Clem. Her flip-flopped feet slopped, uninterested, along the floor.

'He'll have the meatloaf, Jeannie, and I'll have the ribs.'

I was surprised. 'You're not having the meatloaf?'

'Hell no,' he replied. 'Oh, get me a coffee too,' Clem shouted after the retreating figure.

Clem had bought a copy of the local newspaper and was engrossed in its front-page stories. These seemed to be like most papers in the wide interior, filled with rows about water extraction, serial killers and high-school football successes. International events were reduced to single paragraphs somewhere near the real-estate section.

I went to a side room and called my home number to pick up messages, using a phonecard so as not to deplete my tiny reserve of cash. There were eight. The first was from Bleaker, as were the third, fifth, sixth and seventh. They all demanded that I called immediately. Where was I? Grounds for dismissal, serious trouble, no future, very unprofessional. 'Very unprofessional,' I exclaimed back. The second was from Tom Harman. 'Just wondered about Whitney. No pressure of course. Owner seems very keen to find out how you're doing with it. Keeps asking where you are. Bit embarrassing because nobody has any idea. Word to the wise. Might be an idea to call in.'

There was one from Todd, wondering excitedly how I was and where I was and whether I had a view about glass-topped coffee tables. He said that I should call him urgently and gave me a number.

There was a whispered message from Guy Armitage, who 'didn't want to worry me' but 'thought I should know' that there was a rumour going about that I had 'run off with company money'.

I called Armitage first. I don't know why. I probably just needed to hear a familiar voice and it was toll free. '"Ullo, 'Erald."

'Beady Eye, please.' A medley from *The Sound of Music* played before a familiar voice chirruped in. 'Armitage.'

'Guy? It's me. Ollie.'

'Ollie, my dear fellow. Where are you? Listen, let me move to a quieter corner. Colleagues have ears, if you know what I mean,' he said in a theatrically hushed voice. 'Even here.'

There was a pause whilst discretion was asserted. 'I'm in a place called Rayon. Kentucky, I think. It's hard to be sure.'

'Really? What's going on? You got my message, I take it. Stanley's people have been down trying to find out where your friends are in the US, asking anybody who knows anything to contact them. It's most peculiar.'

'Look, I can't really explain. Well, I can, just not yet. I'm in a bit of a mess, to be candid. I've had to leave New York in a hurry.'

'What about these rumours?'

'Not true. Swear to God. I haven't walked off with any of his wretched money, although he might think so. If that makes any sense.'

'Not really, old boy,' said Armitage bluntly.

'Look, he asked me to do something, fix a deal for him out here, then he suddenly called it off. But it was too late, I'd already paid the money over. That's the long and the short of it.'

'How delicious. Good for you. He'd rather lose a leg than dosh,' said Armitage, laughing bitterly.

'It's a little more serious than that, sadly, but I can't talk about it. And Guy, neither can you. You've got to promise not to mention this call to anyone.' There was a pause. 'I mean it. We've known each other a long time. I really need you to sit on this. I promise you, when it's all over I'll tell you everything.'

'Swear.'

'On my next pay cheque.'

'Oh, I want something more probable than that.'

'On my life. On anything you think I may hold dear. It's a great story, worth waiting for. Promise.'

'On your next set of expenses.'

'Oh, all right, then. On my next set of expenses.'

I asked what else he had heard. Armitage said nothing. It was only his own antenna picking up the alarm coming down from the tenth-floor executive offices.

'They wanted to get in touch with your parents,' said Armitage. 'But I said they were both dead.' That was a relief and nearly true. They lived in Godalming.

'Can I do anything for you?' he asked.

I wondered. What I needed more than anything was money. 'I'm pretty broke. Stanley's stopped my salary and my credit card has been cancelled.'

'No! Well, this sounds a fair risk,' Armitage replied. 'How much?'

'A thousand,' I said hopefully.

'Dollars, I assume. You'll have to get me details of where.'

I told him I would try to find a branch of Western Union and call him with the details so he could wire the money over. He gave me his mobile number and told me to leave the information there.

I called Todd next.

'Hey, man. Where are you?' he asked eagerly. Before I could answer, he went on, sounding agitated. 'Listen, can I ask you something, dude? I gotta problem.'

Todd had a problem. This was all I needed. 'I haven't got long. Can it wait?'

'Not really.'

'All right, then. What is it?'

'I went to a coffee place yesterday, Cool Roasts on Seventh, and had two javas, right.'

'Yes. And?'

'So, I leave and everything. Now, I happen to be walking back along the same street today when I got took short, if you know what I mean. I really had to whizz, man.'

'OK, with you so far. Look, Todd, could you move this along? I'd really appreciate it.'

'Sure, sure. Anyway, I go into Cool Roasts and say all polite, "May I use your rest room?" and the guy says "no".'

There was a silence.

'Is that it?' I asked.

'Yeah, that's exactly how it happened. So my point is this: I had two coffees in Cool Roasts the day before, but I never had a piss. So I reckon they owe me one, probably two pisses. One for each cup.'

'Is this going anywhere? I mean, we're not talking life and death here, are we?' I said, exasperated.

'Oh, sure,' he replied, unmoved. 'But do you think I've got a case? Could I sue for the pees they owe?'

I exhaled loudly. 'Jeez, Todd. I don't know. I'm not a lawyer. I'll have to think about that one as I race across the country pursued by mad bastards with guns. This is really the sidetrack I need, something to take my mind off the tedious subject of survival. Let me get back to you.'

'OK, man, relax.' He sounded hurt. 'Just wondered what you thought.' It was his turn to sound aggrieved.

'You're right. Sorry, mate. I'm just a little frazzled right now. Distracted. I'll give it some thought. Promise.'

'Great,' said Todd. 'So, where you hanging?'

'I'm in a place called Rayon. It's somewhere in Kentucky. Listen, have you got any more money yet? I hate to ask again, but I'm pretty desperate. I've got a free ride as far as Nashville, but nothing after that and only twelve bucks and something from Venezuela to buy it with.' I remembered lunch. 'Make that about seven bucks.'

'Shit, no. Haven't sold a thing. The Goth never came back. Maybe that pitch isn't quite right.'

I brought him back to the panic in hand, anything to avoid another meander. 'It's fine, Todd. Look, I really need some cash, badly.'

He sucked in his breath. 'I don't know, man. Listen, call me back later this afternoon. I'll see what I can rustle up, OK? But I got zip in the bank and my credit cards are maxed. But I'll go hard to the hoop for you. You bet.'

I told him I would call later. He asked me not to forget about the glass-topped coffee tables.

Back in the restaurant, our food had arrived. Clem, I noticed, had nearly finished his ribs, reaching the soaking-up-gravy-with-bread stage. My meatloaf sat congealing gently opposite.

'That was quick,' I said, wondering why he hadn't asked the waitress to keep mine warm.

'Sure is. Get in there. It'll be gettin' cold,' he said, burping loudly.

'It's already got,' I said pointedly, pitching my fork into the mass of meat. It really was quite good, some indiscriminate beef and onion combination with a layer of sweet coagulant running through the middle. Three crisp rashers of bacon lay across the top. A dollop of mashed potato clung to one side of the meaty mound, beans on the other. I poured on the gravy, which was still piping hot.

Across the room, I noticed the two-headed American eagle, a happy early experiment in gene therapy, staring sternly from its perch above the nation's Latin motto E PLURIBUS UNUM, which translates, very roughly, as 'All you can eat or drive at less than one mile to the gallon'.

I definitely felt better after gorging. Armitage and Todd between them should be able to help, I told myself.

'Is there a Western Union here, Clem?' I asked with my mouth full, just to be sure he understood.

'Nope. Nearest'll be Nashville. We'll be there in a few hours, 'fore nightfall anyways,' he said, slurping his milky coffee.

That would have to do, I supposed, although the wiring service would probably be closed by the time we arrived, given Clem's erratic sense of time. It looked like another night of uncertainty ahead.

'You going on much further?' he asked. It was the first genuine expression of interest in two days.

'Heading out to California,' I said.

'In a suit?'

'I had to leave in a hurry.'

'I left Indiana in a hurry once,' Clem recalled. 'Fucking phone companies.' There was a silence as he watched me eat.

He was impatient to leave and folded up the Rayon *Bumble and Trumpet* as soon as I had finished.

'Here, I'll get this,' he said, picking up the bill.

'No, please. Wouldn't hear of it.'

'Ain't no big deal,' he insisted gruffly. 'It was my idea to stop here. You shouldn't have to pay for it.'

I thanked him. He had obviously worked out that whatever was behind that suit and strange accent from Londonengland did not include money.

Murder, theft, statutory rape. Could it get any worse?

*   *   *

I sat on my haunches holding a tree bough as the vomiting wrenched me through awful, back-arching spasms. A pool of acid-smelling bile lay a few feet away. My brain had sent an emergency evacuation order about fifteen miles outside of Rayon. I felt light-headed, dizzy. Huge ructions rumbled through my lower intestines, an advancing tank army blasting open its valves. I asked Clem to pull over, told him something was definitely not quite right. Vomit birthing had begun. The contractions were down to every few seconds. Worse, I sat on the stink bombs I had taken from Scotter, filling the cab with the foul, sulphuric stench of rotten eggs. Clem didn't notice, but it tipped me over the edge. 'Stop, stop now,' I yelled through dry retches.

'Awfully sorry,' I said, throwing myself out of the idling cab down a dirt embankment before doubling over to purge myself of the best sweet meatloaf south of the Masquatach. I had never, ever felt so ill. I could barely move. Clem eventually came down to help me back to the cab, the crippled victim of some terrorist atrocity. It felt as if a crude appendix removal had been undertaken with a particularly blunt knife and without the courtesy of an anaesthetic.

'That meatloaf gets you every time,' Clem said cheerily.

'It does? Why didn't you warn me?' I demanded, savage with rage.

'Well, it tastes so darn good,' he replied breezily. 'No idea what they put in it. But it's a hell of a fine loaf. Hate to spoil it for folks.'

'Spoil it? That would be except for the crippling sickness and death spasms.'

'Stop your frettin'. It'll pass,' he said, as if addressing a petulant child. 'Besides. Sounds like yours may've been just about decent. Sometimes, I ain't even made it past the town limits before I'm throwing up everywhere. Heard one guy was in the hospital for two weeks.'

He was right about the pain. It did gradually subside as we headed through the low, lush green hills towards Nashville.

'So, you enjoy the homestead?' Clem asked.

'The homestead?'

'Where we was last night. You ain't forgotten already?' He laughed. How could I forget the scene of my second crime of the month?

'Oh, the farm. It was wonderful,' I replied neutrally. 'Lovely country.'

'Ain't it. Cody took it over when Pa died. We couldn't both be making a living off it, so I headed south, got into truckin'.' A piece of the veil was lifting. 'It's a hard life for him and the kids, no doubt about that. Still, I helps when I can. One day I'll end up back there, build a place. We'll go into business together. At the moment I just does the collecting.'

The mysterious collection that still dared not speak its name. So, Cody was his brother.

'What was Destiny on about when she said a sproat took her mother? Sounds like something out of a ghastly fairytale.'

Clem shook his head sadly. 'Oh, that's just what we told the kids when Babel ran off with the tractor-parts salesman. Jus' disappeared one night.' His eyebrows knitted at the memory.

'How terrible,' I said.

'Yeah. Damn near broke Cody's heart, her leavin' jus' before hog-breeding time.'

'And the sproat?'

'Destiny was too young.'

I understood. 'For a moment, you know, I really thought some strange mythical creature was lurking in the woods back there.' I laughed with relief.

'I don't know about missikle,' Clem said seriously, eyes firmly ahead. 'Sproat we shot last spring coulda felled a horse.'

There was nothing to say. The mysteries of a vast, untapped interior, that wild, strange land far from the noise and neon that is the heartland, was sitting beside me, only partially confounding Gibbon's Second Law. This states that an American City is never as exciting as the song associated with it. Minneapolis/St Paul, the twin cities serenaded by Everything But The Girl, are a vast slab of sprawl, Soulless twinned with Nowhere, each with a desolate and pointless centre. The Mall of the Americas, on the outskirts, is a place of spirit-crushing size so big that cops fight gangs of Crips and Bloods trying to claim sections of the air-conditioned microculture for themselves. And anyone twenty-four hours from Tulsa is dangerously close. Do you know the way to San José? I do, but I keep that dark secret to myself. Nashville? Home of country music and demolition gangs. The Grand Ole Opry sits becalmed in a sea of cheerless hotels, and stratosphere-scraping office blocks of numbing functionality. The convention centre squats close by, a designless incubus dominating a thin strip of old red-brick shop fronts and bars, all that anyone had bothered to preserve of the town and its musical heritage. Gibbon's First Law? Don't worry – stay still for five minutes anywhere in Manhattan and the lunatic will find *you*.

I looked across at contented Clem, barely detached from his world of sproats and shine, hidden forests and families, weird towns and curious foods. It seemed quite appealing. I wanted to be off the map too.

He drove into the centre, past knots of sightseers looking for something worth taking a picture of, then forged out to an anonymous stretch of warehousing on the outskirts of town, the sort of place Dolly never sings about. The rig heaved spasmically to a stop, an old dog reaching the fireside after a day out hunting. 'End of the line,' Clem said, dropping out of the driver side. 'Wait awhile. Just got a bit of business to do.'

He walked to a glass cubicle built beside a wide, corrugated-iron gate. I watched him shake hands with a man in blue overalls. The sign above the gate read COHORT LIQUOR SUPPLIES. It seemed an unusual destination for a wagon filled with pork bellies. I watched as a fork-lift truck emerged from the side of one of the buildings. Curiosity took hold. I felt like John Speke discovering the source of the Nile. The collection. I walked carefully around the side of the rig. Guilt, I suppose, at invading some private world.

Clem was back at the glass cubicle. Something was handed over. I walked and watched as the fork-lift truck lifted a wooden pallet, one of three hidden by pink, eviscerated pig carcasses. Each was piled high with clear bottles filled with a pale bluish liquid. There was something familiar. Then I recognized it as the drink of my night with Destiny. I felt queasy again.

'Now I gotta trust you,' said Clem, shouting at me as he headed back.

I spun around. 'I'm sorry?'

'This here's what Cody and the boys make up at the farm,' he explained. 'Old great-grammy Louella first started makin' it, passed the recipe down. It ain't legal, but Cody met this fella who said it would go down a treat in them fancy bars opening up everywhere.'

He spat chewing tobacco out of the corner of his mouth. 'They're puttin' it in bottles with the damnedest names.'

Shine, it transpired, was being sold, variously, as a base for flavoured vodkas from the Ukraine, a sweet liquor from the monks of Belgium and a fiery schnapps from the burghers of Austria. 'Folks don' know the dif'rence,' Clem explained, laughing softly. 'I'll bet old grammy's shine has even wet the tonsils of senators.'

I smiled. 'Sounds like a grand business to me, Clem.'

'Yup, it surely is,' he agreed. 'Ain't a fucking phone company, that's for sure. Cops don't often stop pork-belly trucks on account of the freezer needin' to be kept at the proper temperature. Means they gotta impound you, get a health inspector over. Lotta paperwork. Ain't worth their while. So I jus' brings it up here for distributing on my way delivering the hogs. Cousin Hollis there smoothes the way, so to speak.'

'Perfect,' I said. 'Listen, I really appreciate the ride. And you know, the secret's safe with me,' I added reassuringly.

Clem chuckled. 'Oh, I know it is, boy. Knew when you got in the cab you was on the run, safe to have you on board. Suit was a give-away. Don't come across hitch-hikers in that finery.'

Of course he knew. Why else would he have dared to take a complete stranger to Hooch Central?

'You're right. I really needed to get out of Philly fast,' I said.

'I'm being chased, frankly, and I'm horribly short of cash. Don't really know where the next meal's coming from, truth be told.'

'I'll bet it was a woman,' Clem cackled slyly. 'Slick fella like you from Londonengland.' He reached into his pockets and pulled out a wedge of notes. He licked his thumb and flicked through. I realized what he was about to do.

'No, really. I couldn't.'

'Hush now. It ain't much, just fifty bucks. But it'll get you a bed and a meal tonight. I know you was hoping to get to Western Union today, but we're too late for that on account of the sickness. Anyways, I know you won't gab if you take some of the profits. That makes you an accomplice, don't it?' He winked, laughing.

'I guess it do, does,' I replied.

We stared at each other. Two people with secrets. It was a bond of sorts, one that we both knew would never be tested. We would never meet again. It was the American way.

'This is a good country to run in,' he said. 'I dunno about where you is from. But here a man can lose hisself for ever if he has a mind. You could go jus' about anywhere and nobody'd find you.'

Clem drove into the centre of Nashville, dropping me near the Ole Opry. He told me the name of a family-run hotel. 'Say Clem sent you. They'll treat you right,' he promised as he waved, heading off into the distant mass of roads and opportunities.

Shania had a birthday in two days' time, and he was on a promise to get home for that. He hated driving at night, but would do three hours. I felt that ache single people have when they meet others firmly, happily attached to responsibilities. To love.

22

The Teadrops were tireless hosts and I seemed to be the only guest. Not that this proved any deterrent to their nightly entertainment: a melancholy review of once-lively pop standards. Herod played guitar whilst Rosalind sang. She had long auburn hair and shook her head in time to a tambourine. The encore was a moving version of something originally sung by the Spice Girls. I sat politely.

Earlier, they had shown me upstairs to a neat, self-contained suite. Fifty dollars didn't buy folded lavatory paper, I was pleased to note. My room had a television.

Although the world I inhabited was imploding, the one lived in by everyone else seemed to be muddling along through this season's concocted crisis, if a quick flip through the news channels was to be believed. The newsreaders were handsome and chirpy or handsome and solemn, depending on what came next on the autocue. They were all called Bill or Natalie.

The Cube Ranch was still on answerphone. There was no reply from Todd, despite his promise to be home waiting for my call. God, he was impossible. I left the hotel number on his voicemail.

The receptionist tapped me on the shoulder halfway through a country-modified version of 'Stairway to Heaven'. There was a call for me. I could take it in the booth by the door.

I squeezed myself into the tiny cubicle. 'Hello?'

'Hey, man, it's me.'

'Todd. Thank goodness. Listen, have you got me any money?'

'I've done better than that,' he said, sounding satisfied, even smug, which I had learnt through experience was the moment just before the scaffolding fell.

'Really?' I asked slowly. 'And what could be better than that?'

'Well, I went around to your place, just to check on Hughgrant.

You know, feed him and so on. Hey, before I forget, that old lady in the basement is looking after him. She said something about colouring, dude. Does that mean anything to you?'

I'd forgotten about Hughgrant, of course. Mrs Crazy again. Hell. 'Yes, no. I mean great, great. Thanks,' I said impatiently. 'What precisely is the better thing you've done, Todd? Quickly.'

'You're never going to believe this,' he said, taking a deep breath. 'On the door was a note with a number saying "Call such and such for the $2,000 I owe you. I've got the cash now."'

I froze. 'Tell me you didn't call the number, Todd,' I said, chilled as something cold inched towards my heart.

'Sure I did. I mean, why not? You need money, right? And here was this guy who owed you wanting to pay up. How amazing is that?'

'In a nutshell, Todd, too bloody amazing, that's what it is. Where are you now?'

'I'm back in Manhattan. Called the guy with the money. He promised to wire it out to any Western Union as soon as I knew which one.' There was a pause for dramatic effect. 'Soon as I got your message I told him you were in Nashville, gave him the number.'

I waited a moment to collect my thoughts, or rather to harness the two flying around unbridled: Panic and Anger were their names.

'Listen. Nobody owes me $2,000. Do you understand?'

There was a pause. 'No shit? They don't?'

'No, they bloody don't, you world-class, ant-brained, walking-to-the-North-Pole-the-hard-way idiot. Don't you think I might have mentioned it?'

I sink into a silent, furious anger.

'I'm sensing some hostility here, dude.'

'Did you get a name for the guy you were talking to?' I asked finally.

'No,' Todd admitted, before going on to mimic Scarpesi perfectly.

'Oh, lord,' I said, exasperated. 'So you gave my name and where I was staying to complete strangers. Just like that.'

'Hey. I thought you needed the money real soon and this was a great way to help you out.'

I moaned. 'Look, Todd. I need money, sure, but not that particular money. I'm now going to have to get out of here fast, see the world on five bucks and something from Venezuela.' Then a thought occurred to me, breaking through the sound of my thumping pulse.

'Do they know who you are?' I asked.

'Definitely. Gave them my name, address, just in case they needed any more help.'

Great, I thought. Bloody great. That degree in niceness was going to kill him one day. But I knew it was my fault. I should have told him back in New York who was chasing me.

'You've got to make yourself scarce too. Those guys you were being so helpful to are after me, probably to kill me. When they don't find me here, they might try to sweat you. Head out to California and the Cube Ranch. I'll find you there. Check into the nearest motel. Got it? The nearest motel to the ranch. That way I can figure out where you are.'

He tried to protest. I could imagine his jaw going up and down, the two-legged guppy of Manhattan. But he promised to leave straight away.

I looked at my watch. It took about two hours to fly from New York to Nashville, assuming there was a direct connection. Allowing for traffic and delays, it was quite possible that Fat Angie and a newly acquired stetson would be here before midnight, that is, if there was no local gang of mobsters he could call up. The feared Folkia, I thought gloomily. They controlled all the maudlin lyrics east of the Mississippi.

There was nothing for it. I was going to have to leave the Teadrops. I could have killed Todd. How could anyone be so naive? Then I thought about my desperate, elliptic plea for money and his agonizing. This was as new to him as it was to me. He was a furniture salesman, at the end of the day. It was typical of him to remember Hughgrant, about whose welfare I had completely forgotten. Homicide, statutory rape, theft. But at least not peticide again.

I thought about calling Fishlove, confessing everything, pleading for help. But I knew what would happen. He would call his foreign editor and somebody would call the *Herald*. The official word would come down, off the record, of course: Gibbon has cracked, run off with company money or something similar. We want to find him. It would be in all the papers. Scarpesi would only have to sit at home and wait for each morning edition. It was hard enough evading gangsters; it would be even harder hiding from Fishlove. He knew all the tricks and would find out about Gina immediately. Always find the girlfriend, boyfriend, best friend. He would head for California and Fat Angie would follow. It was too awful to contemplate.

I checked out quickly and without fuss. The same could not quite be said for the Teadrops, who wondered whether it was the room? The food? I assured them it was neither. 'Y'all come back and stay again,' said Herod Teadrop uncertainly, adding that, regretfully, he could refund only half the deposit.

There was no point in heading to any obvious points of exit. Fat Angie would have those covered. Men with tasselled shirts and small arms disguised as fret boards would be scouring departure terminals already.

Perhaps the best thing was to stay in Nashville. But where? I had no money to speak of. Scarpesi would probably assume that cutting off my cash supply meant that I would check in, as I had, to the cheapest rooms I could find. I was also, surely, beginning to smell. The same clothing for nearly three days was beginning to take its toll. Skunks were crossing politely to the other side of the road.

I was last man at the crease, the goalie in penalty time – frightened, fed up and lonely. This was more than I was equipped to deal with, as were most things in life, it seemed: doing an honest job, keeping gerbils, girlfriends, looking after dogs or choosing reliable friends.

I wandered towards the centre of town and thought about hitching a ride. Too risky. There was little traffic so late, anyway, and I could end up flagging down a mobster ('Hey boss, he's waving at us. Ain't that considerate').

Gloom enveloped me. I seemed to have nothing, nobody, to turn to. More than anything I needed money. I passed a hoarding. Whitney Houston was playing in town tomorrow night. I bet she didn't need money. Bloody Fishlove. I found myself wondering if the puzzle-obsessive spent a fifth of the time worrying what I was up to as I spent panicking about his scoops and contacts. Of course he did: it was a congenital condition that all reporters shared. 'Yes, he does,' I found myself saying aloud slowly. 'Yes, he bloody well does.' It wasn't ideal, but I was desperate and I could control his interest, I was sure of it. I found a pay phone and a spare teenager and called Fishlove at home, imagining the dialling tone disturbing the clinical aesthetic of his apartment, gently trembling the tidy, clear desk and its two heavily laden document trays, each marked EXCLUSIVES PENDING.

'Come on, come on,' I said under my breath. He picked up on the second ring.

'Ah, Fishlove. It's Ollie. How are you?'

'Good, thanks. You?'

I tried to sound relaxed, hack-about-town casual. 'Yeah, fine. Pleasant night, anyway.'

'Pleasant? What are you talking about? It's pissing down.'

'Really? Not here it isn't.'

I detected the change instantly. Good. 'Where are you, then?' he asked.

'Oh, nowhere in . . .'

I dropped my hand at the teenager, the cue. 'Tickets for Whitney Houston. Best seats in Nashville . . .' he shouted. I thrust $10 into his hand and waved him away.

'. . . particular. Look, I've got to go, Fishlove. Love to chat. But you know how it is. Is that the time? Hell. People to see.' I put the receiver down quickly and suddenly felt the need for a drink.

He would come, I was certain. He would assume I was angling for an interview with Whitney and try to get in first. I would tell him that my wallet had been stolen, that I needed to get to California fast. Personal reasons. Gina. We're having problems. He would hope it all worked out for us and, secretly, wonder what he could do to take advantage of his rival's distraction by a personal crisis.

I looked up and down Main Street, which was seared by the sound of sad guitars escaping from its bars. I needed a busy one, even though what I craved was silence, time just to think. If Fat Angie found me, once thing was certain: I was not going to disappear without a great deal of noise and struggle. My kidnapping would be a one-man band of noise, I vowed.

The Lonesome Moon was one of the few places without a plate-glass frontage, the sort that hookers in Amsterdam sit behind for passers-by to assess the talent. It was bright and packed, boisterous and beery. I found a stool and ordered a lager. It was nearly 10 p.m. Fat Angie would be in town soon, probably with a crack squad of fellow trenchermen even then working their way through the airline meals, the Fat Gunmen of the Apocalypse.

I ran through a checklist of assets. What exactly was there positive to tick in the box beside Ollie Gibbon, reporter, liar, lonely heart, desperado and gerbil killer, at this precise juncture in his life? It came down to the price of a few beers, as it transpired, once the last nickel had been counted.

I watched a group of conventioneers gathered convivially. They wore bright red name stickers on their shirts, maybe so they wouldn't lose each other or get mistaken for Martians. Theirs was the forty-third annual gathering of the Malleable Castings Manufacturers of North America. I wondered if they knew they had met with the Probable Site of a Mob Hit Convention of one. Maybe I should pin a sticker to my shirt, OLLIE GIBBON. VICTIM, just to break the ice with myself.

Their talk drifted over and was of impossible orders fulfilled and metal casts made with tiny fractures picked up only at the last minute. 'I hate to think what would have happened if that thing had actually gone off,' said a small, mean-lipped, sharp-eyed man who looked as if he rather liked the idea of what might have happened if that thing had gone off.

After about forty minutes, the crowd started to thin as the labels tipped out into the cold, autumn night, back to their hotels for a nightcap and oblivion before the tedium to come: the flow charts, sales targets, exciting-new-developments, team-bonding river-raft trips, business opportunities, formal dinner and, doubtless, keynote speech from some long-dead executive from the world of metal castings.

I felt bitter and miserable. Two Rolling Rock beers but still not one plan. I switched to a club soda, hoping the iced water would give me some clarity, some hope, some more money. Then another beer came.

'This one's on me,' said the soft, Southern female voice. 'You look kinda low, and I always make a point of buying the saddest-looking man a beer when we finish the set.'

'Thanks, thanks. Kind of you,' I muttered, struggling to muster a social grace. It proved impossible. But she was persistent.

'I'm Mobilene,' she said, reaching out a hand. I looked up and shook it without thinking. Her hair was Sun King yellow.

'Ollie, Ollie Gibbon.'

'Well, now, same as the guy who wrote *Decline and Fall of the Roman Empire*. Interesting.'

Now that did startle me. 'Gosh. Most people don't get the connection.'

'Oh, my pa was a real readin' nut. Said Edward Gibbon was the finest writer in the English language.'

'Really?' This was actually intriguing. 'And what did your father do, exactly?'

'Oh, this 'n' that. Mostly chopping timber over in the Okanogans. Built us a cabin. We was all raised there.'

'How come he got to hear about an eighteenth-century English writer?'

'Through his friend Cameron, I think,' said Mobilene. I opened my mouth to press with a follow-up. But she was distracted, staring down the long reach of the bar to the guy polishing glasses at the far end. 'Hey, Andy. Bourbon. Straight up. Thanks.'

She turned back and stared at me through pale blue eyes. 'So, what brings you to Nashville, babe?' she asked. I guessed from her back-of-the-bar voice that Mobilene was probably in her thirties. But, as I had learnt from experience, appearances were deceptive in the South. She was probably eleven.

'Business, a bit of collecting,' I replied without thinking.

'You with the Malleable Castings bunch?'

'No, not at all. I'm a newspaper reporter, actually. Writing a travel piece about Nashville.'

'Wow, a writing man.' She lit a cigarette. 'I could tell you a story or two.' I glanced at my watch. She blew a cumulus over the bar.

Cue escape plan. 'That sounds great. Maybe we should get out of here, find somewhere quieter,' I said on a whim. The bar was silent and empty except for ourselves and the barman, now busy stacking chairs on tables.

Mobilene smiled and tossed her hair. She must have heard that line every night. But it seemed to work. I noticed deep, dark roots as she drew a hand languorously through the thick growth.

'Well, I do happen to have a full fifth of sippin' liquor back at my place. Could I tempt you with that? Might help your research some.'

It was nearly midnight. Fat Angie, his friends and the Folkia would be scouring the hotel and motel registers soon. Someone would have been told to check the bars.

'You certainly could,' I said determinedly.

'Good. See you, Andy,' she called over her shoulder as we walked out. Andy barely bothered to look up from sweeping the floor. 'See you, sweetheart,' he said to her swivelling hips.

We walked for about twelve blocks, leaving the downtown area. Mobilene talked about the cabin where she was raised with two brothers and an elder sister. Her parents still lived there and wished she did too.

I kept stealing glances over my shoulder, watching for dark cars, dark glasses, shots, Uzis.

Finally, we reached a small, wooden house with white shutters. 'Home?' I asked.

'Sure is. Nothing fancy, but it's where my heart is, as they say in the song.'

We walked around the side of the house to a small porch at the rear. She fitted a key into the lock of a door, turning on a light as we walked in. I followed. It was a sitting room, but only just. Every surface was covered in soft toys, lurid, pop-eyed, simpering creations. There were dogs, cats, bears, cartoon characters, a whole life on earth. The sitting would be hard.

Mobilene went over to a wet bar at the rear of the room. It resembled a Spanish galleon or an Indian dhow, with curved prows at each end. 'What's your pleasure, sir?' she asked coyly.

'That bourbon would be great,' I said. The only place to sit was a small sofa. Mobilene squeezed in beside me as she handed over my drink. Our thighs touched. I felt myself flush and shifted awkwardly.

'Sorry, it's a bit squashed,' I said.

'Friendly, I'd say,' she replied.

'Yes, quite, and that,' I replied, noticing that several buttons down the front of her top had somehow opened, exposing the sort of cleavage they fly tourists through if the Grand Canyon is fogged up.

'All natural, one hundred per cent organic,' she laughed, catching my stare.

I felt myself redden. 'Ah, yes. I was just, just –'

'Catching an eyeful,' she said, smiling. 'You naughty boy.'

'Well, no. I mean, yes. You know. I mean they are certainly.' I found myself staring at the anatomy she pushed forward. 'Incredibly incredible, if you don't mind my saying.'

'Ah. Well, I thank you, kind sir. These are the only assets I got from my ma, apart from a rhinestone necklace, but they done me good.'

She had been in Nashville for some years, arriving starstruck with a good voice, some tunes, a guitar and ambition. 'I was gonna be the next Dolly Parton, have me a theme park called Mobileland. Yes, sir, I had it all worked out. Only it didn't. If you see what I mean.'

'What went wrong?' I asked, thinking that at least one part of the Dolly Parton experience had been fully realized, as it heaved a few inches from my eyes.

'I had talent, sure, but that grows by the sidewalk in this town, baby. I was a sucker. Trusted the wrong people. It's the old story.' Her lips pursed. 'It ain't purty. Got into handing over my savings to cut a CD, couldn't get it played nowhere and couldn't get any management that didn't involve me sleeping with some guy and sometimes not just the guy,' she said.

'In the end, I got the gig at the Lonesome. Been there ever since. Four years nearly. Kinda sad, ain't it? Like a song.'

'No, not at all,' I replied softly. 'At least you're doing what you want in life. At least it's honest.'

'I guess that's the truth. I can drink to that.' She raised her glass in a silent salutation.

I suddenly felt very tired and very dishonest. My night with Destiny, my lasciviousness towards Mobilene. Gina. I thought about Sol Goldblam. Poor sod, however many awful things he may have done. Dead because I didn't have the balls to stand up to Stanley.

The sippin' insinuated its way into my head, seducing it into a luxuriant calm. I knew there was probably little more of this living lyric that I could take, however kindly I felt disposed towards Mobilene, my latest saviour. But neither did I want to be thrown out.

'So, tell me about the reporting game,' she asked suddenly.

'It has its moments,' I said, compelling myself into coherence. Mobilene looked at me blankly. I thought for a moment.

'Well, it's a strange life, chasing human excess and natural disasters a lot of the time,' I said wearily. 'Sex, celebrity and slaughter.

We're the people who drive into those messes that everyone else is fleeing from.'

'Sounds like an adventure.'

'Plain stupid, more like.'

She twirled her glass. 'You're like me – whatever else happens I got my songs, my babies. You got your words.'

'It's not quite the same, believe me. We steal from other lives. It's not creative. We're sponges, good at soaking up facts and spitting them out in a few hundred ordered words. That's it.'

She seemed disappointed. People still liked to think the media was driven by righting and writing. Only in the movies, I told her.

'You got a little lady in your life, Mr Reporter Man?' she asked lazily.

'I hope so. I mean, I don't know at the moment. It's all very confusing, since you ask. Part of the reason I'm heading out to California is to find out.'

I told her about Gina, the bust-ups, a relationship that had flat-lined into rows about fish. I even told her I was being chased, but spared her the details. It was a work thing, I said. She clearly thought there was something honourable about my fleeing.

'Wow, you've really ruffled some feathers by the sound of things, fired up the bad guys,' she said admiringly.

'You could say that.' I must have triggered some country and western gene, the one about helping the lost, lonely stranger find his way. I told her about the money, that I was effectively penniless. She seemed sad.

'Maybe you should pay me for the story as an advance against royalties for when the song you write about tonight is a big hit,' I joked.

'Maybe I should do just that,' she replied. I told her how Gina and I had met in New York (verse three) and how I hated myself for picking fights to release work frustrations (four). Mobilene sat, engrossed. She must live for this kind of stuff, the stranger with a sorry tale of woe. Maybe that was why she always bought the last person at the bar a drink. Its recipient was probably sad, lonely, desperate or all three.

'Anyway, the long and short of it is that I'm broke, anxious to get to California and I'm being chased by some terrifying hoods who want to kill me. Apart from that, it's basically been an average few days.'

She laughed, a long boisterous ripple through the night air. 'I like you. You're funny. You truly are. Here. This may make you feel better.'

With that, she leant over, grasped my head and kissed me passionately. I responded in kind. I was getting good at Southern hospitality. I could see the headline: DESTINY SENDS WORD AHEAD.

We eventually came up for air.

'Feel any better?' she asked, sounding concerned about whether the therapy was working. It was and I did, diving back for seconds, knocking fluffy toys aside with abandon.

'Hush,' she said suddenly. I stopped dead. Not a sound.

'It's Andy,' she said firmly.

'What? From the bar? What's he doing coming here at this time of night?'

'I hope he ain't got nowhere else to go to, honey.' She laughed gently.

'Why's that?'

'He's my husband and I'd get awful jealous.'

'Christ!'

I rearranged my clothes, closed shirt buttons and moved across to a side chair, straightening my hair just as the door opened.

'Hey, darling,' said Mobilene. 'You remember . . . What's your name again, honey?'

'Ollie.'

'Ollie from the Lonesone tonight.'

Andy grunted either yes I do or not a clue.

'Pleased to meet you,' I said, reaching out my hand and smiling strongly, hoping that brilliant integrity shone through. He took it, shaking with barely a glance at me. Perhaps this happened every night. He swept, she snogged.

I wondered what I was going to say to explain my presence in his sitting room at two in the morning. His wife, I noticed with horror, had barely bothered to rearrange herself from our spasm of passion.

'Ollie here needs to get out of town tomorrow and head west,' said Mobilene, as Andy moved to the wet bar and poured himself a whiskey.

'That so,' he muttered, heading upstairs with the glass. ''Night, mister.' He hadn't looked at me once.

'He'll have a plan by the morning, you see,' said Mobilene confidently. 'I could tell he was workin' on it.'

'You could?'

23

The plan arrived over coffee and I tried to look on the positive side. My own suit was the wrong side of filthy, it was true. The smell of Brit was probably hitting air-pollution detectors across the nation. Even so.

'You'll look great, hon,' reassured Mobilene as Andy brought out the ensemble.

'What I like 'bout this one,' he said matter-of-factly, 'is you've got several choices. The full rig, which is kinda hot to travel in, or various parts. You got your tail, whiskers, ears and paws,' he said. 'That's still a lot of squirrel options to go for and in a washable, thin material.'

I nodded my head earnestly, the eager student to some strange Druidic rite.

'A lot of folk go for the all-in-one. Now that's fine, of course, but very impractical in hot climates or where you might expect temperature changes.'

'Quite,' I replied. 'Yes, I can see that.'

Andy and Mobilene, it transpired, were Plushies, people who enjoyed dressing up as furry animals. But nothing was surprising me much by then. My precarious hold on life already owed everything to an amateur clown and a bootlegger. Why not throw in a squirrel impersonator?

Mobilene showed me her own costume, a bear. She said that Andy enjoyed dressing as a rabbit these days. They attended conventions around the country. It was where they had met. Mobilene was invited to sing sometimes. It was a thrill to entertain a roomful of furry animals, apparently. 'They're good people, Plushy folk,' she said, catching my sceptical expression.

Andy had had his big idea overnight, as promised. A Plushy

convention was due to take place in northern California. They were not going themselves, but 'Doc Bear' was and might just be able to take me in his private small aircraft. 'He's a fine man,' said Andy. 'You'll like the Doc.' I was to travel with him and mingle, disguised, at the event until I was sure the coast was clear.

Mobilene said I should help myself to a book to read on the journey. I wondered where the bookshelves were, but thought it impolite to ask. There hardly seemed room for literature in such a repository of cuddly toys. Eventually, I found what constituted the library. It was in the downstairs lavatory. Four shelves of reading. There were a couple of Grishams, a Collins, a Bible, some biographies of country stars. My eye hit upon *Cube Nation* by Depak Firman, MD. I sighed, but it was a chance to connect with Gina. I found myself staring at the famous mystic with the marketing touch. He stared back, reassuring in his surgical whites. I turned the book over and, out of habit, looked at the price. Mobilene had paid $20 for this Cube nonsense. I noticed that the spine was unbent. I decided to take it. Mobilene seemed relieved.

The convention began tomorrow and Doc was heading out to tonight. Mobilene said she would drive me to 'the spread', which was fifteen miles out of town.

I crouched in the rear of her aged Buick. Paranoia had found me and was nuzzling at my fears. I expected to see Fat Angie lurking at every street corner. But there was no sign. There was only the Todd trail for them to follow, I thought irritatingly. Clem would by now be far away, not that there was ever much chance that anyone would find him. Mobilene stopped for petrol on the outskirts of town. I began to feel a strange relaxation drift over me. If I could just get to California and Gina, capable Gina, things would be fine. She would know what to do. Mobilene told me that Doc Bear owned a cattle ranch. I allowed myself a grim smile of satisfaction. Find me now, you numskulls.

'You know, this is so good for me,' she said.

'How so?' I asked.

'It's that country music thing. Life's a bed of pain, a snatched rose. It's a comfort to know that others are often a whole lot worse off. People like yourself.'

'Glad to help. No charge.'

She laughed.

I told her how much I appreciated what she and Andy were doing. I promised to get their Plushy costume returned, dry-cleaned if possible. She said not to bother, it was an old one from their 'rodent moment, very nineties'. On our way to the 'Doc', I asked Mobilene to find me a pawn shop. My watch was all I had left, a gift to myself when I was first posted to New York. I knew it was worth about $500, but accepted $100 from the grizzled man behind a layer of protective glass. There was no haggling. 'Take it or leave it, friend,' he said. I had little choice. I lost time, but gained time. It was a neat paradox. Mobilene looked sympathetic. That was worth another verse, I knew.

He was waiting for us at the end of a bitumen drive the width of a runway. Later, I was to discover why. It was the runway.

Doc Bear was a round, avuncular man. To my surprise, there was also a Mrs Bear. They were introduced to me as Bruce and Wanda Goosebalm. Both shook my hands warmly. I was expecting something odder than the respectable-looking Rotarians in front of me.

Mobilene kissed me on the cheek as we said our goodbyes. She thrust a wad of notes at me.

'Advance royalties,' she said. I tried to force them back.

'Look, I couldn't. I was only joking.'

'I wasn't and it ain't much anyway. You've given me some great material. The story's almost as important as the tune in country, you know.'

It was $150. I smiled. 'Thanks, Mobilene. I owe you.'

'No, you don't. But promise me one thing: let me know if you get back with your girl. It may alter my last verse.'

'What are you planning?'

'Well, as this is country, I'm thinking of a broken heart. But, as it's you, I may come up with something upliftin'.'

'Thanks, I need all the help I can get,' I said, smiling ruefully.

I watched her drive off and thought of Clem and his also unbidden help. For every Fat Angie there was a Fat Clem or a Big-Hearted Blonde.

The Goosebalms guided me to the house, a brick colonial with white shutters and a veranda wrapped around the lower floor. A thin, painted colonnade supported a second-floor balcony. Plump, lush wisteria seductively encircled each column. The place was clearly cherished.

I half expected to be offered some apple pie.

'You'll have a slice of pie,' asked Wanda kindly.

'I'd love one. Thanks.'

Only Bruce was a true Plushy. Wanda stayed home and looked after the mansion, but would attend 'conFurences' occasionally, she said. 'I go as Babs Bunny.'

'That's just, just fantastic,' I said. 'Fantastic.' I was suddenly beyond exhaustion in some place where adrenalin and strange chemicals flow as stimulants, legal and unbidden. I wanted to sleep after a restless night alone on Mobilene's sofabed, but was eating apple pie instead.

I called my home telephone for messages. There was just one. It was from Fishlove.

'I wouldn't bother buying those tickets to see Whitney, if I were you,' he said drily. 'She's cancelled the Nashville concert because of a throat infection.'

Sod it. My plan to lure Fishlove down and, without giving anything away, shelter behind his credit cards had failed miserably. Time for a quick audit. I was in Nashville, where I had been turned into a song, preparing to dress as a woodland creature and waiting to be flown across the States by a stranger who preferred to be a bear. A normal day.

Fortuna, California, was surely twinned with Irony. Never could a place have been less honestly named. The Inn of the Mountain Gods was its triumph, a monument to the values of corporate optimism over design sense, a bizarre, sharp-angled concrete monster, the *Battlestar Galactica* landed in a soft artificial parkland of wood-chipped flower borders set just beyond the town limits.

We were valet parked by an Inca king, befeathered and bespectacled. An Aztec warrior in Ray-Bans, identified as 'Ramon' by a brass breast plaque, took my luggage, a large carrier filled with squirrel.

Above the reception desk hung two banners: 'Welcome to the Western States Fifteenth ConFurence' and, more ominously, 'Welcome to the 65th Army Reserve Division'.

I glanced anxiously at Bruce, wondering if he was thinking what I was. But he was too excited, a Plushy finally amongst his own. 'Hey, Cas Coyote, how ya doin',' he yelled, as a mountain creature strode across the atrium carrying a gym bag and Diet Coke.

'Hi ya, Doc, just gonna work out. Catch you later, yeah? There's gonna be some scritching tonight.'

'You betcha,' said Bruce enthusiastically.

'Scritching?' I asked, as we headed to the lifts.

He winked at me. 'You'll see. It's a lot of fun. We should get ready. There's a welcome reception at the Ritual Sacrifice Bar in the penthouse at 7 p.m.'

I was on the fifty-fourth floor. Bruce had got off two time zones lower. 'Don't forget your handle.'

'What?'

'Let's see. How about Sammy the Squirrel?'

'How about Ollie the Brit?' I countered.

'No real life here, that's for Mundanes. Well, you choose. See you in the bar.'

I put my squirrel down by the far wall, a bas-relief of a Spaniard beheading a Native American, and took a shower. It seemed sensible to wash at every opportunity. Bruce had proved a generous tour guide. There were many, sometimes hair-raising detours to view sites he thought worth catching. These were never architectural or natural marvels in the conventional sense, but landscape features that reminded him of places and people.

'Hey, we'll just head over to those woods yonder,' he said, pulling the Cessna sharply to the right. 'There, see it, see it,' he said, pointing enthusiastically.

'What exactly, Bruce? Sorry.'

'Down there, there,' he shouted, exasperated. I stared hard.

'The rocks in those trees, ain't they the image of Elizabeth Taylor!'

This way we passed the time between Nashville and Fresno, stopping on the way to refuel at dusty pumps all, it seems, worked by an aged, weathered man named Al. I saw, or rather missed, Marilyn Monroe's face on the side of a cliff, the leaning tower of Pisa in a wooded copse and the entire chorus line from *Chicago* represented in a clutch of cacti. He flew through a land of sheet lightning so far distant that there was no thunder, above landscapes of cottonwoods, clumps of grama plants. The small, twin-engined aircraft had shuddered, tossed in timeless, mistral winds that seemed to toy with us as we flew determinedly towards some unreachable horizon. I would occasionally glance over a wing, watching for Fat Angie behind the cockpit of a requisitioned Harrier.

The shower in my room had been 'sanitized for my convenience' with enough tape to deter asylum seekers. One day I really was going to carry a can of spray paint: 'This room has been graffitied for your offence.' I called room service to take my stinking clothes for cleaning. I was dozing when I was woken by another tap at the door. 'Room orientation,' said a voice.

'Hold on.'

A small, round-faced man, who introduced himself as Michael, was waiting beyond the door.

'Room orientation? Because if I've got a choice, I'd like mine to be female and giving because I've been a bit lonely lately. Is that at all possible on my rate or would I have to upgrade?'

He looked at me uncertainly. 'I don't think so. Maybe at the concierge desk,' he said, trailing off. 'I just got to show you how the room works, sir, to maximize your comfort with us here at the Inn of the Mountain Gods.'

I sighed and let him through. He seemed relieved, pointing out the air-conditioning system, the heating centre, the home theatre with surround sound, the dozen shower-pressure options. I listened in a daze and thought life had come to this: a hotel room had more choices than me.

Andy was clearly a rodent size smaller than me. The crotch pulled tight and I also had problems attaching the tail, which resisted all my efforts to bend it into a reasonable resemblance of anything natural. The body suit was full, except for the head, which left an oval hole for the human face to fill. But at least I was a red squirrel so the blushes wouldn't show.

I padded over to the lift. The feet were huge and furry, more flipper than paw.

"Tenshun, Woodland Creature aboard.' The three young uniformed men clicked their heels in unison and smirked hard as the lift doors closed. I decided on a display of studied indifference, even as my face brightened to car-stopping crimson.

The door opened straight into the Ritual Sacrifice Bar and safety. It was as if every cartoon character ever invented had turned up for cocktails and canapés. A white duck offered a cigarette to an ostrich. I checked in at the reception desk by the door. 'Pet Squirrel,' I announced confidently. The red setter writing out the name badges looked at me oddly and sighed wearily. 'You sure? OK, then, Pet Squirrel it is. I'll have it printed in the directory.'

The murmur of conversation carried me to the bar, as I pinned the name tag to my fur. I ordered a beer and began on the pile of nuts, not just to keep in character. I was really very hungry. There was no sign of Bruce.

Then someone scratched me on the neck, repeatedly.

'Excuse me,' I said pointedly, turning sharply.

'Hey, no offence, just scritching.'

So, that was it, a tribal greeting.

'Oh, right,' I said, relieved, staring at the kangaroo.

'I'm Skippy,' he said in a deep Southern voice.

'I'm, er, Pet Squirrel.'

'Well, good luck,' he said, winking, a surprised smile spreading across his lips. 'Those days are way behind me.'

Skippy was wearing large, red-framed glasses. His body suit even contained a pouch. 'Don't remember seeing you before.'

'First time.'

'I come every year. This is one of the best. You've chosen a good one.' He glanced over my shoulder.

There was an awkward silence. I had reasonable social skills. I could talk blandly for hours. I may not be brilliant, but could, to paraphrase Dr Johnson, be agreeable. I still struggled to find the entry for conversation. The economy? Mid-term elections? Third World debt?

'So, have you seen the *Lion King*?' I asked eventually.

Before Skippy could reply, he had found his own exit from the awkwardness. 'Ah, I can see my lovely lady has just arrived.'

I followed his gaze towards a creature with ash-blonde hair. 'You're a lucky man,' I said. 'She makes a quite delightful skunk.'

'Don't she. Ellen certainly dresses to kill. I'll catch you later. I'm sure we've got some things to discuss with a Pet Squirrel,' he said, emphasizing the word 'pet' and winking again. I winked back. Why not? This was their world.

I met an assortment of soft coatings. Some were pleased when I approached introducing myself; others seemed to move away. Maybe squirrels had a reputation for stealing nuts?

Bruce was chatting with Cas the Coyote when I found him by the picture window. He introduced me as a new convert to Plushiedom. 'He's borrowed the gear, haven't you? Still, you should get your own by next year.'

Next year? 'Right, yes. I decided on Pet Squirrel as my handle, by the way.'

Cassy's eyes popped open and she stared at my badge. Bruce looked worried and winced.

'What's wrong?' I asked. 'I mean, I thought it sounded practical, descriptive.'

'Oh, it's descriptive all right,' said Bruce. 'It just sounds like you want a great deal of a certain kind of sex.'

'What?'

'My, you really are new to this, aren't you, sweetheart?' said Cas. 'A "pet" is the subservient role in a sex act in our little world. You're basically telling everyone you want to be, ahm, involved with another animal. A lot of folks don't like that. They'll be calling you a furvert.'

'Oh, terrific.' Visa fraud, conspiracy to murder, theft, under-age sex and now soliciting bestiality.

'Doc Bear, you have been naughty,' said Cassy. 'Shame on you, sir. You shoulda told him.' She turned to me. 'Take Tiger Cowboy over there,' she said, pointing to a man dressed in stripes and whiskers sipping a bourbon. 'Now he likes to be led around on a collar and lead, so he's a "pet". Obviously, one thing often leads, if you'll excuse the pun, to another. I guess what I'm saying is, you may want to change your handle to something a little less suggestive.'

I was ahead of her. 'Squirrel Nutkin?' I ventured.

She scrunched her eyes in thought. 'Still sounds kinda soft to me. How about Spiked Punch? Nobody'll mess with you then.'

Fine by me.

The conFurence was to last for two days. It was obvious to me that nobody could have picked up my trail here. Mobilene and Andy could be trusted. I decided to spend the night at the Inn and leave tomorrow, slipping away before the main events, which seemed to be a fashion parade and some sort of revue featuring the Reindeers singing Motown.

Drinks turned into a buffet supper and, after a while, I found myself slipping comfortably into the role of Spiked Punch, soft on the outside but tough as nails underneath all that fur. Nobody asked me to be their pet for the night. I drank beers manfully, certainly squirrelfully, and talked about the Mets and the Yankees, the Chiefs and the Tomahawks. There were quite a few no-nonsense furries. There was barrel-chested Mike, a turtle, who worked in information technology, he said, which turned out under closer interrogation to involve attaching plugs to the mains cables of personal computers.

'I was in 'Nam. But I got out.'

'Really? See much action?'

'Sure did,' he said. 'Them North American Muppets know how to have a good time.'

He looked around. 'But these,' he said, sweeping his flipper. 'These are basically some sad bastards,' he said, surveying the room. 'Me, I gotta life outside of here, you know. I support teams, go to sports bars. For them, this is all they got. Know what I'm saying?'

'Absolutely,' I said emphatically. 'I couldn't manage without teams.'

'Government are gettin' in on this,' he said, leaning over and speaking more softly. Mike, it transpired, was also in his local Wyoming militia and resented the federal authorities, especially those parts relating to liquor, tobacco and guns.

'Heard they're using this DNA genetic engineering stuff to create the perfect killing machine, a hybrid human.'

'Really?' I said, as he warmed to his theme.

'You won't read about it, of course, but they got an installation out in Montana and they're workin' on a whole load of shelled men and, so I hear, alligator folk, basically trying to make creatures that'll do anything they're told.'

'What? Like armed beagles? Pretty clever,' was all I could find to say.

'Clever indeed, my friend. Clever indeed. Now me, I would only take part if they'd kinda turn me into a mountain lion. Don't get me wrong, I love turtles but not in a combat situation. No, sir.'

We had the run of the Ritual Sacrifice Bar until 10 p.m. when it was closed, just as the serious drinking and scritching was beginning. We were hustled, complaining, to the lift, which would take us down to the main lobby bar. Mike and I were amongst the last to leave.

By coincidence, the 65th Army Reserve Division had been ejected from their reception, in the Machu Picchu Suite several floors below, at the same time. Natural camouflage fought for space with unnatural versions. The men in combat fatigues could barely contain themselves. Then someone made the mistake of scritching the neck of a severe-looking army captain, who turned quickly and lashed out, punching a racoon hard in the shoulder. He or she yelped.

'Careful, man,' said Mike, who at about 180 pounds and six feet, emerged as the natural spokesman from our company.

'No, you watch out,' said the fresh-faced soldier, his neck muscles rippling in anger, head jutting forward. 'I don't need to be felt up by some perv in an animal costume, OK.'

There was a murmur of anger from the furries. 'Stop being so anal, soldier boy. He wasn't feeling you up. Anyway, your costume's pretty wild too,' said an unidentified voice from the back.

There was a murmur of appreciative laughter. I winced. Inflaming the military muscle in the lift seemed a bad idea. I looked anxiously at the number display. Twenty floors to the lobby. What was that – a light year? We were all heading there, apparently. Not that it took a military strategist to work out why. The main bar in the hotel was the only one still open to residents.

The mood was getting ugly. Three soldiers began to press backwards against the jam of fur, pretending not to know what they were doing. There were rumbles in the animal kingdom as we tried to rearrange ourselves. A 'ping' announced our arrival on the ground floor.

'You are really very rude,' complained a Canadian goose to one of the uniforms, a 'Bedermier', according to the stencilled name on his chest.

'And you're a weirdo. Wanna make something of it?'

Mike was clearly reaching some sort of combustion point, buoyed by his commanding authority in the lift and fuelled by cocktails. There was a steely determination about this turtle, striding purposefully towards the man who had punched the racoon.

'Hey, pal. You with the attitude, I'm talking to you,' said Mike, reaching his target and spinning him around. 'What gives you the right to behave like an asshole? You're a disgrace to that uniform.'

That was it. The man pushed Mike hard. He lost his footing and fell to the ground. Within a second he was on his feet, demonstrating remarkable agility and helped by the spring-like padding on his back. He bounded over and hurled himself at the soldier. They flew into a display of tropical palms. It was nothing less than a call to paws. When I heard someone shout 'call the cops' I realized it was time to leave.

I slipped back into the lift and pressed my floor. Within a minute of entering my room, I remembered where my clothes were – spinning somewhere deep in the Mountain God's bowels.

There was no question of my risking the police and a trip back to New York, to Scarpesi and his basement. I doubted Fat Angie would be so careless the second time.

I sat on the bed. Todd would be on his way to the Cube Ranch by now. What would he do if I didn't show up? Blurt something to somebody. I had to get there and fast.

He might even have arrived, checked into his motel and be waiting. Would he make contact with Gina? I hoped not. I wanted to call him on his mobile. But he had proved such a blabber-mouth, it wasn't worth the risk. What would he tell her? The thought of my partially explained experiences going through the strange filter of his brain was deeply alarming.

What would I tell Gina, for that matter? And would she believe me? There was a California state map in the room. The Cube Ranch was outside Santa Barbara, about two hours' drive away. There was another stumbling block. I had just enough money to hire a car and pay for my night in the Inn, thanks to a mighty discount the conFurence had negotiated for its wildlife. I called reception. A car would be no trouble at all, said an Aztec. Perhaps any early departing furries were to be encouraged. The Hertz hire office was at the back of the hotel and still open. There was nothing for it. I was going to have to persuade a receptionist to rent a vehicle to a squirrel.

She was named Sarah and didn't stare, smirk or ask a quizzical question as we went through the long mechanics of form filling. I had a current driver's licence, no endorsements and money. So what if I buried nuts in the garden? America can be very forgiving that way.

I was soon on the road, heading towards I-5, the interstate that runs up the spine of California, and my uncertain fate. I felt good, elated even. For the first time in a while my fate wasn't dependent on the kindness or violence of strangers. I was my own person, a squirrel in my own right, a rodent of the road. I whistled a happy tune.

By the time I reached Santa Barbara it was nearly one in the morning. I was overcome by exhaustion and wanted to sleep. I had hired the smallest car available, a compact, and regretted the financially sensible choice. I needed to conserve my small bundle of money, not least because Todd was an unreliable cashpoint and probably had little money himself, unless the Goth had come back with cash. But I was not going to hold my unpierced tongue for that to have happened.

I found a vacant lot and tucked the compact inconspicuously near a row of dumpsters that serviced the El Viejo Mexican restaurant next door.

I couldn't sleep, so dipped into the Cube book I had taken from Nashville. It worked. I curled into the back seat, tucked my tail between my legs and slept instantly.

24

Santa Barbara is old by American standards, which means its history predates the first McDonald's drive-thru. Franciscan priests defined it as they spread Catholicism and sensual architecture up the West Coast in the eighteenth century. It is rich and famous. The place is white. White houses, white people and egg-white omelettes, because the alternative involves yolk, which is yellow. It was quiet except for the mournful lowing of water buffalo tethered in backyards. A famous Hollywood actor had one as a pet, and they were now highly prized.

'Hey, buddy, you looking for nuts?' yelled the driver of a croissant delivery van, unloading plastic pallets of baked goods outside a coffee shop just before 7 a.m.

'No, breakfast. When does this place open?'

'Around 7.30, but they may make an exception for a squirrel,' he said, hopping back into his cab. 'Sure must have been quite a party. See ya, buddy.'

I waved him off and sat on a wooden bench outside the coffee shop. It was tempting to steal a croissant or a bagel. I resisted. It was probably grand larceny in Santa Barbara, and I didn't want to add that to the criminal rap sheet. People stared, but not too many. This was California after all, State of Odd.

It wasn't completely clear to me what the next step should be. Clothes, of course. By the time the sun had risen on another perfect Californian day, I was the only person queuing outside a discount clothes outlet. Inside I trudged up the aisles. I was getting adept with the tail, keeping it out of the way of other people, stopping it from snagging in the wheels of trolleys. Children pointed. I scooped up t-shirts, a formal shirt and two pairs of trousers, trainers and a supply of underclothes. On impulse, I raised the bundle to my nose and inhaled the new, fresh smell, savouring the moment in the way others might test an avocado for ripeness. It felt good, human. This was as close as I was going to get to actual possession.

I reached for my wallet. Jesus and Mary. I let my hand perform a panicked dance around the tiny, and apparently empty, pouch pocket. I went out to the car, fear welling inside me. This really was bad. I searched everywhere. No sign. For a while I just sat motionless behind the wheel, stunned. Even my wallet had deserted me, deciding it had a safer future at the Hertz office, by the road somewhere. Anywhere else.

There was nothing for it. Santa Barbara tourist information helped me locate the Cube Ranch. It was a short drive out of town. They also identified the closest motel, the Meaningful Experience Inn, which was about two miles from the entrance to the ranch.

'I hear they've got a big gathering there this weekend,' said the coiffured matron behind the information desk. 'You attending?'

'Yes. The clothes, isn't it?'

She nodded that it was. 'I just love your accent, by the way, so elegant.'

'Thank you, you're very kind. They've got them on sale at Marshall's, by the way. You should check it out,' I said. She followed me with a baffled stare.

'I might just do that,' I heard her say.

The Meaningful Experience was off a country road and surrounded by huge pines. A wooden board announced that continental breakfast was included in the rate of $29 a night. A water buffalo grazed placidly near the entrance. There was no other car parked in the courtyard, towards which all the rooms on the two linked floors seemed to radiate.

The reception area was festooned with things meaningful. Framed quotations from great texts hung off the walls. The Bible, the Koran, Oprah and, of course, Cubethink were all reflected in small, easily digestible homilies. On the desk was a small plaque announcing that the duty manager was Mr Patel.

'May I be helping you, sir?' asked a voice, bringing my attention down from the walls.

'Yes, please. I'd like a room. But first I want to check that you have another guest here by the name of Todd Bowman.'

'Ah, yes, the movie gentleman,' said Mr Patel, cheering at being able to help. 'He has just this very minute or two gone to Pitstop Grill.'

'Great. Listen, I'll tell you what. I'll come back and check in later. I really have to see him first,' I said, hurrying out.

Thankfully, the framers of the Constitution had included a requirement that nobody should be more than five minutes' walk from a folding laminated menu and a five-course Happy Heart Attack Meal, so the restaurant was close. Todd himself was all but obscured by a Pisa of pancakes tottering in front of him, his head buried, surprisingly, in the local newspaper.

'Dr Todd, I presume,' I said jauntily, pleased and amazed that he had actually managed to work out where to stay and followed my instructions.

'Hey, Ollie the man, good to see you,' he said, rising quickly. I slid in opposite and prepared to tell of my Odyssey. But he got in first, burying his head back in the print, just as my mouth opened.

'Guess what, dudester. They're saying here that the number of swallows heading back to San Juan Capistrano every year is going down. One day, they may never show up at all. What do you think of that?'

I was determined not to be thrown by morsels of Todd inconsequences. 'Much as I'd like to get my head around the swallow problem, perhaps we could leave that to another time,' I said.

'Sure, man. Whatever you say.' He folded the newspaper, pushing it to one side and began a full, UN-sanctioned attack on the pancakes. 'Here, want some?'

'No, you go right ahead. I'll watch, see if the defenders fight back.'

He came at them from all sides, pushing his fork into one flank whilst thrusting a spoon into another. The pile never had a chance. I watched, awed as ever by the Todd eating-machine, a medical miracle. I flipped idly through the newspaper. No sign of me, which was reassuring.

'So, what's the plan?' Todd asked finally, leaving his fork and spoon spreadeagled across the empty plate. He seemed eager as a puppy.

'I'm not sure. You made contact with Gina yet?'

'No, thought I'd wait till you got here, like you said,' he replied. 'Only got here myself last night,' he said, drinking noisily from a coffee tankard. 'Didn't want to screw things up, so thought I'd better keep schtum.'

'That's good, very good. Well, I think we should just head up there, see if we can find her.'

'Great plan.'

'So, how was your trip?' I wasn't quite ready to tell him about mine, worrying that it could just overload him. I needed Todd with what passed for uncluttered judgement.

'It was the deal. Outstanding. We had the greatest chicken meal. It was with some potatoes in a creamy sauce and had a kind of noodle side dish. The bread roll was amazing. Just right. Really bad turbulence over Tahoe. Some guy got flung out of his seat. They did his leg up best they could and sedated him. Bone sticking out and all.'

'Amazing news about the bread roll, Todd.'

'Wasn't it? Anyway. let's hit the trail.' He slapped his hands together. 'It'll be so great to see Gina again.'

'Stop, stop,' he suddenly exclaimed as we walked over to the compact. He moved in front of me. He looked at me, moved to one side, rubbed his chin. 'No, no, don't say anything. I got it, I got it.'

'Got what, Todd?'

'You're in a squirrel suit.'

'My God, are you sure?' I feigned surprise, patting myself down in amazement.

'Yeah. Hey, you're kidding me, right.' He wagged his finger, smiling. 'I mean, it's definitely a squirrel, whatever they told you at the store. I'm telling you, man.'

'Actually, it's deliberate.'

'Like a disguise, right?'

'Well, like a disguise. But it isn't one because I can tell you from personal experience that dressing as a squirrel in public means attracting a good deal more attention than if you don't.'

'Now you know,' said Todd, suddenly serious. 'Take that as a lesson. Next time you could go for something like a rabbit or a gopher. People are more used to seeing them.'

I wasn't really up to Todd or immersion in that shallow puddle he passes off as wisdom, so stayed silent as we drove back to the motel.

'Or a mule, maybe. Or would that have too many legs?'

I needed to think. 'I'll see you at the reception desk in twenty minutes, OK?'

'Sure,' he replied cheerfully, heading off to his own room. 'Say, I'll check the *Yellow Pages* for mule costumes.'

'You do that,' I replied. Why fight it?

I needed a strategy, but none was presenting itself. I had to make contact with Gina, secure the protection of the ranch and then . . . what? My mind was blank. This was not what journalism was supposed to be about – some lunatic exodus across the country pursued by mobsters and employers. This was not what I'd signed up for.

Todd had a little money but not much. It also turned out that the only clothes he had were the ones he was wearing. He had taken my advice and left New York immediately, probably stung by my rebukes. We had to get into the ranch fast.

I tried calling again. No answer, just some twaddle about the enlightenment festival taking place, which meant no contact with 'the outside' until Monday to ensure maximum 'energy retention' within the grounds.

I luxuriated in thoughts of khaki trousers and a short-sleeved summer shirt. In my reverie, I gave the squirrel outfit to house-keeping to clean. It would return folded, inanimate and ready for return to its home in Nashville.

The motel was not, as it transpired, empty, but filled with people attending the great Cube think-in. They had all left early for a sunrise gathering on a hilltop. Mr Patel turned out to be full of information.

'Oh, yes, indeed. Many, many people from all over world here for this most great gathering,' he said.

'Good for business, then.'

'Most. Dr Firman is a visionary,' said Mr Patel, waving his hand in the air as if to challenge anyone or any god who might deny this assertion. 'I learn much self-confidence from his teachings. We are all cubes, Mr Gibbon. That you must not forget.'

'I remind myself of that very fact at least once a day, believe me.'

'Yes, yes,' Mr Patel said excitedly. 'I also. I no longer have sugar cravings. No, sir, all gone.'

Where was Todd?

'Fruit is answer, much of it very good for temper, spleen and small part of pancreas, which is so often ignored by conventional teachings on nutrition.'

Perfect. This was all I needed in my life, another fruit nut.

'Except the kiwi fruit,' I interrupted.

'I'm asking your pardon?'

'The kiwi fruit. It's a vicious little bastard. Turns people into monsters, megalomaniacs, over-bronzed Napoleons.'

'My goodness. No?'

'Trust me. I've got practical experience. There's a piece in this month's *Bastards Today*.'

Todd emerged, still weirdly unmoved by our circumstances.

'You look distracted,' I said, as we walked to the car.

'Yeah, man. Those swallows. Tried to ring the bird sanctuary down there. Couldn't get through.'

'I wouldn't worry too much about them today,' I said sharply. 'They're not being pursued by the Mafia.'

'That's true, I guess.'

The ranch was near by. A small sign discouraging visitors was covered by a poster making an exception for invited guests this weekend. The drive curled gently up a slope to reveal a magnificent white wood mansion sitting on the crest of a hill. A herd of water buffalo grazed a huge, rolling pasture that ran almost to the main entrance. The Pacific was visible in the distance. And so was Gina on horseback.

The laughter reached us first. 'Good grief, Ollie, I know you hate leaving cities, but it is safe in the country, you know. You don't have to look like an animal.'

I smiled stiffly. 'Hi, Gina, it's a long story.' I suddenly didn't know what to say. 'How are you?' was all that came out.

She smiled. 'I'm good,' she said, dismounting. God, she was beautiful. 'I'm pleased you've come. Really. It means a lot.'

We sat on a hillside, watching Todd on her bay, whooping and hollering, as it trotted around the meadow.

She looked at me and put her arm around my shoulder. 'It's a long way, and I know how you hate flying. But you flew across a continent for me. I'm touched.'

I coughed awkwardly. 'Well, it wasn't just for you.' I felt her stiffen. 'Mainly for you, of course,' I added quickly. She was staring at me. I had nothing to lose. This was the moment. I told her everything. This time she seemed to believe me. Maybe, it was the presence of Todd or the evidence of her own eyes. The squirrel costume alone pointed to at least some plausible disorder in the Force.

Todd testified to my frantic phone calls, pleas for cash. I clearly did have a problem, of the sort even her father could not expect to solve. She trusted what Todd said, I thought wretchedly. Only anything from my lips was suspect.

'I can't believe you've led them here,' she said, as we sat on the hillside and watched the calming sea swells. 'Looking like that. I mean, Ollie.'

'I don't think I have brought them here,' I insisted. She knitted her eyebrows and nibbled a fingernail. These were encouraging signs.

'Oh, come on. How long do you think it's going to take them to work it out?' she said. 'Look, the centre has a huge event this weekend. There are Congressmen here, for goodness sake. The governor is expected.'

'But that's great. I mean, I doubt the mob are going to just march in and take me, assuming they've even made the connection, with all that going on.'

Gina snorted derisively. Todd did the same, which was particularly infuriating because I knew he was just following her lead. I made a mental note to raise it with him later.

'Look, sweetheart, I'm sorry. Really I am. I just didn't have anywhere else to go. I thought this would be safe, give me a chance to sort things out, try to find a way out of this. I wanted to make things up with you, of course, too.'

She gave me the look traditionally reserved for a dying animal. 'I'm sorry. I just wish you'd called. This, well, it complicates things. I left you, remember.'

'We all make mistakes,' I said, adding quickly: 'Just joking.'

'Aren't you always? Why didn't you call, anyway?'

'I did. Nobody seems to be answering the phones here.'

'What about my mobile? You could have left a message.'

I didn't want to admit that I was scared she might turn me down flat, block off my one retreat. Oh, why not.

'I thought you might say no, tell me to bugger off after our fight, and God knows I would have deserved it. The truth of it is that I didn't have anywhere else to turn and I was frightened.'

She smiled. 'Well, I've missed your craziness too. I guess we're making progress. Hey, the truth isn't so hard now, is it?'

I smiled back thinly.

'You could even get good at it, dude,' said Todd unhelpfully. I glared at him.

Gina took control brusquely. She was worried that Scarpesi would turn up at the ranch and disrupt proceedings; she wanted to avoid 'a scene', especially with her father there. We should stay at the motel. It was an order. I loved it when she was commanding.

'Listen, if Scarpesi and Flat Angle, or whatever his name is, do come to California, they're going to come here, right? Not to the motel down the road.'

I could see her point.

'Yeah,' said Todd enthusiastically. 'And they might get Ollie confused with those other Brits staying there.'

'What other Brits?' I asked slowly.

'The guys on the plane with me.'

'What did they look like?' I asked.

'Well, one was short with a round, bald head and, come to think of it, so was the other one. And they talked kinda weird, like "noy woy, moy, moy mate" kinda thing.'

Todd said they were 'real friendly', asked him where he was going, bought him a beer at the bar at La Guardia.

Gina and I looked at each other, two intelligent life forms trying to work out if their less able friend was ever going to make it out of the swamp to fulfil his evolutionary potential.

'It could be nothing,' she said, sounding unconvinced. I nodded in agreement. 'In fact, it's probably nothing,' she said finally, firmly.

Todd said that although he told them where he was going, they seemed only mildly interested. They said they were tourists, just planning to drive around the state, check out Disneyland. It was possible, two guys on the razzle on their own. He knew he had to be careful, especially after the roasting I gave him from Nashville.

'Anyway, they were a great laugh, so I told them where I was heading,' said Todd.

I felt the foundations of my mental home, precarious at best, start to crack and crumble.

'Great lobotomized monsters,' I exploded. 'Just great. What did I tell you, you mentalist? Do the words "Don't tell anyone" ring any bells in that cavernous belfry you call a brain?'

He blanched. 'Sure, man, but –'

'No buts. So what do you go and do? You only tell the first random people who show an interest in talking to you. Unfuckingbelievable.' I paced around in frustration. 'Why don't you get one of those "ask me" shop assistant badges?' I yelled. 'It could say: "Looking for Ollie Gibbon? I'll Help."'

'Hey, listen. I just thought they were Brits, you're a Brit. It might be good to hang out.'

Gina tried to intervene. I wasn't finished.

'Good to hang out! Todd, in case it's slipped your mind, wherever that might be hibernating for the winter, I'm actually on the run. Not a fun run, a three-legged race or a five K for charity. I'm running for my life. Got it?'

Gina stepped in. 'Hey, calm down. Don't worry, Todd. It was probably nothing. It could have been just a chance thing. Ollie, it could, really. Plenty of British people visit California.'

She was right, of course. I was still furious, but it was hard to direct my rage entirely at Todd. We stood around awkwardly for a few moments, avoiding each other's eyes and staring out at the Pacific.

Gina looked at her watch, and said quietly that she had to help her father host an early-evening reception for the assembled supplicants.

It was not safe to go out buying clothes dressed as a squirrel, she warned. And she definitely did not want me in the house, just in case her father saw me. 'God, honey. He'd write a whole book about you looking like that,' she laughed. 'But he'd really give me the third degree, let me tell you. I've already spent a lot of time defending your mental state to him as it is.'

She would get some of her father's clothes sent to the motel later. In the meantime, she gave me $100. It would pay for the room.

It seemed a sort of plan. Todd had recovered and fell in alongside me as we headed for the car.

'How you feeling?' he asked.

'I'll feel a lot better when I've got into some proper clothes.

Look, I'm sorry I snapped at you. I know I got you into all this.'

'Hey, no problemo, dudester. It's great to be here, you know,' he said, breathing deeply.

'I know, the redwoods, the clean air.'

'Right,' he said, genuinely content with life. 'They totally kick ass.'

'Someone should bottle you,' I said grimly. 'Essence of optimism. Use sparingly.'

He slapped my back. 'Listen, I'm not saying you don't look great in the squirrel stuff, don't get me wrong, but it must be kinda weird being something you're not.'

'Don't worry, I'm used to it,' I said. 'Occupational hazard, pretending to be something I'm not, like genuinely moved, upset or concerned with something other than the size of my name on the page.'

'Man, you shouldn't be so down on yourself. You're a good guy. We like ya.' He was staring out at the ocean. 'I guess Gina is right. We just take it easy for the rest of the day. Chill out, head for the ranch later. Gina'll know what to do.'

It was probably a judgement often made in their college days. What Todd wasn't saying was what I was feeling: how good it was to be revolving around Gina, to have her making decisions, seeing things clearly. And she looked fantastic on her horse, slim, rhythmic and controlled. I really had missed her. I thought about Destiny, wondered what she would make of her knight in squirrel costume making up with his fair maiden – I looked across at Todd as we headed back to the car, the picture of serenity – and his Fool.

Back at the motel, Mr Patel was busy at the front desk and I decided not to bother asking whether any bald-headed bruisers had turned up. I was tired after my compact night. It could wait.

25

'What the!' I blurted. One of them leapt up from the bed and slammed the door shut, pushing me against a wall.

'You was a long time, wasn't you,' said Tweedle Dee, who was sitting in the one chair, his feet on the bed. 'Telly's crap and all,' commented Tweedle Dum.

'I'm Terry and that's Kev,' said Tweedle Dee. 'Sir Derek sent us.'

'What for, dare I ask?'

'He wants us to bring you home,' said Kev.

'Not to New York, I take it.'

'Nah. London. Remember? A place where you is loved.'

They laughed. I grimaced. 'When?'

'Soon as, mate. Soon as,' said Terry. 'In fact, we'll make the call now, just let him know we got you.'

Kevin said that I had caused 'a lot of grief' and 'the boss' was worried about what I was up to. 'Says you're a rogue reporter, 'e does. You're like one of them soldiers that goes mad in them Vietnam movies, incha? But don't tell us. We don't want to know, awright. Safer that way. For us and you.'

These were Todd's drinking companions. I sat on the bed. They were uncannily similar to each other, the hair on their heads shaved to bristle length. Their faces were round, without any obviously defining features.

'How did you find me, if you don't mind my asking?'

'Not so hard, Oliver, not so hard. We just staked out your gaff, talked to the neighbours. A lovely little old lady, Mrs Ratfinkle.'

'Romstein.'

'Anyway, she said your old lady had been calling about the dog. We got the number and just did a reverse directory thing on the internet to get the address. Simple. Figured you must be out here.'

'Quite a guess,' I said.

'Well, then your mate turned up, also worried about the bleedin' dog. Kev followed him, watched him leave his gaff in a hurry. Anyway, we knew we was heading this way, so we thought we might as well follow him to the airport and see where he was going. We'd have split up if he'd gone somewhere else.'

They booked on the same flight as Todd when they discovered he was also heading for California. They chatted to him in the bar. I sighed. Todd would never tax the resources of a squeamish torturing regime. Ask him anything. He'll try to tell you what he knows.

'He was going on about meeting a friend in California, another Brit like us,' said Kevin. 'A reporter. We was chuffed to hear that, wasn't we, Tel? I think we should try and head out tonight. What do you think, Tel?'

'Sounds like a plan,' said Terry.

'Don't matter what you think, I'm afraid,' said Kevin to me. We would drive to Los Angeles, about two and a half hours away, and catch an overnight to London. I felt despondent. They had even remembered to pick up my passport.

After all this, I was being returned to Britain and some private hell, that job covering local government. He'd be too cruel to sack me. Stanley would want me where he could see me. 'Said something about you owing him some deposit money,' Kev explained. So, that was why he had stopped my pay.

The squirrel suit was a problem. If I didn't mind, they might suggest something more casual. 'Don't think they like wildlife at customs,' Terry explained. They both laughed, loud men-at-the-bar laughs. I cracked them up.

They were still laughing when the door was kicked in.

Under other circumstances this would have been a moment to savour, a grand meeting between London thugs and the mob's finest. Fat Angie was in front, looking fat and angry. He had two fellow refrigeration units with him. It was really no contest. The Americans were dressed better, I noticed.

They pushed Kevin into Terry, grabbing both of them. Neither had a weapon, which was a mild surprise. But you could still get a head bang through customs, I imagined. Even these days. Angie, of course, was playing at home. He had a pistol that he waved at us all.

'You'se a hard man to track down,' he said glacially. His two sidekicks were tying up Kevin and Terry. I felt rather sorry for them.

'Hey, leave it out, will you?' complained Terry as he was bound.

'What a bleedin' liberty, eh?' said Kevin, appealing to me. I shrugged in agreement.

'Anyway, what's your game, pal?' Kevin asked Fat Angie accusingly, as thick duct tape was ripped into two mouth-sized strips.

'No game. We just want this guy here,' he said, pointing at me.

'Yeah, well, wait your turn,' said Kevin, outraged. 'We got 'ere first.'

Fat Angie strode over and stared Kevin in the face. 'I ain't gonna say this again, so listen good. This guy is mine. There ain't no line, got it? He's done a bad thing, owes money to an important man.'

'Did you hear that, Tel?' said Kevin. 'Blimey, mate, you owe money to important geezers everywhere.' He turned to Fat Angie. 'As it 'appens, he owes money to an important man in my country.'

'No, I don't,' I found myself saying.

'Oi, less lip from you, OK.'

Emboldened, I felt like some revenge. 'Well, only one of us is not tied up.'

Kevin turned to Angie. 'Are you sure you've got the right guy? I mean, it's a bit of a bloody coincidence, we all turn up at the same place for the same guy. You got to admit. I mean, he don't even sound American. How can he owe you money?'

'It's a contract,' said Fat Angie.

'What would that be?' piped up Terry. 'A squirrel-dressing contract?'

Fat Angie scowled at them and then at me. He nodded to his cohorts, who began undressing Kevin, to his deep distress, after finally taping up the two Cockney mouths. Kevin was left in his underwear.

'Here, put these on,' ordered Fat Angie, as a goon handed over trousers and a t-shirt. I unzipped the squirrel outfit.

'You realize you look ridiculous in that, don't you?' Fat Angie said.

'Seemed like a good idea at the time. How did you find me?' I found myself asking once more.

'Followed your dumb friend,' said Fat Angie, smiling. 'He gave us his home address. It was easy.' Of course it was.

Where was Todd to answer these slanders, accept my punch to his chin, call the cops, or do something useful?

'He's talking to some bird place,' said Fat Angie, as if reading my mind. 'He was saying something about swallows.'

Bloody Todd. How could he, at a time like this? Kevin and Terry were left tied in my room. I was facing torment, death, who knew. Todd was puzzling about bird-migration patterns. I was bundled into a Lincoln Navigator with tinted windows. It was early afternoon.

By the time Gina realized what had happened, it would be too late. I would be at Los Angeles International Airport, on my way to supporting a freeway bridge. The goons on each side of me stared impassively ahead as Fat Angie roared out of the motel courtyard.

We drove for about an hour. I tried to make conversation, but soon gave up.

'Hey, you guys wanna stop for something?' said Fat Angie eventually. 'There's a Denny's ahead.'

'Sure, boss. Sounds good.'

'How 'bout you, chipmunk? You want something?'

'Squirrel,' I said petulantly through pursed lips. 'And I'm not hungry.'

'Your choice, pal,' said Angie. 'Take my advice, always be hungry and eat. You never know when your next meal's coming. Or, in your case, if.'

They all laughed. I was bundled out. Inside, Denny's was doing a desultory business. One family group and a clutch of elderly couples, hunched and vulpine, picking silently over early-bird special meals, all oblivious to the new party of four. Fat Angie ordered ribs. His friends did the same. If he decided to juggle bagels, so would they.

'You bin a bad boy,' said Angie, pointing his fork at me. 'The boss is very unhappy.'

'I'm sorry to hear that. But,' and I dropped to a stage whisper, 'I can't get him money I don't have. Doesn't he get it?'

'Oh, he gets it all right,' said Angie through a mouthful of bread. 'And so will you, my friend. He's had it with all this. You gonna disappear.'

I suddenly felt drained, dizzy with fear again, empty and powerless. My only allies were either oblivious to my fate or, bloody hell, trying to find ornithologists. I thought about screaming, but it seemed futile. Half the diners would probably have suffered coronaries.

I barely noticed the police car pull up hard in front of the diner. Fat Angie tensed as two deputies from the sheriff's department got out, unclipping the guards on their holsters. They headed into the diner. They were joined at the door by a tall, bald figure and I felt my heart begin to pump in excitement as I recognized a familiar shape. Relief washed over me. The trio looked around, finally settling on our table. I couldn't help myself. 'Hi,' I shouted.

Fat Angie and his hoods looked at each other and carried on eating.

One of the deputies came over clutching a piece of paper. 'You Oliver Gibbon?' he asked.

'I'm Ollie Gibbon, that's correct, officer,' I said ecstatically. He looked at the image in his hand, then at me.

'You know you were reported missing in New York?'

'Really?' I said. 'I'm not, as you can see. Right as rain.'

The deputy looked at Fat Angie, who managed a small wave. 'Are you with these gentlemen?'

'No, not at all. We've just met, haven't we?' I said to my companions, who nodded in agreement, poison in their eyes.

'Perhaps I can help, officer,' said Fishlove smoothly. 'Mr Gibbon was probably working undercover on a story, weren't you, Ollie?' he said pointedly, looking intently at me.

'Yes, yes. That's it. I mean, that's right,' I said enthusiastically.

'Is that so?' asked the deputy.

'Happens quite a bit in our business,' said Fishlove. 'You go off for a few days, try not to let your competition know, next thing somebody reports you missing.'

'Well, sir. Can I recommend that you go with him and contact your people in London, tell them you're fine and in future make sure you don't just disappear, OK?'

The deputy called headquarters. It was the missing Brit, he said. Yes, seemed fine. Was it OK to release him to his colleague?

I walked out with the deputies, glancing over my shoulder. Fat Angie and his gang were huddled, rigid and powerless. They left money on the table and began to hurry out.

'We're going to have to move fast,' I said quickly to Saint Fishlove.

'I would imagine,' he said coolly. 'How are you, by the way?' he said, his pate glistening in the California heat. 'Didn't like the look of your new friends.'

'How did you –?'

'Oh, that. Easy.'

'Not Todd again?'

'Who?' asked Fishlove.

'Never mind.'

'I talked to that guy Leopold and realized it was obviously you who'd fixed it. I mean, that porn mag arrived the same morning. I couldn't think who else would send me a World Media delight. It isn't actually available over here, incidentally.'

'Oh, I can explain that,' I started to say quickly. Fortunately, before I had to discover whether I could, Fishlove had moved on.

'Don't worry. I thought it was a clue, an interesting challenge, a taunt. So when lovely Leopold described who you were with, I smelt something. I just put two and two together and hoped for four and a good story,' he said.

'You did?'

'Yes. I thought from the description that you might be meeting Whitney's bodyguards, I must admit. Then that call from Nashville. I was worried they were taking you somewhere for an exclusive chat. Thought you might be trying to throw me off the scent.'

We were heading fast down the highway.

'But how did two and two equal California, not that I'm anything other than eternally grateful, of course?'

Fishlove smiled. 'I thought even you would have found out that Whitney cancelled that concert days ago. And why were you calling me for a meaningless chat? I called your library and just asked what was the last set of cuttings you'd asked for. Talked to some chap called Bowker, who said he'd sent you some stuff on Frank Scarpesi. It all started to get very intriguing, especially when Whitney's people called about setting up an interview and swore blind they hadn't met with you. I thought you must be on to some amazing scoop, something linking the mob and pop worlds. It worried me a little, especially after your Mafia series. I got a bit bollocked for that.'

He had staked out my apartment, he said. 'It was when the terrible twins turned up wearing WE LOVE BILLERICAY t-shirts that curiosity really got the better of me,' he said. 'There had to be a connection, so I followed them out here. Fascinating puzzle, absolutely fascinating, Ollie. I couldn't work out how any of the pieces fitted. I was hooked. Couldn't think of anything else. But you know me, once I get the bit between my teeth.'

'I'm impressed anyway,' I said, glancing over my shoulder to see if Fat Angie and company were on our tail. So, he'd got bollocked, had he? I felt a small flush of satisfaction.

'Then this wire report came over. I got it faxed to me. Here.'
I read the single sheet of paper. 'British Reporter Kidnapped,'
ran the headline.

Fears are growing for the safety of British reporter Ollie Gibbon, who
has disappeared from his New York apartment.

Gibbon, 34, had just completed a three-part series on the workings
of the Mafia for his newspaper, the *Daily Herald*, and was believed to be
preparing for an interview with singing star Whitney Houston.

Police sources said they were not yet treating the disappearance as
suspicious, but were alerting agencies around the country following a
request from his employer.

'We're most concerned for his safety and state of mind,' said Trevor
Bleaker, a spokesman for the London-based *Herald*. 'We know he's had
financial troubles and are very worried that these may have overwhelmed
him.'

I handed it back without comment. 'So, how about the real story,
now I've got you out of your hole?' asked Fishlove. 'Because I'm
not making any sense of this at all.'

I was rather enjoying his predicament. It was rare for the shoe
of wonderment to be on the other foot. 'I can't tell you anything
yet. But I will.'

'Just tell me it isn't Whitney and I'll relax,' he said, sounding
strained. He had saved my life. I owed him.

'God, I wish. No, it isn't about Whitney. It's a much better story,
in fact.'

'Good,' said Fishlove, relieved. 'That's all I need to hear. As long
as there is a story. I was a bit worried I might have flogged out
here for nothing.'

'Apart from saving me, of course.'

He smiled faintly.

'Quite. Hang on, I think we've got company,' he said, looking
through the rear-view mirror. The Lincoln Navigator was on our
tail. Fishlove coolly roared away. 'Persistent sods, aren't they?'

The road was straight and the sedan Fishlove had hired was powerful. We managed to keep a distance from Fat Angie. Fishlove proved fearless and fast. Was this man bad at anything?

It was obvious we couldn't go back to the motel.

'Let's head for the Cube Ranch,' I said. 'It's just up the road. It's where Gina lives whenever we bust up,' I said.

'Sounds good to me,' replied Fishlove calmly. The Navigator was gaining on the narrower, winding roads above Santa Barbara towards the ranch. I saw the complex of buildings ahead, a beacon of wonderfulness on top of the hill. I never thought I would ever be so grateful to enter Cubeworld.

'There it is,' I yelled. 'The entrance is somewhere around the next couple of bends. Watch out for water buffalo. You'll have to slow down – if we miss it, I doubt we'll get time to reverse back.' The Navigator was less than a quarter of a mile behind. There were the gates. We turned in hard. I looked over the seat back. The Navigator had screeched to a halt at the entrance. Fat Angie needed small spaces and no crowds for his work. This was neither. I was safe for the time being. We pulled up to the front of the house. A small cavalcade of cars was dropping off guests for the reception. We pulled around to one side.

Gina was in a main hall area. She rushed over when she saw me. 'Ollie! I've been frantic. Todd called about an hour ago, said you'd just vanished.'

'Really? He was so busy worrying about swallow-migration patterns that I'm surprised he noticed.'

'Are you OK?' she said. There was definitely moisture in her eyes. We hugged. It was kind of goofy and we shuffled apart, embarrassed.

'I'm fine, fine. But only thanks to Fishlove.'

'Hi, Fishlove,' said Gina. 'I might have known you'd be on the trail.'

'I can smell a story at ten paces, Gina. It's a curse. Turned out it was the wrong story and I still don't know what it is. But I'm on a promise.'

'I know. Ollie always says you're brilliant. It quite freaks him out, you know I think he's jealous.'

'There's still the small problem of how we get out of here,' I said tightly, changing the subject. 'Those bastards chasing me will be waiting outside your property right now.'

But that could wait. The hum of a reception reached us in the hall, a quiet engine of conviviality and clinking glasses. 'Going well?' I asked Gina.

'Great. Daddy's having a blast. Lots of new business, I expect,' she said, smiling at me, but I could see she was anxious, biting her lower lip. 'I don't know, Ollie. Couldn't we call the cops? I don't like the idea of those guys hanging around out there, and you can't stay here for ever.'

I took Gina to one side. There was a limit to how much I wanted Fishlove to know.

'What would I tell them? It all sounds ludicrous or, worse, that I'm somehow mixed up in a crime. I'll end up being deported or held by Immigration. They already suspect me of porn smuggling and visa fraud. What would your father think, anyway, if California's finest suddenly turned up?'

Fishlove came over, said he wanted a hint. Had I taken money from Stanley? Word had got out, he said.

'Fishlove, look the answer to that is no. But it's a long, complicated story.'

'And it's got my name on it, right?' he said. I wondered how much choice I had. After all, this was my rescuer. Fishlove could go to find a telephone now.

'It's got your name on it, yes. But not a word until we're out of here. Deal?'

He thought for a minute. It was.

I went to the bathroom. I just needed some time to collect my thoughts. Gina was charming Fishlove, I noticed, when I came back. He was obviously wondering where this particular game of chess was going, a game where, so far, he hadn't been able to move a single piece.

She really was good at public relations and seemed determined to work her skills on him. He must have been tempted to head for the nearest telephone. But what did he know? He knew I was wanted by my newspaper and he had found some vague mob connection and a glimmer of Whitney Houston. But what he couldn't do yet was link it all up. I smiled to myself, despite everything. Of course he was going to hold fire. None of the competition was here, and he had only half a story. I had the whole one. What he must have worried about was sending over what little he knew, only to find my version in the *Herald* far more lurid and eye-catching. Then he'd really get a bollocking. It can be a delicate, vicious game.

Gina suggested I change into clothes that fitted. 'Let's see what I can find upstairs. And that t-shirt, what does it say "Arsehole" or –'

'Arsenal, it says Arsenal. It's a football – soccer – team.'

'Really? Well, it looks kinda scuzzy, so I think that'll have to go as well. Wait here.'

She was right. It was originally white, but was now stained by age, blood and, undoubtedly, gallons of London Pride.

Fishlove, of course, looked unruffled in his suit and uncreased white shirt. His tie was barely out of place. He had been prowling.

'Quite a pad. Must be money in cubes.'

'Yeah.'

We sat down on a wooden bench in the vaulted hall, reporters in repose.

'Much else going on?' I asked reflexively.

'No,' said Fishlove.

'Any luck with Whitney?'

'Not yet. Like I said, thought you'd cracked it. Got me a little worried. One minute her people were all over me, the next, nothing. I bet they're trying to stitch up something with one of the Sundays.'

It was good to relax. 'You must be knackered,' Fishlove said.

'Too right. It's been quite a rush the last few days.'

Fishlove nodded. 'This is going to be a belter of a story, isn't it? I can feel it. There's definitely something going on here.' He looked intently in my eyes, for commitment and clues. 'You won't forget our agreement?'

I reassured him. It was exquisite to watch the usual professional insecurities playing out even in Fishlove, who always seemed so in control.

'What did you tell your foreign desk?'

He said that he was sure there was a good yarn, something to embarrass Stanley with. The library cuttings sealed the decision to send him on my trail. 'I must say,' he said, 'that guy Bowker couldn't have been more helpful.'

I bet. I had a hunch that Bowker knew something was going on and was hoping for the same as Fishlove, something to deeply embarrass a proprietor who threatened three generations of filing systems.

Gina reappeared, carrying a bundle of clothes, and pointed me to a door. 'You can change in there,' she said, assured, protective. 'Then we should talk.'

I came out dressed humanly for the first time in days. I pulled at the cuffs of the cotton shirt, felt the seams of the trousers. This is what my life had become, a frantic search for the human.

'Fishlove, do you mind if I have a word with Ollie alone? Just for a few minutes. You should go in and grab some food.'

Fishlove left us, perfectly happy so long as his quarry – myself – remained more or less in sight. I noticed him staying firmly at the door as I stood with Gina.

'This is a mess, Ollie,' she said bluntly.

'That would be an understatement.'

She said that she realized I had been telling a sort of truth. I apologized for bullshitting generally. She was right – it wasn't worth working for a dangerous, volatile man for a lifestyle.

'You need more self-respect, Ollie,' she said passionately. 'That's all I've ever wanted for you. Now look at you. Good grief, you've managed to get away from the mob, not just once but twice. You've got balls, loverboy.'

I smiled. She sounded impressed and giggled back. 'But you,

we, do have a problem,' she said. 'This lot will leave soon and I'm willing to bet that's all your mob friends are waiting for.'

I suggested smuggling me out in a car; they couldn't follow everyone. 'But what's the point? You're just on the run again and they'll hunt you down. No, somehow, we have to resolve this here.' She bit her lower lip, eyebrows knitted in concentration.

'Maybe your father could help?' I suggested.

'Don't be dumb, Ollie. If he found out what was going on, he'd kick you out the door. He's got an image to protect, remember. And Mafiosi hanging out at the end of his drive don't fit with it. I'm in PR, trust me. He'd be pissed.'

I glanced into the reception room, where mounds of food were laid out in a gaudy fiesta to spell the slogan THINK TO FEED THE HUNGRY. There he was, tall, angular, telegenic, concerned, immaculate and basking in the cubeness of it all. Great teeth. I could see what Gina meant.

We tried to come up with a plan. But nothing seemed to make sense. It was a mess, made more so with a report from the front line. There were at least three cars parked outside, waiting, said Gina after a scouting mission. She had gone out on her horse with a digital camera. Fat Angie would be pleased with that one of him forcing two doughnuts into his mouth simultaneously, I thought. The reception was starting to thin as people left. I could see Gina was anxious, weighing up at what point she would have to tell her father that the house was likely to be attacked by the mob and hoping to avoid having to do so altogether.

Fishlove, meanwhile, had enjoyed his wine and exposure to Cubethink. 'Amazing, really, whole new way of looking at the world,' he said rosily. It would have been good to include him in the council of war but too risky.

I happened to glance at the front door as it was opened by a sandal-wearing Filipino. The blood drained from my face. Scarpesi strolled through.

He saw me instantly, locked in with his eyes and smiled warmly.

There was nowhere to run. Cornered. He appeared to be alone, which was some small consolation. I wondered why. Perhaps some instinct for discretion.

'Ollie Gibbon, how good to find you,' he said, striding over before I even had a chance to warn Gina. Scarpesi had his hand outstretched. We shook. He put his arm around my shoulder and guided me away. Gina stood watching, confused. She had no idea who he was. Fishlove watched quizzically, but kept his distance. I doubted that he'd ever seen a photograph of Scarpesi. I was skilfully steered into a corner.

'You have given me the runaround,' he said, grinning in a disconcerting way. 'Clever too. It's been interesting. We lost you after Nashville. Fortunately, your friend, Todd, isn't it? He was most helpful.'

'Wasn't he,' I replied tightly. 'What made you walk in here?' I asked.

'Fat Angie is, how shall I say it, good in the muscles department, less good when it comes to brains. I came when he told me about the other people looking for you. And we knew about your girlfriend, of course. The West Indian gentlemen in the apartment below yours were most helpful too.'

Scarpesi was dressed in a summer suit. Very Californian. His shoes were immaculately white trainers. On his head, a pair of Armani shades perched above the hairline. His t-shirt was a rather absurd pink. Here was the Immaculate Deception, resembling almost anything but a mob boss from the East.

'I thought to myself, "Somebody must be very worried to send out muscle from England." They must have been worried and also without very good connections over here. It's always better to use local talent, Ollie. Less obtrusive.'

I grunted in some sort of agreement. 'What happens now, then?' I asked, resigned.

Scarpesi let a tight grin spread across his face. 'The person you work for has money, I know. He owns a newspaper. Get the money from him. A telephone call will save your life.' He looked back at Gina and Fishlove and smiled at them. 'Maybe theirs too.'

'Hey, they've got nothing to do with this,' I snapped.

Scarpesi shrugged. 'But they've seen me, you see, and I'm sure you've told them some of our story. They probably know my name.'

I asked Gina for the telephone, but didn't respond to her questioning look. It was late in London. I called Bleaker's mobile number. At least I'd get to wake him up again. Small pleasures were starting to count.

'Hello,' said a groggy voice.

'It's Ollie Gibbon.' That woke him.

'Where are you? We've been trying to track you down for days.'

'I know. Your goons found me.'

'Oh, did they?' Bleaker said, with a hint of satisfaction.

I plunged the knife. 'Then they were found by the mob people chasing me. Last I saw they were tied up in a motel room. Only one of them had any clothes on. Hope they didn't have your name and address on them.'

There was a pause as Bleaker digested the news. I ploughed on. 'So, here's the situation. I'm cornered in a house in California by a Mafia kingpin, a genuine Mr Free Meals in Every Restaurant, who is threatening to kill me. Ring any bells? He wants his money or I probably die and so does my girlfriend and, are you listening, a reporter from the *Sentinel*.'

'What?'

'What did you expect, putting it about that I'd somehow walked off with Stanley's money? I'm surprised there aren't more hacks out here.'

'That's how we see it. You stole from the company. The chairman wanted you back before you caused any more trouble.'

'That, as you know, is utter cobblers,' I said. 'So, what are you going to do?' There was a long silence. 'Call Stanley,' I said, emboldened. 'Tell him the game's up. He'd better cough up this money or an already bad situation will get a whole lot worse. I know stuff, remember, and I've got someone I can tell.' I glanced over and uttered the dread invocation: 'Fishlove'.

Bleaker was surprisingly calm. He mentioned libel and slander but did say he would call Stanley. I was to call back in three minutes. Scarpesi watched me, arms folded. There was a bulge under his jacket. It was either a gun or an ambitious penis transplant. I settled for the gun. No running for it, I realized, and where would I have gone anyway? Gina was right. I looked at the watch I no longer had. I guessed the minutes and called Bleaker back. He answered swiftly.

'Sir Derek says that you're obviously ill, delusional.' There was a pause. 'He wants his money back, the money you were given to help set up a business operation in New York under instructions from the company here. He also wants you back in London.'

I breathed hard. 'Listen, Bleaker. I'm going to blow the whistle on this, you creepy, sanctimonious git. I'm about to get shot and so is my girlfriend, a furniture salesman and another journalist, because that stupid, ignorant, selfish bastard we work for won't pay his debts.' There was silence on the line. 'Hello? Are you still there?'

'So, everyone who knows anything will be dead,' Bleaker said softly.

'Yes, yes, everyone,' I answered impatiently. At last, Bleaker seemed to be getting it. There was hope.

'How convenient. Good luck, Oliver.' The line went dead.

'Hello? Hello?' I said urgently into the telephone. Scarpesi was frowning in my direction. I played for time, mouthing words into the receiver, scrabbling for a plan. This was harder than inventing stories.

An idea was forming, just a germ, really. I dialled the *Herald* and asked for the library.

'Yeah,' said Bowker after an insulting eleven rings.

'Bernie? It's Ollie Gibbon. Fine, thanks. Listen, I need a favour and fast. Yeah, life and death thing. Literally, since you ask. I need those cuts on Frank Scarpesi. That's him. There was one about his business interests. Something in the *Sunday Times*, I think. He was under pasta recipes in the end, or maybe it was under Frankie Goes to Hollywood.'

There was a pause. Come on, come on. I willed Bowker on like a barracker in the terraces. 'Got 'em,' said Bowker. 'Some bugger had filed him under "Scarpesi, Frank".

'Let me have a look now.' I could hear him muttering headlines under his breath.

'Stop,' I shouted. Bowker had read the magic words 'Mafia Goes Mainstream'.

'Read the first few paragraphs,' I said.

'"Organized crime leaders in America are trying to diversify into legal businesses in an effort to protect their fortunes.

'"The FBI task force in charge of breaking the Italian Mafia is convinced that shareholders are being made offers they cannot refuse.

'"Frank Scarpesi, widely regarded as a spokesman for the five crime families of New York, confirmed the FBI claim in an exclusive interview.

'"He said that the days of shake-downs and extortion were numbered. 'The real money is out there in the so-called legitimate business world,' he said."'

That was it. All I needed. I thanked Bowker and put the receiver down.

Scarpesi was in animated, almost friendly conversation with his next three victims. It was quite chilling.

'Can I have a word?' I asked.

He came over. 'So?'

'Bad news, I'm afraid. They won't pay.' I didn't wait for a reaction. 'But I have an idea that may make you even more money.'

He looked at me carefully and motioned. We moved to a corner and an old church bench.

We were bathed in sunlight. To the casual observer we might have been old friends, deep in conversation about life, Cubethink, the Lakers' last game. At one point Scarpesi even laughed, clapping his hands together in delight. What must we be talking about, I could see Gina thinking.

Fishlove, ever the professional, was near by and had one eye on me. But he knew not to get too close. Why risk the story?

We sat for about fifteen minutes as the plan took root, grew and eventually flowered. What seemed at first absurd soon became incredible and eventually settled down as merely outrageously possible.

I just let it flow. We finally rose, smiling, and shook hands. Scarpesi put his arm around my shoulders. Gina had her mouth open, gaping. It was impossible. It couldn't work. It was ingenious.

I needed to square Fishlove, which might be hard. But people are often tempted by new challenges, more money, better security and an easier life. Especially journalists. I doubted even the *Sentinel* could erase those instincts from its staff. In the end, he was a pushover.

Gina was harder, thought it was all too clever by half. 'This is the sort of thinking that got you into all this shit in the first place.' But I could see she was unsure, tempted. This was a way to thrust me into professional significance, which was alluring. The job security would be welcome too. So would the chance to set up her own agency. Yes, she did love the apartment. There would be a big new account for her fledgling company. 'It just seems so, what's that word you always use? Preposterous,' she laughed, despite herself, tried to staunch the flow of giggles but couldn't contain them. Scarpesi had insisted that everyone 'be squared', and they were.

He made it clear that the rewards would be great for everyone. But the penalties could, quite literally, be fatal. Scarpesi left the house and made calls on his mobile. We had all been squared in the midst of cubes, which was also mildly satisfying. What would the great Depak Firman make of it all?

'We're bound together in this,' Scarpesi said on his return, as we walked down the drive. 'I can now trust you because the risk you carry is the same as what I carry. We are bound for ever. Capisce?'

We capisced in chorus. He was right. This was dangerous, probably illegal and certainly the stuff of which outcries are made. There would be parliamentary inquiries at the very least.

26

We flew to London first class. Scarpesi had insisted. Fat Angie and two other hoods were with us. 'I think it's important to give a good first impression,' he said, as we sipped champagne. 'That's what they teach you in business school.'

'Size matters,' I agreed.

He looked at me. 'Well, the owner of your newspaper has people he can call upon. It's important he understands how serious we are. That I too have people at my disposal.'

Scarpesi was still holding Kevin and Terry, doubtless languishing in some Los Angeles basement. I wondered what Kevin was wearing. Maybe they'd given him some lurid Hawaiian shirt and, hopefully, a pair of humiliatingly yellow culottes.

I called Stanley's office as soon as we arrived at Heathrow. He was in a meeting, said Trish, the World Traveller. I called Bleaker.

'I'm back,' I said simply.

There was a gurgling on the line, the sound of vocal cords struggling.

'With friends. And we need a meeting with Stanley today. I don't care how many kiwi moments or kick-boxing meetings he's got with the circulation department. This afternoon. I'll be in touch.'

It was amazing just how empowering it was to have the mob at your elbow. I called back in half an hour. Some people are reassured by credit cards. Scarpesi and Fat Angie had arranged to meet a London 'friend' in Paddington who would give them guns for the duration of their stay. It was quite enough reassurance for me. That'll do nicely, sir.

I was tired but excited and wanted to call Gina. But she would be asleep. Todd too. Definitely Todd. He had, of course, turned up at the Cube Ranch and, in his inimitable way, actually went up to Fat Angie and asked him whether he had spotted a Brit-dude heading in. We scooped him up on the way out. He had flown back to New York with Gina, who promised to explain it all on the way. Incredibly, Todd promised to listen.

We had a few hours to kill, to coin a phrase. I sat in a Starbucks and thought about the useful fruits of globalization: skimmed milk lattes and shirts that shrank evenly in Indonesia and High Wycombe, not to mention the Mafia outreach programme.

Scarpesi and Fat Angie went to meet their friend. We agreed to regroup in Fleet Street. We could walk from there to the *Herald*. I thought about going to the Old Printers' Nark. But it was too risky.

The meeting was fixed for 2 p.m. I was looking forward to it, powerful for once: in charge of something, or at least on the bridge for the first time in my life. Stanley must have been amazed at my presumption, the 'fucking nerve' he probably said. But he had agreed to see me. Bleaker had picked up on my resolve and sensed trouble, something over his head. It was exhilarating. This was the sort of thing Cubes went on about. I was glad to have read the book borrowed from Mobilene and its chapter about assertion, about how self-confidence is a weapon. I felt armed in a Schwarzenegger kind of way.

There was no coffee or kiwi fruit or drum roll when we arrived. In fact, there was no sign of Decca at all. We were buzzed, unfrisked, through the two outer security doors. Bleaker led the way. He was visibly confused by the Americans. After perfunctory introductions, Scarpesi simply said that he had a 'proposition' that he felt sure Stanley would want to hear. Fat Angie and the two hoods stayed silent, menacing.

Stanley was, as usual, dripping with sweat. He was businesslike, shaking no hands but pointing to chairs arranged around his desk. Not a word.

'You've got a nerve,' Stanley said evenly in my direction. 'Where the fuck have you been? I should kick your spine through your hat.'

I looked straight at him. 'I don't think we're in a spine-kicking situation here, Sir Derek. Didn't Pinky and Perky call? They found me. How stupid. Of course not. I bet you haven't heard from them either,' I said calmly, glancing at my fingernails, something I noticed Scarpesi did at moments of intense significance and, yes, I'm fairly sure, Marlon Brando affected as Don Corleone.

'Go on,' Stanley said slowly.

Scarpesi stood up and walked over to the window.

'What an amazing view. I can see, what is that?' he interrupted casually. 'The breast thing.'

'St Paul's Cathedral,' I said.

'Ah, yes.'

'Excuse me,' said Stanley, 'I know we've just met. But I haven't got the fucking foggiest idea why.'

'Why?' said Scarpesi serenely. 'Forgive me. I was just so enraptured by the view from this office. The carpet will have to go, of course. And I've never liked leather. We Italians like darker woods, you know. It's in all the movies.'

Stanley was thrown. He stared at Bleaker, who shrugged his shoulders, then at me, searching for clues. I hoped his eyes saw an impassive face, but his ears were not detecting my rapidly beating heart.

Scarpesi was evidently a beast in his preferred habitat, prowling confidently around the huge office, picking up objects, stroking chair tops. 'Neat drums,' he said before coming back to his chair. 'I'm more a piano man myself. Bach, Rachmaninov, Barry Manilow.' He was still smiling, enjoying himself.

'Kevin and, who was it, Terry? Yes. Kevin and Terry. What talkative people, Sir Stanley, or may I call you Derek?'

'As you like.'

'Well – Derek – my associates and I have a proposition for you, a business proposal.'

At this Stanley leant forward. This was familiar territory, a battleground on which he felt comfortable. 'Go on,' he said.

'I read in *Business Week* that you paid, what, a hundred million pounds for this newspaper a year or so ago. I will buy it from you for, say, seventy-five million. How does that sound?'

There was a pause. Then Stanley laughed, loud and in disbelief. This was the funniest thing he had ever heard in all his years of clawing his way up through pantylines to national newspapers to tea with the prime minister. 'In your fucking dreams. Well, good to meet you. But I've got a newspaper to run.' He started to rise. But Scarpesi was quicker and pushed him back in his chair. Not something they taught in business school, I thought. The chairman of World Media was stunned. Nobody had ever done that before.

Scarpesi stared straight at him in the same way that he had locked on me, mesmerically, in the Central Park toilet.

'That is the deal. Take it or go to jail. It's that simple, Derek. You see, thanks to our mutual friend here and your two unfortunates, both are fine, by the way, thanks for asking, I know things.'

'What do you mean?' asked Bleaker, controlled and analysing.

Scarpesi paused, probably for dramatic effect. 'Poor Sol Goldblam. Sure he was a sleazebag, but he was a friend of ours. Some people are very angry. They would want to do harm to whoever was behind his death if they were ever to find out it was something other than an accident.'

There was a long silence. Cue dripping pipe, I thought. Stanley looked at Bleaker and then stared at me, his expression cocked and ready to fire. I remained impassive, but only on the outside.

'I am sure that to avoid prison and the destruction of your reputation, not to mention the complete ruin of your newspaper, you will agree. Otherwise, I go to the authorities and you are through.' Scarpesi drew his hand across his throat. An unnecessary emphasis, I thought. 'This way, you sell for a sum that, publicly, we'll inflate so it looks as if you've made a dazzling profit. So, you leave with your reputation intact and just a little out of pocket. You will, naturally, retain your other titles.'

Scarpesi explained how simple it would be for him to point the FBI towards London. 'I have a certain reputation as a go-between and have excellent contacts,' he said. 'I will also have your two employees and the testimony of Mr Gibbon here. His experiences were witnessed by a reporter from another newspaper. They will all provide interesting statements.'

'Could bugger tea with the prime minister,' I found myself adding.

Stanley glared at me. 'Is that the thanks I get?' he spat in my direction. 'You ungrateful little nobody. I gave you the status you had as a foreign correspondent and this is what I get back. Disloyalty.'

'Let me stop you there. First, the *Herald* has no status. Down and outs have stopped using it as loo paper since you took over. Second, you gave me an outrageous task, one that I fulfilled, and then you backed out. That's why we're all here today. You were too bloody tight to honour your debts. And these people' – I glanced at Scarpesi – 'worry about honour and debts more than anything. I was loyal. Too loyal. I tried to tell you.'

We sat in strained silence for what seemed hours. Stanley looked thoughtful, unrushed. For the first time some of his confidence appeared to fade. He swivelled his chair to look out of the window, an escape from the eyes boring through him.

'You know, I always dreamt I'd own a newspaper one day,' he said to nobody in particular. 'I thought, look at all those prats, rich bastards inheriting the keys to the kingdom, and all that. I didn't come from much, you know. Started out with the gas board, reading meters. But I saw a world of power out there. Money and power. That was really all I wanted. I made a lot of money with the magazines, got toasted by sanctimonious twats. But respect. I never got that.'

He turned in his chair to face us. 'I've got three kids. They'll inherit everything. I don't want to include anything they'll be ashamed of. There'll be other newspapers.' He got up. 'I'll recommend your offer to the board, Mr Scarpesi.' He turned to Bleaker. 'I propose selling the *Daily Herald* to this bloke here. All those in favour, raise their arm.'

Bleaker raised his arm.

'Passed. It's all yours.' And that was that. Scarpesi produced a banker's draft for seventy-five million pounds and handed it over.

'I'm impressed. You're taking it calmly,' said Scarpesi.

'Yeah, well, win some lose some. I've made money stripping this place of its fat for the last coupla years. And also,' he dropped his voice, 'you don't know how much I really paid for it, do you? You got that figure from the newspapers, didn't you? You should never believe what you read in them.'

Stanley smiled for the first time and I knew then that he had made a profit. Not that Scarpesi minded. He had got exactly what he wanted: the perfect vehicle for laundering Mafia cash.

Regulators stay clear of scrutinizing newspapers and so do politicians, I had pointed out to him back at the Cube Ranch, as my plan came hurtling out, a grand, prefabricated cathedral of ideas, its flying buttresses designed to keep myself, those I loved and even Fishlove alive.

'How do you think someone like Stanley could ever get approval to own a national newspaper in the first place?' I told him.

Scarpesi, the business-school graduate, had seen it immediately. 'This could be perfect for us,' he mused. 'A legitimate business that nobody ever dares to challenge.'

'Yes, yes,' I went on, wildly constructing the crypt and nave. 'And the thing about newspapers in Britain is that they all lose money. It's perfect for any money, er, disguising you might need to do. You just announce you're going to spend ten million on an advertising campaign, for example. Nobody ever checks, but there it all is, reported in the business pages. Press releases hide a multitude of sins. Gina could help with all that.'

After the deal with Stanley was done, Scarpesi and his crew went to meet more 'friends' that night. I was left alone in the city. The deal had been struck rapidly. Derek Stanley had sold his dream before 5 p.m. I wondered what he would tell his wife.

'Hello, dear, nice day at the office,' she'd say as he walked into the kitchen, probably after being frisked.

'Yes, sacked a few people, swore a lot, sold the company to some

American mobsters. What's for dinner? Not pasta, I hope.'

Scarpesi had booked us all into an anonymous west London hotel, one of those white-stuccoed buildings that look magisterial from the outside but that had interiors degenerated by cheap refits into small, odd-angled rooms and were usually filled with foreign-exchange students or family groups from Bucharest. Fat Angie was looking forward to the cooked breakfast. He still watched me, confused and suspicious of my change from dead meat to business partner before you could say 'whack'. I sympathized. It was hard for all of us.

I called Gina and told her the good news. She was ecstatic. 'I'm really, really so proud of you,' she said. This was code for pleasure at my doubled salary and the weighty column I would write each week.

Fishlove was also bought off. He was to join the *Herald* on a ludicrously large salary to do all the features and news items that I had so singularly failed to deliver but that he lived for.

I arranged to meet Guy Armitage in the Old Printers' Nark. He was surprised to see me but could barely contain himself.

'They say we've been sold. To an Armenian corporation. Have you heard?'

'Yes, as a matter of fact. I know all about it and it's an American corporation, by the way. Stanley gave me money to entertain high rollers over there. You know, expensive weekends at spas and so on. I was supposed to try to find him a bidder. He just got pissed off when there weren't any results, thought I was wasting his money. I did a bit of a runner to get away from him, clear my head for a while. I couldn't tell you at the time, of course.'

Armitage nodded. It wasn't a watertight story, but I banked on his not inspecting it too closely for holes. What mattered to him was the change in ownership.

'So, that's what it was about. It all makes sense now,' he said. 'Can I put the goss around?'

'Be my guest,' I replied. We sank several pints, of brandy in

Armitage's case. He was beside himself over the news and constantly on his mobile, tipping off rivals. I stumbled back to the hotel that night, drunker than I had been for a long time.

27

I would hear occasionally, usually from Armitage, about what was going on. He was particularly pleased that the library had been reprieved. Perhaps not surprisingly, the new owners – never identified, but hidden behind a network of overseas holding corporations – quickly sold on to a British company. They were a front, of course. Scarpesi remained in charge, running the money side of the business, which was all he cared about, from New York. The circulation started to rise thanks to a series of exclusive crime stories.

'It's great,' Scarpesi said over dinner at Swanky's one night. 'We're clearing out all the competition.'

His people were feeding tips to the crime reporter, anonymous packages filled with incriminating evidence. The police would get involved and, as Scarpesi would say, 'another problem disappears'. Whole crime gangs, rivals in London and in the rest of the country, were busted. The holes they left were filled by Scarpesi's British 'friends'. Money that needed to be 'purged' was taken to the *Herald* and laundered through its accounts and offshore subsidiaries.

I was busy on a book. I got a sabbatical – on full pay – to write it. The story was about a reporter who tangles with the mob and gets chased across America. Fiction, naturally.

Scarpesi promised that the *Herald* would serialize it and pay lavishly for the privilege. He just wanted the ending changed. Gina now had her own firm and was handling the publicity. (Her clients included a number of construction and waste disposal companies; she had overcome her objections to the mob with remarkable speed.) She said the prospect of serialization should guarantee me a publisher.

'They love books by journalists. They know their buddies will review it. You're rolling,' she said, planting a big kiss on my cheek.

We were back together, firmly. I had achieved all that any New York woman wanted in her man: success, security, a Polish cleaner, a loft.

'You're actually getting ahead, Ollie,' she said one night over a bottle of Californian red, which was all we seemed to drink these days. 'You were so down, so lost, so cynical about everything. Now you're back. You found yourself. I'm so proud of you.'

The Jamaican builders were still on a promise to sort out the water. We had made up at Mrs Romstein's marriage to Mr Kapachutski. It was a low-key civil ceremony held in a small East Village bar. As Mr Kapachutski explained: 'I still have enemies.'

Hughgrant, who was Best Dog and carried the wedding ring in a small box attached to his collar, is blue this season.

Todd has been enjoying the fruits of a strange connection. Scarpesi had put him in touch with someone named Ralphie Knuckles on the West Coast.

'It's amazing, dude,' Todd said one afternoon. 'I get all this stuff straight from the sets. No hassling. No studly stuff.'

'Amazing,' I replied.

The telephone rang late one afternoon. Gina picked it up. 'It's Whitney Houston's people,' she said.

'Give them Fishlove's number,' I replied.

Acknowledgements

Thanks to Sharon Krum for lighting the blue touch paper in New York and to Mary Mount for keeping it burning. Peter Straus and Tony Lacey worked their inimitable magic to make sense of the explosion. Donna Poppy Knows Everything should be on t-shirts. Zelda Turner, another Penguin star, saw it all in four perfect words. This owes much to Rowan Routh, who works with Peter at the Rogers, Coleridge & White agency. I am grateful to Richard Addis for sending me to Manhattan, Rosie Boycott for keeping me there and James Gandolfini for the chat on Jane Street. Hugh Willis gave encouragement over many years. I've been blessed with the support of family and friends, both in and out of the Mafia and journalism. Finally, Laurel Ives nourished tirelessly with enthusiasm, affection and insight, which is why this is for her, forever.